The Wolf Mirror

Caroline Healy

The Wolf Mirror

Caroline Healy

Published by
Fire and Ice
A Young Adult Imprint of Melange Books, LLC
White Bear Lake, MN 55110
www.fireandiceya.com

The Wolf Mirror ~ Copyright © 2017 by Caroline Healy

ISBN: 978-1-68046-427-6

Cover Design by Caroline Andrus

While thoughts exist, words are alive and literature becomes an escape, not from, but into living.
Cyril Connolly, The Unquiet Grave.

For another CC, Colette, this book is for you. Like a lighthouse is to a ship, your beam keeps me on the straight and narrow.

Chapter One

~ Cassie ~

Cassie lit a cigarette and inhaled deeply. Smoking on school property was strictly forbidden.

Who cares!

A black Mercedes waited for her by the gates. News of Cassie's suspension had travelled fast. She walked down the stone steps and across the green, her satchel swinging from her slim shoulders.

The Principal must have phoned Cassie's mother straight after *the Incident*.

She narrowed her eyes at the dark car. Justice Miller of the Queen's Bench had sent a driver. Irritated, Cassie flicked the half-smoked cigarette onto the manicured lawn.

At Winchester Abbey Girls School, no student had ever been caught fighting. It was unheard of. The principal had spent a good twenty minutes lecturing both Cassie and Becky 'The Troll' Travers.

"My ladies should never lower themselves to that of brawling delinquents." Mrs. Pritchford's glasses slid down her nose as she gesticulated in annoyance. "You have a reputation to uphold for the junior girls. Your behaviour is inexcusable," she sniffed. "Now, would one of you care to tell me what is going on?"

Cassie had remained tight lipped. To confess that they had been fighting over a boy, a flaker like Dwane Rubens, was not an option. It didn't matter anyway. Becky 'The Troll' Travers was the Vice-

Principal's niece. Cassie was as good as done for as soon as she threw the first punch.

Frustrated, she yanked open the door of the car and slid into the back seat. She buckled her seat belt and turned to stare out the tinted window, ignoring the driver. They changed all the time anyway, so what was the point in making conversation?

The trip across London passed in silence. Cassie daydreamed about having a full-time job, her own car, independence. All she wanted was to finish her exams. Then she would be free. Maybe she would go to France, visit her Dad. That would really piss her mother off.

The car turned a corner and pulled into a tailback of lunchtime traffic. The chauffeur muttered something under his breath.

"A few minutes more Miss," he said, trying to catch her eye in the rearview mirror.

Cassie grunted, resenting every second spent in the confines of the Mercedes's plush leather upholstery. A chauffeur was the sole perk of Judge Miller's job that she allowed her children to partake of.

A normal upbringing is important, that was her mother's philosophy.

Bullshit!

How can you have a normal upbringing when your father lives in another country and your mother is a workaholic?

"I'm in the middle of a case, Cassie, I can't take holidays now." That was the excuse, every time.

Sixty hour working week, constant meetings, never-ending phone calls with clients, a nasty habit of forgetting important details, like the birth dates of her own children; Justice Miller was a *perfect* role model.

The whole thing made Cassie shake with anger.

No wonder her father had married a French tart. She felt the prickle of tears to the back of her eyeballs but she ignored it. She hadn't cried in over two years.

Cassie picked at the black varnish on her nails, trying not to think, concentrating instead on the sharp pain to her lower back.

The car wound its way along the embankment, parallel to the brown waters of the Thames, before taking a turn to the left.

The driver pulled the car smoothly to a stop in front of the Royal

Court of Justice.

"Here we are, Miss."

Cassie glanced up at the building before unfolding herself from the confines of the car. "Have a lovely day, Miss Miller." The chauffeur called after her, his voice eager.

Newbie, thought Cassie, as she banged the door closed. She didn't bother to say thanks.

Tugging her blazer into place, she hitched the strap of the satchel over her shoulder. It was too hot for this crap. The collar and tie around her neck were strangling her.

"Screw this," she said out loud as she stomped up the limestone steps to the main entrance.

The building was old and built of squared, grey stone. To the casual observer, it could be mistaken for a church, complete with turrets, spires and a rose window. The only hint as to its real purpose was the milling of people in and out of the bowels of the building.

Cassie hated coming to '*The Office*'. She stood out like a sore thumb in her bottle green uniform and formal grey blazer. The security guard eyed her lazily as she crossed the marble tiled foyer towards the lift.

She pushed the button and waited, her foot tap-tapping with impatience. Eventually the doors opened. In the privacy of the lift she adjusted her skirt, rolling the material up at the waistband. She opened the top button on her shirt and pulled her tie askew. If she was going to get in trouble she may as well make the most of it.

As the elevator ascended to its final destination, Cassie brushed her long mahogany hair away from her shoulders. She fingered the piercings at the top of her ear, a habit she unknowingly performed. The base of her back burned fiery red so she shifted the satchel to her other shoulder, trying to ignore the discomfort.

Keith Dobson, her mother's aid, was standing at the reception desk talking quietly to a receptionist. Dobson glanced up when the lift doors opened.

"Cassie," he said warmly, as he moved forward to greet her, his hands outstretched. "Oh my! Your mother mentioned something about your hair, but she didn't say it was so," he paused, "bright!"

Cassie smiled at him. The ends of her long hair had been dyed pink these last two months. Her follicle antics had lost their ability to irritate her mother so Cassie was considering a trip to the hairdressers for an undercut.

"Hi Dobson. How are you?" She unceremoniously dropped her satchel to the floor.

"I'm fine, thank you, Cassie. How are you, more to the point?" Somehow, he managed to waggle his eyebrows, a trick Cassie had tried many times but failed to master.

"I'm great. I've just been suspended from school and summoned to my mother's place of work. I'm just perfectly peachy." Cassie's shoulders slumped.

The door at the other end of the reception area opened and a meek looking secretary exited, scurrying down the hallway, past the reception desk. She glanced over her shoulder, her gaze lingering on Cassie for a moment.

Cassie felt a stab of pity for the secretary. Justice Miller was a hard lady to work for. She turned her attention back to Dobson, "What should I hope for? Sunny temperament? Happy disposition?"

Dobson lifted his shoulders in a slow, lazy gesture. "Your guess is as good as mine, sugar plum. But when the phone call came through this morning," he leaned in, so only Cassie could hear him, "I think I heard her use a bad word."

Cassie fumbled the retrieval of her satchel from the floor. She swallowed loudly; her mother must be mad, really mad.

Straightening up, Cassie spied the receptionist looking at her, a fleeting look of distaste crossing her otherwise marble features. It was enough to rally Cassie's fighting spirit. She gave a quick toss of her head, the motion causing her pink-tipped hair to flick back over her shoulders. She walked briskly down the hallway, her heart rate accelerating. Best get this over with, she thought, as she pushed open the heavy door. Cassie didn't bother to knock.

Justice Eve Miller sat in a burgundy, leather-backed chair, behind an impressive mahogany desk. Along the walls were a number of bookshelves, crammed with files and folders of various shapes and sizes. A tall, green lamp stood in the corner of the room, next to a large sash window. Cassie could make out the grey limestone facade of an office block across the courtyard.

The rest of her mother's office was relatively ordinary, a sparsely populated coat rack stood sentinel at the door. There was a seat, positioned just in front of the desk. Cassie made her way to it and sat down heavily, dropping her satchel at her feet as she stretched out her legs in front of her. She hated this chair, it was low and creaky and to keep her mother's gaze she had to strain her neck upwards. Cassie concluded that her mother liked it that way, towering over her underlings.

Justice Miller was scribbling on a notepad, seemingly unaware of Cassie's presence. Eve Miller was good looking, Cassie supposed, for a woman her age. She was forty-five years old, sharp grey eyes, an auburn bob to just below her jaw line. Cassie stared at her, willing her to speak. The sound of the pen scratching over pale cream paper filled the space around them.

Chipping week-old polish from her finger nails, Cassie began to tap her right foot, conveying her impatience, hoping it would annoy her mother.

"Are you deliberately trying to irritate me, Cassie?" Sometimes Judge Miller had a freaky habit of reading Cassie's mind.

"No."

Her mother stopped what she was doing, put the lid on her fountain pen and laid it gracefully on the sheet of paper in front of her. She looked up at Cassie, her steely eyes cold and still as water.

Oh no, thought Cassie, she is really mad. "Mum, I…"

"Forget it Cassie, I don't want to hear it." Her mother held up her hand, magically cutting off Cassie's ability to speak. "The principal phoned me this morning in the middle of a chamber session telling me that it was urgent. I thought there had been some kind of an accident, only to find out that you had been caught fighting with another student."

Cassie snorted. She wasn't sure if her mother was put out by the fact that her daughter had been suspended or that her own chamber meeting had been interrupted. Either way, Cassie resigned herself to the fact that there was no point in trying to explain. Her mother would believe the principal, whose version of events had been tainted by Becky 'The Troll' Travers' lies. She slumped back in the seat and gazed over her mother's

5

shoulder, out into the autumnal day.

"Do you have anything to say about your behaviour?" her mother asked.

"No." Cassie continued to stare blankly out the window.

"Nothing to put forward in defence of your actions?"

Cassie bristled, hating the fact that her mother was using legal jargon on her. "It's not like you would even listen to me anyway." She picked at her hair, examining it for split ends.

"So much for justice being blind," Cassie continued petulantly, "It looks like you have made up your mind, so there is no point giving my side of the story. You're as bad as that lot at Winchester." Cassie looked at her mother, challenging her to disagree.

"The facts are pretty conclusive, Cassie. You were caught by your biology teacher in the hallway of your school…scrapping!"

Cassie said nothing, just shrugged her shoulders.

"Do you know how this will look on your record? Do you know how much that school costs me? How many strings I had to pull to get you in there after your last episode?"

Cassie bit back a smile. She found it amusing when her mother referred to her expulsion from the Greystone Girls Grammar as an episode. Shortly after the divorce, things had gotten a bit messy.

Biology class, her one-time favorite subject; she had been etching graffiti on her desk with a black pen when her lab partner dared her to mix the chemicals in the test beakers. On a whim Cassie had added salt to see what would happen. The fire had been an accident. She hadn't meant the solution to ignite. No one believed her when she tried to explain.

Judge Miller was glaring at her across the desk, her face stony.

Cassie nodded her head, if only to move things along and get the lecture over with.

"Your actions reflect badly not only on yourself but on others too. Did you ever consider that?"

Subtext, Cassie wanted to add, my actions will reflect badly on your standing as a representative of the law.

Experience told her to keep her mouth shut. This would be over sooner if she just kept quiet.

"Do you have anything to say?" asked her mother.

"No." Cassie just wanted to go home. This whole day had been a disaster from start to finish.

Her mother threw her hands up and sat back in her chair, sighing heavily. "Fine then."

Cassie waited. Fine then what? She had expected the usual sentence. No phone for a week, no internet, no going out, having to babysit her brother. But her mother hadn't mentioned any of these things. A finger of dread brushed along Cassie's spine. The silence was making her twitchy. What was her mother playing at? If Cassie was to get out of here she was going to have to capitulate.

"Fine what?" she asked sullenly.

"You leave me no choice. We are going to Ludlow Park."

Cassie almost jumped out of the chair, "NO! Mum, come on. I hate it there. It's ages away. There is nothing to do, no WIFI, no way of contacting my friends..." Cassie was panicking, gibbering on like an idiot. She stopped listing off the disadvantages of going to Ludlow Park, aware that these were the exact conditions, in her mother's mind, to constitute an appropriate punishment.

"We leave first thing in the morning. Until then, you are duly grounded. Your phone will be confiscated, no internet, no television."

Cassie started to complain, to fight her corner but her mother held up her hand, the action bringing instant silence. "You will go home, pack your things and make dinner. Your brother will be in from school shortly, and I have given Mrs. Jenkins the afternoon off. I will be home from work early. I want you to take this time to think on your actions. When we get back from Ludlow you will go into school and apologize to your principal, your teacher and that poor girl who you attacked."

Cassie's teeth clamped together. She felt the burning of dry tears behind her eyes. She could practically taste her anger. She was duly dismissed, as Judge Miller had returned her attention to the paper work on the table in front of her.

"Oh, and Cassie," her mother said as she looked up, "Leave your mobile with Dobson."

Cassie wasn't able to say anything. She knew if she opened her mouth she would probably start to scream. She turned with as much composure as she could muster and walked steadily from the room, her fists clenched by her sides.

Dobson was waiting at the reception area. He held his hand in her direction and wrinkled his nose in distaste. "Sorry Cassie honey. Boss's orders. I'm going to have to take your phone."

Cassie felt a sudden kind of pressure, like a golf ball stuck in her throat. It pushed against her esophagus and larynx making it both hard to breath and hard to speak at the same time. A flash of Becky 'The Troll' Travers' face after Cassie punched her came into her mind and for a moment she thought the whole thing had been worth it. She slipped her phone from the front pocket of her blazer. "Dobson," she asked, her voice raspy, "one text. Just one?"

He glanced at the solid door to her mother's office and hesitated.

Time to drive it home, thought Cassie. "Please," she begged, looking as dejected as possible.

"One text," he conceded. "Quick now. You have five seconds."

Cassie fumbled with the key lock, her fingers feeling large and clumsy in her haste. She scrolled through the menu, frantic in her hurry. Who should she text? Dwane wasn't exactly top of her list at the moment and Tallulah was probably still fuming after the bust up in the hallway. Cassie bit her lip, knowing she did not have the luxury of time to overanalyse. She typed the words quickly, her thumbs flying across the buttons.

Being sent 2 Ludlow—Hell ☻Will try 2 contact u soon. Cx

She pressed send and waited for the delivery before dragging the key lock button and slowly, ever so slowly, handing her phone to Dobson. "Thanks D."

"No problem, C. Now I have been given instructions to get you home and to do a pit stop at the shops. You are on galley duty this evening, cooking for your brother. What's your poison?"

Cassie shrugged. She may have to cook for the little rug rat but it didn't mean that it would have to be nice. "Macaroni and cheese."

Dobson looked disgusted. "If you say so sweet pea, rather him than me. I'll have a car brought around. Say hi to Jonah."

Cassie moved slowly through the reception area towards the lift, her shoulders sagging under the weight of her punishment.

Dobson followed her and pushed the button. "Hey, don't worry." He tried to sound cheery. "It might not be that bad. It's always nice to go on a holiday."

Cassie nodded and smiled a tight smile as the doors of the lift opened. She stepped in and waved half-heartedly. A holiday was not how she would describe her punishment. Dobson had obviously never been to Ludlow Park, never had to spend time in the depths of a communication black spot and more importantly, he had never met Mrs. Rivers.

Chapter Two

~ Cassie ~

Cassie could see the corner of her mobile phone. It was peeking out from her mother's handbag; tantalisingly close. She desperately wanted to check for messages. The last sixteen hours of technology withdrawal had been hell. No Facebook, Twitter, emails, text messages; even a phone call to Tallulah had been off limits.

Now, here they all were, the happy family, driving out of London.

The prospect of being stuck in their exclusive company was a depressing one.

"Did you tell your teacher about the squirrel you saw in the park?" Cassie's mother chatted sporadically with Jonah, ignoring Cassie completely.

"Yeah. She asked me what colour it was. I told her pink, 'cause it was a girl squirrel." They both laughed. Jonah turned his attention back to his Nintendo, her mother to the road.

Cassie stared out the window, silent, her fingers rotating the silver sleeper in the upper cartilage of her ear.

Communication with her mother was clipped, all interaction brief. Their communal exile to Ludlow Park was not in Judge Miller's best interests either. She had, no doubt, a very full schedule. The lack of reliable internet connection and phone would set her back a few days. Cassie got some pleasure in knowing that *her* punishment would inconvenience her mother also. She sighed, the scenery flying by as they

10

joined the motorway.

"How long, Mum?" Jonah shouted from the back seat, the beep of his computer game beginning to irritate.

"We should be there by six."

"Six! That's ages."

"Ludlow Park will be worth the trip." Judge Miller's voice was bright and positive, the lie sounding dubious.

Ludlow Park was Judge Miller's family home. It was over two hundred miles from London, and in the middle of a dead zone; the Bermuda triangle for communications and I.T. They rarely made the journey.

Cassie sighed. It was going to be a long two weeks. She began to shift in her seat. Her back was particularly uncomfortable today. The pain changed depending on the way she was sitting, what clothes she was wearing, how tired she was. Right now, it was a thumping kind of ache, increasing in spasms every time she moved. She bit her lower lip and tried to distract herself from the discomfort, counting the road signs. The car wound its way off the motorway, going deeper and deeper into the countryside.

"Hey, Cassie." Her brother kicked the back of her seat. She winced. "CASSIE. Cassie." Again, he pummelled the headrest. She knew that he wouldn't leave her alone unless she turned around.

Her younger brother by nine years, Jonah was all the things she wasn't. He was fun, even-tempered, made friends easily and their mother actually liked him. She shifted around in her seat and glared at him. "What?"

He waved his Nintendo at her. "Level twelve!"

"So? That game is for retards."

"Cassie!" her mother chastised, taking her eyes off the road, "you know better than to say things like that."

Cassie made a face at Jonah before turning back to stare out the front window. She wished for the tenth time that she had her iPod. Flicking on the radio, she rested her head back against the seat, her eyes half closed, comforted by the thump-thump of the deep bass. Suddenly, with a click of the tuning button, the nasal tones of the Radio Four news reader hijacked her listening pleasure.

"News time."

Cassie glared at her mother whose eyes were trained conscientiously on the narrowing road ahead, a hint of a smile on her face.

You are so infuriating, fumed Cassie silently. She crossed her arms and closed her eyes, settling gingerly in to her seat. She was determined to ignore her family for the remainder of the journey.

About an hour later, as the car jolted over a pot hole, Cassie woke. The sky was black and sullen, angry clouds gathering all along the horizon. Cassie looked at her mother. She was hunched forward over the steering wheel, a frown of concentration marring her features. Jonah was asleep in the back, snoring gently. The Radio Four lady voice drifted in and out as the car bumped its way along the muddy roads.

"...Severe weather warning for parts of...and east...poor conditions..." The radio signal was crackling so much Cassie was surprised that they could make out anything. She leaned forward and flicked it off.

Her mother glanced at her. "You're awake."

"Yeah." *Obviously.* "Are we almost there?" she asked, looking out the window, trying to distinguish any familiar landmarks.

"Yes, another ten minutes or so should see us…" A crack of thunder echoed off the hillside. Cassie held her breath. Two seconds later a bolt of lightning lit up the sky. Then the heavens opened. Torrents of rain lashed against the windscreen battering the wipers, which whipped back and forth across the glass, furiously trying to keep it clear. Her mother muttered something under her breath and hunched even further over the steering wheel, peering into the darkening evening.

Cassie found herself gripping the edge of the seat as the car lurched over every bump and pot hole.

The road took a sharp turn to the right and there it was; the entrance to the estate. Blocks of fluted limestone, over two meters tall marked the gateway. Once-elaborate carvings of two fierce wolves adorned the top of the pillars; their muzzles pulled back, their vicious teeth exposed. She had nightmares about wolves for weeks as a child, every time she came to the estate.

Cassie shivered as the car passed beneath their watchful gaze.

The driveway to the main house was as she remembered it, lined

12

with oak and chestnut trees as far as the eye could see. It was a big estate, built at some stage in the 1600's by the first Miller. Her mother had attempted to impart the family history many times but Cassie was not interested. In fact, she actively ignored any conversation raised on the ancestral home. It was one of the reasons her parents got divorced. She despised the place.

They rounded a bend in the driveway, and in the blink of an eye she could see it, rising up from the growing darkness; Ludlow Park.

You could not help but be impressed, simply by its size. The house consisted of three parts, the main building and two wings, one to the east and one to the west. Pale grey limestone steps led up to a thick, deep-set door of heavy mahogany. Doric pilasters stood to attention on either side. The walls were a mix of light grey and cream blocks of limestone, interrupted by huge sash windows.

It was as if the house, decrepit from years of neglect strained towards them, welcoming the wanderers home. Cassie averted her eyes, the large windows looked eerily vacant.

The car came to a stop as close to the front door as possible. "You and Jonah make a run for the front door." Judge Miller raised her voice over the din of the rain on the roof. "Mrs. Rivers should be expecting us. I'm going to gather up a few bits and pieces from the boot."

Cassie rolled her eyes knowing full well that her mother was going to stand in the downpour, hunting around for her work folders in case she got a spare minute.

"Now please, Cassie." Her mother's tone was not one to be argued with.

"Come on, Jonah," Cassie called as she reached back to shake her brother awake. "We're here." She gathered up her bag and pushed open the car door, streaking out into the rain, taking the limestone steps, two at a time.

Jonah squealed as he followed her. Once on the steps beneath the portico, he shook his head, spattering rain drops on them both. "Quit it!" complained Cassie.

The front door groaned on its heavy hinges. Cassie and Jonah both froze, before turning in expectation. The door inched open. Cassie held her breath and reached out her hand, pushing against the dark wood. In the dimness of the hallway, Mrs. Rivers stood still, watching them.

Ever since she was a little girl Cassie had been terrified of the housekeeper, of her severe stares, her prolonged silences, and her disfigured face. Mrs. Rivers was as synonymous with Ludlow as the green pastures. Cassie had memories of her as far back as she could remember.

The housekeeper was in her mid-sixties, apparently never seeming to age, stuck in time like the very stones of Ludlow Park. She was tall with broad shoulders, wearing a self-imposed uniform of shapeless, tweed skirts and stiff, starched blouses. Wrinkles colonised her face and silver was the dominant colour in her once dark hair. She wore it scraped back into a bun at all times.

Her eyes scared Cassie. They were deep set and of a dark green, the colour of a cloudy sea on a dull day. Whatever Cassie did, no matter the importance, those eyes would scrutinise her and she would shrink under their steady gaze.

There was also the scar. It ran the length of the right side of the housekeeper's face, from her hairline to the middle of her cheek. It stood out, a line of angry pink on her aging visage.

And now here they were, the three of them, standing on opposite sides of the threshold. Cassie didn't know what to say and she could feel Jonah's trepidation at the prospect of stepping into the hallway without their mother. Cassie risked a glance over her shoulder. All she could see were a pair of legs, her mother's frame blocked by the opened boot. She would be drenched by the time she rooted out her stupid files.

Serves her right, thought Cassie, as she shuffled forward dragging Jonah with her.

She swallowed nervously. "Hello, Mrs. Rivers. We got caught in the beginnings of the storm. My mother is just getting her things from the car, she should be with us in a moment…" Cassie's voice trailed away into silence, breaking under the scrutiny of Mrs. Rivers' gaze.

A wet hand gripped her shoulder from behind. Cassie jumped, stifling a scream.

"What are you doing standing there in the cold?" Her mother was behind her, dripping water on the stone steps. She crossed the threshold into the hallway, her breathing a little heavy. "Mrs. Rivers. We are here,

14

finally." She shook the rain from her hair. "No thanks to that terrible weather."

Mrs. Rivers nodded her head, her gaze never leaving Cassie's face. The way Mrs. Rivers looked at her made her feel as if she had done something terrible, something inexcusable. Cassie blinked and glanced down at her wet trainers, hoping that Mrs. Rivers would look away.

Her mother shook out her jacket, depositing files, and folders onto the dry area of the tiled floor. Cassie risked a quick look around, dropping her bag. The old place hadn't changed much. The hallway, where they stood, was long and cool, floored with a chequered tile, in black and white. A grand staircase swept up to the next floor. The timber was golden in tone, the wood worn shiny in places. Along the walls of the staircase, a range of portraits from various periods were hanging, their faces stern. She shivered, even though the heavy, mahogany door had been closed against the darkening evening.

"I'm going to see if the T.V. is working." Jonah wandered off into the reception room.

Cassie noticed that the furniture in the entranceway was covered in a light film of dust. Her mother had informed her once that it was Queen Anne style, whatever that meant. If it was a queen who had designed it, then she had horrible taste. Cassie surveyed the space, her interest momentarily stirred. The low hanging chandelier in the centre of the hallway was greying with age. She wondered how Mrs. Rivers managed to keep on top of all the chores.

"…your room…Cassie?"

Cassie looked up, her mother had moved up a step or two on the stairs, Mrs. Rivers dutifully following. "Huh?"

"Your bag? Do you want to take your things to your room and get settled?"

Cassie looked behind her to the doorway and her discarded rucksack. She made her way over and bent down to retrieve it. Immediately she realised her mistake. The hoodie she was wearing had ridden up, exposing her lower back. She could hear her mother's gasp from the foot of the stairs.

Shit!

Cassie turned slowly. Two sharp pin points of red were beginning to form on her mother's cheeks and Cassie could see the anger building. Judge Miller took a step towards her.

"Cassie, what is that on your back?" Each word pronounced with slow deliberation.

Cassie shrugged. "Nothing."

Her mother was advancing towards her. Cassie moved back a few paces before coming in contact with the solid front door. There was nowhere to go. World War Three was about to kick off. Cassie spied Mrs. Rivers standing still on the stairs, observing. It irritated her that they were being watched.

"It's nothing," she said breezily, a tone she knew would annoy her mother even more, "just a new tattoo I got."

Justice Miller's face was turning an unsightly purple colour. "A tattoo?"

Cassie shrugged in acknowledgement.

"Of what?"

"Just some tribal design."

"Just. Some. Tribal. Design… You don't even know what it is?"

Cassie shifted from one foot to another, bristling against the heat of her mother's anger.

"Are you out of your mind? A tattoo is forever!"

Unlike a marriage.

"Really? The tattoo artist forgot to mention that bit, and to think," Cassie's voice was rising to a very high octave, "I thought it would wash off."

The slap came from nowhere. The cracking sound it made echoed off the walls of the hallway. Her mother froze, a look of shock registering in her face. Cassie's eyes watered as she touched her cheek with her fingertips, gingerly pressing against the place where her mother's palm had connected.

Judge Miller called her name softly, a hand outstretched, "Cassie."

It was too late—the damage was done. Cassie pushed past, heading for the stairs and the sanctuary of her room. She tripped on the fifth step, stumbling forward. Mrs. Rivers' bony hand gripped her arm, holding her upright, her fingers pinching. "Stay out of the east wing, mind."

Cassie shook her hand free, trying to mask her distress as she moved quickly. The Japanese room, her room, she needed to get to it. She jogged across the landing, down the corridor and into her bedroom.

Cassie flopped down on the bed and rubbed her cheek, her chest heaving from the shock of what had transpired in the hallway. She felt the prickle of unshed tears burn her eyes. Why was everything such a mess? Her new tattoo itched something awful, and for a minute she regretted it.

To distract herself from the overwhelming urge to cry she looked around the room. Pale cream wainscoting ambled its way around the base of the four walls. Silk wallpaper, imported all the way from Japan, adorned the rest. The pattern of leafy foliage and exotic birds gave the room its antiquated feel. One oriental travel chest with ivory detail sat in the corner, reminding the occupant that they were, in fact, in a house which dated back to the seventeenth century. The rest of the furniture was boringly modern.

Why did her mother always overreact?

Cassie rolled over onto her belly, resting her head on her palm, cradling the stinging cheek.

Okay, perhaps getting a tattoo was a big thing, but lots of people have tattoos, and it was not like it was in a really noticeable place. It could be hidden for the job interview, the college placement, the court appearance for juvenile delinquency. Cassie wasn't a complete idiot. She had, however, been hoping to hide it till she turned eighteen, or at least moved out.

She wished her father were here. He had a way of calming the tension between herself and her mother. But he had a new life now. Cassie picked the sleeve of her hoodie, pulling the thread of the seam apart. The last time her father came to visit he had brought his new wife. Cassie had poured a full bowl of cold custard down the woman's expensive dress. The stupid French tart. What did it matter now anyway? Her father wasn't here and wouldn't be coming back.

The rain pelted on the window, adding its own rhythm to the noises of the house. Somehow the constant patter soothed Cassie's anxiety and the sting in her cheek began to lessen. She slipped into an uneasy sleep where she dreamt of a courtroom in session, with voices shouting and the silent figure of Mrs. Rivers standing somewhere in the shadows.

The grumbling of her stomach woke her shortly after midnight. She sat up on the bed, disorientated. Then she remembered, her hand moving to her cheek. It was slightly tender, as if sunburnt. She ran her tongue around the inside of her mouth, exploring for any unusual sensations. She was dying for a cigarette. The last smoke she had was in her room before they left London, leaning precariously out the open window into the early morning sunshine.

She reached for her rucksack and extracted a box of twenty. She had four left and that would have to do her for the next two weeks. Shops weren't exactly within walking distance and she couldn't purchase a box of fags with her mother around. She was in enough trouble as it was already. Cassie took a minute to weigh up the pros and cons of going downstairs for a smoke. She couldn't open the heavy sash windows without waking half the house. If she went downstairs, there was a chance that she would bump into either her mother or Mrs. Rivers. Neither option was appealing.

Why was it that the only time that creepy woman spoke more than two words together was to give Cassie ominous warnings like, *"Don't go in the east wing."* What was so special about the east wing anyway? Cassie never went there. It was boarded up and had been for years. Maybe they were renovating. The thought entered her head instantaneously. What if it was open now? She could have a smoke in one of the empty rooms and nobody would know. She should go take a look. She had never been over there before. It might be interesting. Better than sitting here sulking.

Cassie pushed herself off the bed, stuffing her box of cigarettes and a lighter into her pocket. She eased the door of her room open, glancing along the corridor both ways. The house was quiet except for the persistent noise of the rain on the windows. She moved with stealth down the corridor, conscious of the noise of her footsteps on the old timber flooring.

The east wing was at the end and to the left along the main corridor. When the house was sealed up all those years ago, the west and east wings became off limits, windows shuttered, dust sheets spread over furniture and a large makeshift door put in to both corridors, sealing them off. There were two sets of keys as far as she knew. One set in her mother's office and the other strapped to a key ring that Mrs. Rivers kept on her person at all times.

Cassie rounded the corner to the east wing and stopped in her tracks. The out-of-place, modern door was as she remembered it. Made from pine, it sat in a makeshift door frame that the carpenter had cobbled together. Cassie tutted, there would be no going down the east wing any time soon. So what was Mrs. Rivers going on about?

A crack of lightening lit the dark sky outside. Cassie jumped, a spike of adrenaline coursing through her. The storm sounded like it was getting worse. She should get back to her bedroom before the electricity... The pale lamp shade in the middle of the corridor flickered, once, twice, then died, plunging Cassie into complete darkness.

"Crap."

She stood perfectly still for a minute to let her eyes adjust. The corridor was dark, the shapes and shadows indecipherable. The tips of Cassie's fingers reached forward as she tried to feel her way slowly to something more solid. She touched the cold pine of the door in front of her, her other hand brushed against the stainless-steel handle. She paused for a minute and pushed downwards. The door did not budge. Cassie shook her head and was just about to move away when she thought she heard a noise from the other side, a sound like soft footfall. She tried the handle again, pushing down more forcefully. The door opened, a loud creaking sound filling the hallway.

Cassie hesitated for a split second before stepping through into the east wing, her desire to smoke forgotten.

It was darker here, the boarded windows blocking any light from illuminating the hallway. Cassie used her hands to pat her way slowly along the wall. She could feel the softness of the old wallpaper as she moved tentatively along the corridor. There was a patch of less dark a little further along. Cassie moved towards it. One of the shutters had come undone, hanging precariously from its hinge. There was a little light coming from outside but it was enough for her to distinguish an old-style lamp, bracketed to the wall. She assumed that there would be many of these lamps along the hallway, just as there were in the main section of the house. She took a few more steps, keeping her fingers in contact with the wall. Suddenly they brushed against something hard, something gilded, timber perhaps, before sliding onto smooth, cool glass.

Another crack of lightning; the corridor lit in brilliant brightness. Cassie stifled a scream. The light illuminated two wolves, carved in relief on either side of her, as if they were stalking prey. They snarled silently before plunging back into darkness. Cassie whimpered, her brain trying to compute.

As if to prove to herself that she was not scared Cassie took a step forward. "It's just a mirror," she said out loud. "It's just the carving on the mirror."

She took a few deep breaths and reached her hand out again, searching for the cold surface of the glass. Another roll of thunder rippled around the house. Cassie held her breath. A flash erupted and she stared at the mirror, illuminated for the briefest of moments by the lightning.

Her reflection, except she was wearing a ridiculous nightdress of mammoth proportions.

Two seconds passed then darkness enfolded her again as the lightning ceased.

"Don't be stupid," she told herself as she stretched out her fingers to feel for the smooth glass. She reached over, leaning her body. She must be further away than she thought. She stretched forward.

"Stupid mirror," she hissed. "Where are..."

Chapter Three

~ Cassandra ~

Lady Cassandra Miller woke with a jolt. The silk, damask cover had slipped from her bed during the night. She shivered in the chill. Ludlow Park was eerily quiet. It seemed as if the house was holding its breath in expectation. Of what, she could not imagine.

Under the covers, she pulled the lace end of her night shift past her knees, down towards her shins, wrapping it around her toes. Winter was coming and the nights were getting colder. She had foolishly ignored Miss Blythe's advice and refused a warming pan, declaring that it was too early in the year for frost. She snuggled deeper in the bed, regretting her decree.

She wished her mother was here. This time of year, coming into the darkness of winter, Cassandra felt her absence the most; her Mama, the exquisitely beautiful Lady Augustine Miller. If the stories of her youth were to be believed, she had commanded the attentions of not three but four prominent gentlemen during her début. Cassandra smiled to herself before twisting around in an effort to get comfortable. The horse hair mattress was lumpy. She would instruct Molly, her new maid, to beat it in the morning.

"How am I expected to sleep in such discomfort?" she said to the darkness before sitting bolt upright, her frustration rising. "Insufferable!" She turned and punched her eider down pillow.

The room had recently been renovated, her furniture repositioned.

Wallpaper had been purchased from London and a new canopy of light green silk had been added to the four posters of her bed. A mahogany writing desk and matching chair had been imported from France. According to Miss Taylor of Upton Manor, they were the most fashionable of furnishings and a necessity in any lady's bedroom.

"Simpering idiot," she said into the dark.

Miss Taylor was very free with her opinion, an opinion that Cassandra usually disagreed with. Much to her dismay, it was her duty to suffer the companionship of the ladies of the neighbourhood once a month. It was a tradition that her mother had established, before Cassandra was born. The gatherings were an opportunity to become better acquainted with the families of the parish.

Cassandra loathed the events. In truth, as far as Cassandra could make out, the occasion was an excuse for gossip, a way to show off the latest fashion and a means of securing a match with someone's brother, uncle or at times, even father.

These thoughts irked her. There would be no going back to sleep now, her blood pumping with discontent.

She reached to the chair beside her bed and pulled a well-worn shawl over her shoulders. If Miss Blythe was to see her wearing such an item of clothing, she would scold her no end. *Oh, Miss Miller, so unbefitting for a lady of your stature.* Her governess still called her Miss, even though by rights, since her mother's death, Cassandra was now the Lady of the house.

However, Miss Blythe, for all her remonstrations, had been a tower of strength and sense in the last three years. She had taken Cassandra under her wing and instilled all the knowledge she possessed. Cassandra had learned to move in polite society, to host social engagements, to handle the servants. In truth, she had learned how to administer a large estate in a relatively short period of time; a fact that she was particularly proud of.

For a simple governess, Miss Blythe's knowledge of society was quite impressive. Yet sometimes Cassandra found her cautious nature overbearing. Every now and then she wanted to throw discretion to the wind, order beef instead of mutton for a dinner party. Or perhaps go out in the carriage without a bonnet. Such recklessness would not be acceptable of course. It would seriously hamper her chances of attracting a suitable husband.

Automatically Lady Cassandra thought of her father.

Lord Miller was dying.

The doctor had tried to spare her from the truth, but Cassandra was not a simpleton. She bit back a sob that threatened to overcome her. There was no use in giving in to one's feelings. That was what Miss Blythe said. It was important to have decorum and poise when it came to displaying emotion. But Cassandra couldn't help herself. She loved her father and could not imagine life without him.

The symptoms of his illness had presented themselves gradually over a number of weeks.

"Father? Are you well?" On his return from a trip to Huxley Hall in London, Cassandra noticed him faltering in the evenings, his head lolling to one side, as the fire blazed in his study.

"I will have Johnson prepare you a tonic." Two days later she sent to the village for medicine.

"Does this evening's meal displease you?" He began to excuse himself from dining, claiming lack of appetite.

"Shall we walk the grounds, Father?" He even began to forgo his daily exercise.

Mr. Weston, the estate manager, had taken over the running of business, so her father rested.

Cassandra began to worry. The final incident happened one evening, at dinner. Cook had prepared a fine feast of grouse, and Mr. Hector Wiggins, a visiting curate from Marshfield, was dining with them.

"My dear?" Her father's voice from the head of the table was quiet amongst the chatter.

"Yes, Father." Cassandra had immediately turned to offer her full attention.

"I regret…" He looked very pale. Cassandra leaned towards him to hear better. "I regret very much my dear, but I…"

And then it happened. Cassandra felt herself colour at the memory. Her father's silver knife had slipped from his hand and clattered to the plate in front of him. There he sat, stunned, a silent *"O"* forming on his lips before his eyes rolled in his head and he began to convulse violently.

He slid from the seat to a crumbled heap on the floor. Cassandra had cried out in alarm, rushing to his side, cradling him as his body trembled, a sliver of spittle sliding down his chin.

She had been terrified that he would die right there.

They waited impatiently for the doctor to come from the village, Cassandra pacing back and forth outside her father's chamber. Upon the doctor's arrival, he had dismissed her almost immediately, ushering her back down to the drawing room, away from his patient. She had reluctantly returned to her guest, knowing full well that by midday the following day, the news would spread around the neighbourhood like wildfire. Mr. Wiggins was not known for his tact and as sure as the sun would rise, he would have cause to accidently mention the incident to anyone who would listen.

After the first seizure, many more came, each one a little worse. Doctor Brown had prescribed tonics, spa water, salts and poultices. All manner of things but nothing seemed to work.

He fell in and out of consciousness; he suffered from hallucinations and night terrors, chills and tremblings. He refused to eat and Cassandra was growing strained with worry. No one could tell her what ailed him.

Miss Blythe, ever conscious of her duty, encouraged Cassandra to keep up her exercise and to eat properly. *It would not do, at this expectant time, to let your looks fade*. There it was; the crux of Cassandra's daily woes, her looks and their fading.

Flinging back the cover, she swung her legs out of the bed and padded on bare feet to the fireplace. In the glow of the embers she picked up the poker and plunged it into the grate, rattling the coals. A plume of sparks flew up the chimney and a wave of heat ebbed towards her. She hunkered on to her heels and lay the poker down, stretching her fingers towards the hearth, enjoying the warmth of the fire.

She looked at her hands. They were slim and well-proportioned, with petite wrists and well-groomed nails. Miss Blythe had tutored her to always wear her gloves when outside, so as to preserve the soft skin. A gentleman, in bending to take a lady's hand would notice such a thing.

If Cassandra had her way she would have callused hands and never marry as long as she lived. But it was not Cassandra's choice. She had a duty. It was her responsibility to pick a suitable husband. If her father's health was as precarious as she thought, then it was incumbent upon her to choose. Unfortunately, given the turn of events she must choose quickly.

As she was an unmarried only daughter, Ludlow Park would go to a cousin, a Mr. Reginald Huxley of Huxley Hall, London.

A gust of wind howled down the chimney and spatters of rain fell on the coals of the fire. Heavy drops hit the panes of the window and the sombreness of the night closed in around her. Outside in the park the trees creaked under the pressure of the romping wind. Cassandra drew her shawl closer around her shoulders and huddled near the glowing embers.

To distract from the noise of the brewing storm, she thought on the list of potential suitors. There was Mr. Taylor, Miss Taylor's insipid brother.

His opening conversation at the summer ball had been, "Lady Cassandra, do you like to shoot?"

His comment had left her unsure how to proceed. Did he mean that he thought her very course and wind beaten, a sure sign that she hunted?

When she did not respond, he continued, "I shot a rather nice deer in the pasture to the front of Upton yesterday."

At this point he proceeded to guzzle red wine, spilling a fair splash onto the white of his dining cravat. She looked on in disbelief as he talked, ignorant of her discomfort. He described the detail of the hunt, the skinning and de-organing of a stag. Cassandra had felt quite light headed at the end of the vivid description. He then asked her to dance and she had to suffer his closeness for a further half an hour. Oh, the shame.

Miss Blythe had been quite animated in his praises, highlighting his good family connections.

After Mr. Taylor, there was Mr. Wrix from the neighbouring townland. He was by far the best choice, he was shockingly handsome, very rich, a good conversationalist yet Cassandra had an uneasy feeling about him. The way the servants scurried when he entered the house, their eyes continually downcast, their tone subdued. This was standard behaviour for any well-trained servant but in Mr. Wrix's company their restraint seemed as taut as a newly strung bow.

Then there was Mr. Fitzwilliam Turner who was not yet sixteen, far too much her junior. Next, Justice Hatfield, the local magistrate, just gone sixty, far too much her senior and extremely rotund.

Her father would not let her go to London, so Cassandra had not had a proper coming out. The pool from which to pick a potential husband was restricted. In truth, she did not mind so much, there was only one man she would truly wish to marry. But that was impossible.

She admonished herself for being foolish, gazing into the amber coals of the fire. There was no point to think on anything except her duty. He was not hers and nothing would change that.

Cassandra touched the chain of cool gold that hung around her neck. A heavy oval shaped locket rested just below her breast bone, close to her heart. The outside was engraved with delicate swirls. The inside contained a miniature portrait of her late mother. It was a present from an old friend. Every now and then she would press the coolness of the locket to her skin and think of happier times.

People said that Cassandra looked like her mother, dark mahogany hair, and strong brow. Her figure was tall and lean, with fair, womanly curves proportioned appealingly. She had her father's grey eyes.

"Perhaps I should check on him." She spoke into the darkness of the night time, as if requesting reassurance. "Don't be such a nincompoop!" She stood up abruptly, fumbling on the mantel piece for the stub of a candle. If she wanted to see her father, then she would do so. She was, after all, the lady of the house.

Perhaps the noise of the storm was keeping him awake. Maybe he would be lucid enough for her to sit with him for a while. She bent to catch a flare to the wick of her candle.

Cassandra paused for a moment and considered her bare feet. To be caught in the corridor by anyone, particularly a servant, bare footed with simply her night shift and shawl would not be appropriate. But Cassandra was not about to ring for her lady's maid to help her dress. She made up her mind and moved silently towards the door, pressing her ear to the solid timber, listening for any unusual sounds. Nothing. The house and its inhabitants were all asleep. She slipped the latch and stepped out cautiously to the hallway, the light of her little candle flickering.

With a bravado she did not truly possess, she began to move down the corridor towards the east wing. Her father's rooms were located away from the main house so he could rest undisturbed during the day. She felt the coldness of the floorboards beneath her feet and hurried along, conscious that she did not want to catch cold. The last thing she needed was to have Doctor Brown attempting to administer to her too.

As she rounded the corner of the east wing something at the end of the corridor caught her attention; a moving shape, two green eyes gazing at her. She gasped, stopping dead in her tracks, a hand to her throat. Then she smiled at her own imaginings. It was just the dog.

"Snap," she called quietly. "Come here, Snap." But the hound would not advance; it remained in its seated position, its head held high, regarding her along the length of its snout. It whined, a desolate kind of sound and Cassandra's wish to see her father intensified. She took a step forward, holding the candle high, shedding as much light as she could along the corridor. A movement to her right caught her attention.

There on the wall was a very fine gilded mirror. It had been in the east wing corridor for as long as Cassandra could remember. Her great grandfather had procured it from a master carpenter, in some small town in the Italian Alps many, many years ago.

At the top corners of the mirror stood two wolves, their lips pulled back, teeth bared. Even in such a stance of aggression they looked regal and assured. Their bodies were angled towards the glass of the mirror. Along the rest of the frame the carving brought to life a myriad of unfamiliar foliage. Leaves and blades of grass intertwined with flowers, creeping up along the frame, wrapping around it, stretching out towards the feet and legs of the wolves at the top. The animal had a special place in the hearts of the Miller family, taking centre stage on their family crest.

Snap whined again, a low, soft sound causing Cassandra to pry her gaze away from the mirror and look towards him. His canine eyes regarded her evenly. She went to move along the hallway but a clap of thunder stopped her in her tracks. The windows lit up with bright lightening. Cassandra exhaled sharply, her breath almost quenching the candle.

Exasperated she looked around her, peering at the mirror which seemed to glow in the aftermath of the flash of light. The gilded wolves snarled at her. She saw her face, a reflection in the dimness of the night, except it was not her face, her hair loose around her features. Lady Cassandra Miller took a step towards the mirror and lifted her hand, her fingertips reaching forward, straining to touch the glass. Another clap of thunder; her candle blew out.

Chapter Four

~ Cassie ~

A tickling sensation on Cassie's cheek woke her. She scratched the itch, keeping her eyes closed, hoping to get back to sleep. She frowned. Her bed seemed extremely hard. Cassie's eyes flared open in momentary panic. She remembered where she was: on the floor, on the landing, in the east wing. What had happened? She pushed herself up onto her knees. It was dark.

Cassie touched her forehead gingerly. "Ouch."

It was tender and a raised, oval bump confirmed her suspicions. She felt with her hands along the floorboards. Hadn't the corridor been carpeted the last time she checked? She crawled in the general direction of the wall. The electricity would be out, no point searching for the light switch. She fumbled in the dark, the lighter in her pocket might illuminate but only for a few seconds before becoming too hot to handle. She should go down to the kitchen for some candles.

Blindly, she patted the floor till she felt the timber of the skirting board and then the wall. She pulled herself up to a standing position and made her way towards the stairs. Her fingers brushed against cold timber, followed by the smoothness of glass. The Wolf Mirror. Cassie pulled her hand back instinctively. She didn't want to touch it. The thing creeped her out.

She shook her head and looked down at herself, unable to see much in the gloomy darkness. She patted her legs, felt the coolness of denim.

In her trainers, she wiggled her toes, confident that her feet were safely encased. Her super dry hoodie was zipped to the neck and sufficiently warm. Under no circumstances was she wearing a nightdress. She rationalised her momentary vision with the disorientation caused by a flash of lighting.

Cassie moved along the hallway and turned down the corridor. Pale puddles of moonlight streamed in the sash windows. The storm clouds must have cleared. Cassie could just about make out the familiar shapes of the portraits along the wall and the odd piece of furniture.

She stopped at the head of the stairs and looked down into the darkness. The first three steps disappeared into black. Cautiously, she dipped her toe into the darkness and felt her way, slowly, down the stairs. They creaked their complaint as she descended. At the bottom of the stairs she bore left towards the open space of the reception area. The kitchen was down a dark hallway, the prospect of which made Cassie shiver. What if Mrs. Rivers was still up?

Her father would have laughed at her aversion to the elderly housekeeper, teasing her for her overactive imagination. Cassie stopped at the bottom step and felt a knot of pain in her stomach. She grasped the bannister, counting to five silently in her head. She would not think about him. But somewhere in the back of her mind was a tiny voice.

He left you behind. He doesn't love you anymore. Who would want you anyway?

"Shut up!" Cassie hissed into the darkness. She could feel the cramps tightening in her belly, her breathing coming short and sharp. She would not think about it. Like the unshed tears, her deepest thoughts about her father's new life were pushed aside.

She needed to get to the kitchen, to get some candles.

Determined, she took a step away from the stairs, her hands held out in front of her, groping across the large, open hallway. Stepping forward she knocked into a piece of furniture and something ceramic smashed to the ground, the noise echoing off the high walls.

"Crap!" That hadn't been there earlier on.

If the inhabitants of the house were not awake they would be soon.

There was a noise from upstairs, the sound of movement. Someone was coming. Cassie's heart beat sped up. Maybe, just maybe, a little part of her was still afraid of the dark. Moving with as much speed as was possible she retreated her way back up the steps to the landing.

She was about to call out, rationalising that it was her mother coming to see what all the noise was. But what if it was Mrs. Rivers? Cassie stopped in the hallway and held her breath, anxiety making her hands shake. The faintest glow of candle light advanced down the west corridor towards her. Cassie waited. The west corridor was supposed to be closed off.

Around the corner came a girl, a year or two younger than Cassie with a long plait of corn coloured hair hanging over her right shoulder. She was small and slim, a cream night shirt of some sort sweeping down her body to the floor. Cassie could see pink toes peeking out from underneath the material. The girl stopped in her tracks when she saw Cassie, the light from her candle flickering.

"Who the hell are you?" Cassie demanded. Had Mrs. Rivers taken on another member of staff? Was there someone visiting, whom Cassie didn't know about?

"Lady Cassandra?" The girl's voice was low, tainted with a hint of apprehension. She kept her eyes downcast.

"Lady who?" Cassie asked, her brow wrinkling in confusion. The girl's gaze jumped to Cassie's face before returning to the floor. There was an expression of disbelief on her features. They both stood in silence.

Finally, the girl stepped towards Cassie, her hand outstretched. Cassie had seen enough movies to know that if this was a ghost, the hand would pass straight through her. She stood stock still and waited. The girl's fingers touched the sleeve of Cassie's hoodie and lingered for a minute, rubbing the material. Her eyes were large and something akin to fear showed in them. They were a deep green colour, strangely familiar in some way. Cassie could feel her breath and see the detail of her face. This was no ghost. "Who are you?" demanded Cassie.

"Lady Cassandra, I..."

"Can you stop calling me that! I'm not a lady and nobody has called me Cassandra since my mum put it on my birth certificate seventeen years ago."

The girl stared at her blankly, her head inclined to one side.

"Well?" inquired Cassie.

"I do not know what to say to please ya, Mistress. I heard a noise, havin' just retired upstairs from pressin' your gowns…"

"My gowns?"

The girl continued hesitantly. "Yes, me lady. Ya requested yer ridin' habit for the mornin' and an evenin' gown to receive visitors. Am I mistaken?"

Cassie thought the ghost girl was about to cry, tears welled up in her eyes.

"I need to speak to my mother." Of all the people in the house, Judge Miller would be able to make sense of the situation.

The girl gasped, a shaky hand coming to her lips. "Me lady, yer mother…yer mother," she said slowly, "…she is dead."

Cassie felt the blood drain from her face. "This is not funny. Take me to my mother immediately."

The girl stepped towards her, a look of pained concern on her face.

Cassie was having none of it. "I will scream this house down if you come one step closer."

"Lady Cassandra," the girl implored, "if Miss Blythe or yer father were to hear ya, I…"

"My father?" Cassie took a step towards the young girl and grasped her by the collar of her long nightdress, "My father does not live here anymore!"

The girl remained still, her breath coming even, she did not struggle, she did not move, her eyes she kept lowered, only raising her gaze when Cassie stopped talking.

"Madame, yer father is here," she whispered. "He is asleep as we speak. Doctor Brown gave him a tonic and he is restin'. Miss Blythe is yer governess and has been these last score years." The girl took a step back, causing Cassie to loosen her hold on the material of her night dress. "Ya are so strangely dressed me Lady and yer hair…" the girl was staring at the pink ends of Cassie's hair, at the piercings in her ears. "Perhaps ya swooned from foul air?"

Cassie looked at the girl and said nothing. Her mind was racing. What the hell was going on? "What's your name?" she asked.

"Molly, me Lady."

"Molly what?"

"Molly Quinn, Madame."

"And who are you, Molly?"

"I am yer new lady's maid, Ma'am."

"Lady's maid?"

"Yes."

"What is that then?"

"Well I have only recently been promoted from housemaid to lady's maid, so I am learnin' as I go. I hope ya are not displeased with me?" The girl's eyes grew round with alarm. Cassie shook her head to signal for her to continue.

Taking a deep breath, she carried on. "I help ya dress in the mornin'. I make sure ya have a fire in yer room. I make sure yer meals are properly prepared. I look after yer wardrobe, yer toilette. I accompany ya if ya wish to go out, if Miss Blythe is busy. I see to it that yer letters are sent or delivered...I...I..." Her voice faded and she looked uncomfortable.

Cassie was staring at her, her mouth hanging open. The wind whipped against the outside of the windows, sounding eerily like a banshee. Cassie thought that the girl must be slightly mad.

"Me lady," she ventured, "perhaps ya should return to yer chamber? I would not wish ya to catch cold."

"You're the one who is running around in that ridiculous sheet," Cassie gestured to the night dress.

"Sheet, me lady?"

Cassie shook her head, "Never mind. The wolf mirror, the one with the carving of the two wolves on it..." began Cassie, hoping that the girl would know something. "I think I..." Cassie paused, unsure if she should verbalise the thoughts she was having. "I think I saw something weird in it."

"Weered, ma'am?" Molly's brow puckered.

"Weird. You know, weird, strange, odd?"

Molly shook her head. "Perhaps ma'am," she said cautiously, "we should retire to yer room?" The lady's maid did a little curtsy and looked at the floor as if afraid Cassie would strike her.

Cassie's lips twitched. The girl was simply making a suggestion.

Was Cassie that scary? "Right, let's go." Cassie began to move in the direction of her room, the lady's maid following a step behind, the flicker of her candle light elongating Cassie's already large shadow. "What are you doing?" she asked, irritated.

"Followin' ya, me lady."

"Yeah, I've noticed, but why are you back there? There is plenty of room to walk beside me."

Molly paused for a fraction of a second. "It is not customary for servants to walk next to their mistresses."

Cassie turned and stared at the girl. The light of her candle cast an eerie golden sheen over her pale skin and Cassie felt herself shiver. She remembered the wolf carvings and how it glowed in the flash of lightening. She felt a stone of dread lodge in her stomach. She half whispered into the darkness, "Molly, what year is it?"

"The year is 1714 Lady Cassandra. Why do ya ask?"

Chapter Five

~ Cassie ~

"Oh, my God, oh my God, oh my God."

Cassie couldn't pinpoint the exact moment when she began to lose the plot, repeating the same three words over and over again. She had a vague recollection of Molly half dragging, half carrying her along the corridor towards her bedroom.

Who was this girl, and why had she told Cassie that it was 1714? Her brain kept trying to make sense of what was going on. The year was 2014.

At the heavy, cream coloured door to the Japanese room Cassie shook herself free from Molly's firm grip. She pushed the door open and reached, out of habit, for the light switch. The palm of her flattened hand came in contact with smooth wallpaper. Molly held up the candle to illuminate the way. Cassie peered in the cream glow at the perfection of the imported silk. It was beautifully bright, even in the dimness of the night time. Cassie could make out the lacquered hair of the workers in the rice fields, bending to pick their crops. The bamboo-like foliage was wispy and delicate. It was only wallpaper, Cassie rationalised, but it took her breath away with its beauty.

Molly was traversing the perimeter lighting candle after candle to dispel the gloom. As the candle-flicker began to illuminate the room Cassie tried to compare before and after. There was a fireplace, small embers of pink glowing in the grate. Last time she checked, it had been bricked up, a plaster board wedged in front of the unsightly opening. Molly bent down and blew on the embers bringing them back from the brink of extinction. The girl reached into the pit of a black bucket, drawing out kindling and sods of earthy peat. Expertly, she arranged them around the coals in the grate.

Cassie began to pace, taking some comfort from the light of the two candles on the mantle, the candle on the writing desk in the corner, and the last one perched precariously on some kind of white table. There was a large circular hole cut in the flat surface of the timber and beneath it, a small shelf. A towel of scratchy linen was draped over the edge.

Shaking her head, she tried to think of possible explanations as to what was happening. Was this person, this lady's maid, completely off her rocker? Should Cassie force her way to her mother's room, tackling Molly to the floor? Should she start shouting for help? She rubbed her hands together, blowing on them. Her room was very cold.

Why was it so cold? It was autumn time for God's sake! She moved to the window and pulled back the heavy peach coloured drapes. The night was dark but on the horizon, at the furthest point of her vision she could make out the hints of daylight. The storm was clearing. The day would be lovely, fresh and bright. What time was it anyway? She had no idea.

Cassie pulled her mobile phone from her back pocket and flicked the screen. Nothing. It was completely dead. She pushed a few buttons but no response. Shaking it in frustration she flung it on the bed and continued her fast, impulsive strides from one side of the bedroom to the next.

"Crap!" she said out loud, to nobody in particular.

Molly stood up from the fireplace and turned towards Cassie, her face a strange mottled red, "Me lady, it is not yer custom to speak in such a manner. May I call somebody? Miss Blythe perhaps? I am beginnin' to fear for ya."

"Fear for me?" questioned Cassie.

"Yes, me Lady," the girl looked uncomfortable, "not that it is my place to say, ma'am. But ya are wearin' the strangest of clothes. And men's clothin' at that."

Cassie looked down at her well-worn jeans and trainers and said,

"What do you mean?" She looked up at Molly, who was shaking her head.

"Lady Cassandra, ya are the lady of the house. If Miss Blythe were to see ya, ma'am, I dread to think." The girl looked positively ashen now in the light of the candles. "Yer mother, ma'am, if I may be permitted to say."

"No, you can't. Be permitted to say. Leave my mother out of this." Cassie expected some challenge but the girl merely bowed her head and uttered a meek apology. Cassie continued, "I know two things. My mother," Cassie rubbed her cheek unconsciously, "is very much alive and kicking. My brother..."

"Brother, Miss?"

"Yeah, Jonah, the little toad—is alive and well, as of approximately six hours ago."

"Me lady, ya have a sister, Miss Elizabeth. She is ten years old." Molly looked at her pityingly.

Cassie took a step towards her. "No. No I don't. I have a brother. My name is Cassie Miller. I am seventeen years old. I live in London. I go to Winchester Abbey Girls School..."

"Ma'am, ya are a lady. Ya do not go to school!" Molly was folding and unfolding her hands. Cassie noticed that they were red and chapped.

"Molly, I'm not Lady Cassandra. You have me mixed up with someone else." She looked to Molly for agreement but the maid just stood there watching her, a look of concern in her eyes.

"See." Cassie grabbed a handful of her hair, shaking it in Molly's direction. "I have pink at the end of my hair. Is that something a lady would do?"

Molly shook her head, silent, glancing past Cassie to the bed and the powerless mobile phone.

"You see this, Molly?" Cassie went to the bed and sat down heavily, reaching for the discarded phone. "It's a mobile. We use it to phone our friends and family."

"Phone?" asked Molly.

"Ring. Call. You know. Telephone?"

Molly shook her head.

"Oh for the love... Okay. Here is what I remember. There was a

37

storm. I got up and decided to go to the east wing."

"To see yer father?"

"No, Molly, I keep telling you. My dad is not here. I went to the east wing to...well, never mind. I went there and the power got cut and I was standing in front of the mirror and then...and then..." Cassie stopped in her rendition of events.

The wolf mirror, the flash, just before the power cut.

Cassie pushed herself back up off the bed and went towards Molly, her eyes burning bright. "Molly, in the mirror, I saw her."

"Who?" whispered the servant.

"*Your* Lady Cassandra. She was standing there, here, somewhere and I saw her reflection for a split second. I couldn't figure it out, she was wearing a similar sheet as that thing you're wearing."

Molly glanced down at her nightdress.

"And she looked a little like me, except with lighter hair and she...well, then she just disappeared, the lights went out and the next thing I remember I woke up on the floor."

Cassie turned her back to Molly and began to pull the end of her t-shirt from her jeans, then glanced over her shoulder. "Look Molly, look. My new tattoo. I can't be Lady Cassandra. I imagine she wouldn't have one of these and you help dress her so you would know."

Molly took a step closer and looked down at the design at the base of Cassie's spine. Cassie noted with satisfaction that the redness had receded and it was healing nicely. In another few days, she wouldn't even notice the discomfort.

Molly was bending closer, her eyebrows pulling together into a frown, her mouth forming an alarmed "O". After a few seconds, the girl straightened up, her face devoid of any colour. "If ya are not Lady Cassandra," she uttered, "then where is she? And how do we get her back?"

Cassie shook her head. "I don't know."

A thousand thoughts were whirling around Cassie's head. She could barely keep them all from spilling out, leaking all over the floor. She needed to sit down.

She stumbled towards the fireplace, her feet failing to work properly.

"Oh my god, oh my god, oh my god."

Cassie sank to her knees in front of the grate and stretched her fingers towards the virgin flame, warming her cold hands. The fire was beginning to emit a small but steady stream of heat, the peat and embers mixing together to fuel the blaze. Molly hovered close by, her chapped hands red and angry looking.

Cassie reached up and tugged at Molly. "It's freezing, Molly, come on, sit down. We need to figure this out."

Molly's face was blank. "It would not be proper, ma'am, for a lady to sit on the floor and less proper for her maid to be next to her in such...such...companionship."

Cassie rolled her eyes. "Really? Your boss is such a snob! She doesn't let you sit with her? She doesn't talk to you?"

"Lady Cassandra is my mistress. I am her servant." Molly looked down at her bare feet, averting her gaze.

Cassie shrugged her shoulders and reached up for the girl's hand again, tugging gently. "Okay, Molly, but I'm not your mistress and I would like if you would agree to be my friend. As of right now, if what you say is true then you are the only person I know, in the whole world. Literally!"

Molly hesitated for a second before dropping to her knees. "Do ya think, ma'am, that Lady Cassandra is where ya came from?"

Cassie inhaled sharply. What if snobby Lady Cassandra was in her room, in her house? What would her mother say? She probably wouldn't even notice that Cassie was missing, probably be glad of it. Cassie pushed the thought to the back of her mind. She needed to concentrate on herself, on her own predicament and find a way out of it.

"What are we going to do, Molly? Who should we ask for help?"

"Pardon, Miss?"

"Should we talk to the guy, the dude..."

Molly looked at her blankly.

"The guy who is in charge?" continued Cassie.

"Guy? I do not know what that word means, ma'am, but the person in charge of this house is Lord Miller." The servant girl looked to the fireplace. Cassie stared at her, waiting. "He is very unwell, me Lady." Molly got up from the floor and walked to the window, her back to the fireplace. Silence descended. The girl sniffed a few times and Cassie wondered if she was crying.

"Molly..."

"Ya do not understand. The future for all of us..." She turned back around and retraced her steps, the glisten of fresh tears on her cheeks. "His lordship is desperately ill. They say... There are rumours that he...that he...might not live much longer. Ya are," she paused, "Lady Cassandra is the oldest child, the heir to Ludlow Park."

"Yeah?" Cassie was leaning toward her, listening intently to every word.

"So that means the house will go to ya, her, on Lord Miller's death."

"Yes? So?"

Molly hesitated, frustration evident in her stance. "Only if she is married."

Cassie tutted, "What? That's cracked!"

"Cracked. Broken. However ya like to describe it, this is the way o' things."

Cassie rocked back on her heels, considering. "So what happens if she is not married?"

Molly was quiet for a minute. Eventually she answered. "The house and grounds of Ludlow Park, an estate that has been in the family for over a hundred years, will pass to a cousin."

"The whole thing? The whole house? And what happens to you?"

"To me and all the other servants who work at the house and on the estate. Well," she gazed in to the flames, "Mr. Huxley can do whatever he likes."

"Fire you?"

"Set fire to us?" Molly inhaled sharply, "No ma'am, whatever stories I have heard about Mr. Huxley, I doubt that he would set fire to us. His lordship has met him a few times in London and says he is a kind enough gentleman."

Cassie smiled. "No, I mean, fire you, let you go, get rid of you."

Molly shrugged her shoulders. "I suppose so, as the new Lord of Ludlow, he can do as he pleases."

They remained silent for some time, watching the flickering fire and hearing the morning calls of the birds.

"So I take it," began Cassie, breaking the silence, "Lady Cassandra didn't have a boyfriend or fiancé or something like that?"

Molly shook her head. "No, the choice...the options were not really to Lady Cassandra's taste."

"The boys are pretty skanky then?"

Molly frowned.

"Never mind. Okay, so the option of marriage is not something that is likely to happen. So we are left with the prospect of Huxley." Molly wasn't paying attention. She was playing with the ends of her nightgown. "Molly? What are you thinking?"

"Nothin' ma'am..."

Cassie swatted at her hand. "Can you stop calling me that? I'm not a sixty-year-old lady. It is Cassie. That is my name. No ma'am, no miss, no lady."

Molly nodded once, a look of resignation crossing her features, as if she was admitting that this strange situation could indeed be happening. "I do not know if I should say anythin' ma...Cassie, but the servants below stairs, they think, they believe. Well the rumour is that Lord Miller has been deterioratin' very quickly, with an illness that nobody has really seen before and for such a healthy man too... It is odd..." Her voice faded.

Cassie's eyes were large, "What are you saying Molly?"

Suddenly the door of the room opened and a thin girl with a soot-blackened faced proceeded into the room. Molly jumped to her feet and stepped in front of Cassie, blocking her view. "Betty. Leave the coal box there. I will see to the fire today," she instructed.

Betty looked sufficiently startled at the sight of Molly that she didn't pay attention to the person on the floor. Molly shuffled her out of the door and closed it after her with such speed that Cassie was unsure what had just happened. She was about to ask what was going on when Molly turned on her, a look of panic in her eyes.

"Ya have to get up ma...Cassie...ya have to get up, get dressed. We have to do somethin' about yer..." Molly looked her up and down, a fleeting expression of distaste blurring her plain but pretty features, "attire."

Another gentle knock on the door interrupted their conversation.

"Oh no!" Molly moved quickly to the door. "Please not Miss Blythe." Straightening her shoulders and assuming a more composed demeanour, Molly opened the door. Cassie could do nothing from her place by the fire except watch in horror as stranger after stranger began to force their way into her fragile reality. The soft conversation at the door would not reach across the distance but Cassie could see Molly's shoulders relax a fraction and she assumed that the person on the other side of the door was not whom she had expected.

Molly closed the door and leaned against it for a second. The morning was evident now, the pale fingers of light creeping under the heavy curtains. Cassie pushed herself up into a standing position. "What's that in your hand?"

Molly was holding a sturdy jug. "Water for yer mornin' toilette."

Cassie squinted. "I don't think I'm going to like this."

Molly moved towards the strange piece of furniture on the other side of the room, next to the window and slipped a porcelain bowel into the circle which had been cut out of the timber. The bowl nestled neatly and Cassie moved forward to peer at the contents. Molly poured the tepid water in to the bowl, dipped a linen towel into it and handed it to Cassie. "To wash yer face and hands with, ma'am, in the mornin' time."

Cassie looked at the cloth. "I don't think so, Molly. I showered this morning. I'm okay for now."

Molly looked at her unmoving, the towel dripping water on the bare timber floor. "Until we figure out what to do, Ma'am, I am afraid the only solution is that ya will have to become Lady Cassandra. And to do that," Molly waved the cold cloth at her, "ya will have to do all the things a lady does. We are stuck, till we figure out how to get ya home and how to get my mistress back."

Cassie took a minute to reflect on what she said and she had to admit the options were looking very slim. "Do I have to wear a dress?" she asked warily.

"Yes, Miss."

Cassie stepped forward and accepted the cold cloth, pressing it fleetingly to her cheek and temple.

"I shall get yer corset, ma'am, and yer hoop." Molly turned and made for the door.

"Corset... Hoop?" whispered Cassie. "Holy crap."

Chapter Six

~ Cassandra ~

Cassandra's toes were pleasantly warm. It was going to be an unusually mild autumn day. She could sense the light of the morning creeping under the curtains, the brightness of it warming her eye lids. Usually, at this time of year, she needed double stockings to combat the chill. She wriggled her toes. They were bare.

Doctor Brown was due and Cassandra knew that she would be expected to be up and dressed, ready to receive him. There was something unsettling about the doctor. His eyes were continually darting from one object to the next, never focusing on her, not even when she addressed him directly.

There was also the small matter of his treatments. Cassandra had entered her father's chamber one evening unannounced to find the doctor administering to his patient. She had almost swooned at the sight. Several leeches were attached to her father's chest and forearms. They were shiny in the lamp light and Cassandra imagined she could hear them sucking the blood from the prone figure in the bed. She shuddered at the memory.

The doctor was not a young man to be sure, small in stature with no great weight to his frame. But he was spritely enough for a man of his age. He had come all the way from London last year to take up residence in a well-equipped house on the other side of the village. Cassandra hadn't passed any notice, what would she need with a doctor?

"I require respite from the toils and torments of London. Country life suits me." That is what he told his housekeeper.

Of course, the village people did not believe him for an instant. Cassandra had heard a string of wild rumours. But try as the local gossips might, they could not unearth any lasting defamation. The doctor's reputation as a competent physician was safe.

"We should order a prime cut of meat for dinner this evening, Miss Miller. The doctor may call." Miss Blythe always advised *'be prepared'*. But Doctor Brown rarely conceded to stay unless to carry out a night vigil over his patient.

"I am indebted to you, Doctor Brown." She had told him so upon their last meeting, and he merely nodded, his wet eyes darting from one object of furniture to the next, never settling.

However, that was not important now. She must get up and get dressed. The servants would need to stoke the fire, for as warm as it felt in her bed, she knew when her toes touched the timber of the floor boards, the cold would nip relentlessly at her feet. She was reluctant to open her eyes, savouring the last echoes of sleep.

A piercing screech interrupted her reverie. Her eyelids flared open. She was momentarily blinded by the morning light. Cassandra's heart was in her mouth, panic welling within her. That noise, that terrible screech, what was it? She pushed back the covers, the material catching in her limbs, pinning her down. There was a box beside her, with numbers, flashing red; the source of the wailing. She stared around her disorientated. She had to make the noise stop. She pushed the box gingerly with her index finger. It edged a millimetre across the bedside table.

There were several buttons on the top of it and Cassandra leaned forward, peering at them. Words that she did not understand were painted on the box. *Snooze, Alarm, Sleep,* and *Radio*. Cassandra gazed at the numbers as they changed, as if they were counting upwards. The red numbers said 7.15. She was unsure how to proceed, so she did the only thing she could. Taking a deep breath, she banged the top of the box with the flat palm of her hand. The noise stopped abruptly.

Cassandra exhaled slowly, her heart rate returning to normal.

She sat bolt upright, her eyes large and focused. Her bed cover was different. She reached for her shawl to put on over her night gown, but the chair next to her bed had been moved. How was she expected to get out of bed with nothing to cover her shoulders? In the first instance, it would be indecent to parade around the place with no shawl and on a more practical level she would catch a chill.

Where was her lady's maid? She needed to dress. At this hour of the day, with the servants and workmen around the estate she could not leave her room unless attired correctly. Her maid should know better. To be thus inconvenienced was unacceptable. She would have to have harsh words with Molly.

She reached beside the bed, fumbling with the material of her drapes searching for the cord of the bell. She was becoming concerned, feeling the pulse in her body beat faster. Keep your head, she counselled herself. Just keep calm.

Cassandra pushed herself forward a little and gazed around the room. The cover on her bed was made from some strange material. The new wallpaper was dull and faded. The floorboards were covered with a striped rug and the drapes at the window were a different colour. In the corner was a Japanese tea chest, something she had not seen before.

Her writing desk was nowhere to be found. Instead a tall box with two silver handles stood on the opposite side of the room, blocking the entrance to her dress closet. A black bag of some sort lay abandoned in front of the tall timber box. She wondered if she could find a shawl or some clothing in there.

Cassandra cocked her head to one side and listened intently, fingering the gold locket that hung around her neck. There was no sound of the servants moving along the corridor, no sign of the girl who came and stoked the fire. Cassandra glanced at the grate. A timber board was positioned across the fireplace.

This was just ridiculous, she rationalised silently. How was she expected to keep warm if someone had blocked up her only means of heat? Her indignation made her brave. She flung back the covers and stalked over to the black bag. She bent down to examine its contents.

It contained an unusual article of clothing made from a stiff, tight-fibred material. She pulled it out, lifting it in front of her. It was some kind of blue trousers, the type a man would wear. She flung it aside.

Next, she pulled out the strangest looking top article of clothing. The material was heavy and downy, yet light to the touch. It had a metal band going up the front and a hood with strings. Cassandra supposed she could wear it as a type of shawl and draped it over her shoulders. Now, what was she going to do with her lower half? She would go to the hall momentarily and call for her maid but until she was someway covered, that action was not possible.

The door to the room opened and Cassandra, determined to chastise her lady's maid for being remiss, turned around. She hiccuped and stumbled back to the bed. A boy, of about eight or nine stood in the doorway, a solid rectangular book in his hand. What looked like tiny ants were moving across the page.

"Who are you?" questioned Cassandra, backing away. "Where is my maid? I demand that you leave my chamber this instant and send me my dress maid."

The boy stared at her. He was wearing the strangest clothes Cassandra had ever seen. Unlike the serving boys from below stairs, this child seemed clean, well nourished. He took a few more steps in to the room. Cassandra backed towards the wall, gripping the makeshift shawl at her shoulders.

"Chill out, Cass. Mum said you were acting weird. But then, what's new."

Cassandra looked at him, remaining tight-lipped.

He moved to the bed and flopped onto it, before stretching out, his attention focused on the thing in his hands, his fingers randomly pushing buttons. Strange music played from the contraption.

Cassandra moved slowly around the outside of the room, the door being her destination. I must not faint, I must not faint, she repeated silently to herself. That was the sort of thing ladies did and surely the current situation was perfect for a spell of nerves.

She was three quarters of the way around the room, the door only inches away. The boy glanced up, his brow furrowed. "What is with you? You are acting really strange. And what happened to your hair?"

Cassandra fingered the end of her braid, hoping that her long hair was still in one piece. She looked at the boy and with trepidation began, "Boy". He snorted at her address but remained silent. "Where is my maid?"

"Your maid? You mean Mrs. Rivers? If Mum heard you calling her that, she would flip."

"Mum?" The word seemed strange on Cassandra's lips.

"Ya dunce, you know, mum…the person you are always shouting at. Your parent."

"My mother is dead," answered Cassandra plainly.

The boy sat up. "Why are you always so mean? You make things rubbish around here, fighting all the time, doing stupid things to get yourself in trouble. If only you would try to be nicer then maybe you and Mum would…" His voice trailed away and he sniffed.

Cassandra looked at him more closely. He was crying. Instinctively, she took a step towards him. "What is your name?" she asked.

"Don't be stupid. You know my name. I'm your brother. I'm Jonah."

Cassandra went towards the bed and leaned against it, not setting her full weight upon it, in case she needed to escape quickly. She looked at the boy and with compassion for his lost mind began to explain, "I do not have a brother. I have a sister, Elizabeth. My mother is not alive anymore. I am Lady Cassandra of Ludlow Park. And you, boy, are in my chambers."

His mouth hung open a little and it took him a minute to formulate a response. "You are Cassie Miller, you're seventeen years old, you're my big sister and your sense of humour sucks. I'm going to tell Mum you are being mean to me." And with that he hopped up from the bed and exited the room.

It took her a moment to gather her thoughts and begin to search for her clothing again. She glanced at the big timber box in the corner and approached cautiously. The handles were some sort of dull metal. She touched them with the tips of her finger before grasping them more firmly and tugging. The doors opened easily enough and inside were several articles of clothing.

It was a standing trunk box. Very strange, she thought. The clothes hung on rounded metal hooks and were an assortment of shapes, colours and patterns, none of which were familiar to Cassandra. She fingered the material dubiously before choosing a long skirt from the far corner of the trunk. It was made from a light material and lined with only one inner layer. There were patterns of pink flowers all over it and it smelled musty from disuse.

"It will be impossible to fashion this over my undergarments," she said out loud. She pulled the skirt on over her nightgown, unwilling to discard anything she was wearing. Next, she undid the makeshift shawl that was draped over her shoulders. She examined the ties to the front, a long band of silver, like interlocked teeth. After some struggle, she managed to get the teeth open. She slipped her arms in to the sleeves and drew the garment tighter across her torso. On the shelf, at the top of the standing clothes trunk, she spotted a piece of ribbon. It was pink in colour and made from some kind of cheap satin. She wrapped it around her waist, cinching in the sleeved shawl, and forming a nice bow at the front. She did not bother trying to slip her feet in to any sort of slippers as there were none in sight. She would have to do as she was.

She turned and looked at the door. It was time to leave the room and investigate what utter madness was going on. She would have an explanation. As she took a step across the room the door opened to admit a woman, wearing pants. Cassandra emitted a startled sound, choking back her surprise.

The woman was in her middle years, with short shoulder length hair. Her eyes were grey and sharp and her dress was anything if not completely bizarre. She wore men's trousers in black material and a shirt of white. Underneath it, Cassandra could make out the outline of some kind of restrictive under garment. Squaring her shoulders, she addressed the woman. "Who are you? And what are you doing in my chamber?"

The woman looked at her in surprise, appraising her outfit. "Cassie…" The woman stepped forward, her hand outstretched.

"Desist in calling me that. You will address me by my proper title. I am Lady Cassandra Miller of Ludlow Park and you, madam, are trespassing in my house." Cassandra did not feel as confident as she sounded, but if Miss Blythe had taught her anything useful, it was how to appear composed and in control at all times.

"Cassie." The woman's voice held a hint of reproach. "You passed out last night. Don't you remember? Mrs. Rivers found you in the east wing. There was a storm."

Cassandra frowned. Yes, she remembered something about a storm. Yes, come to think of it. She glanced at the fireplace. The candles, the embers, she had gone to see her father in the middle of the night. "Where is my father? I wish to see him," she demanded.

The woman was silent for a minute, a hard expression crossing her features, "Your father is in France, Cassie. You know that."

Cassandra moved towards the bed and sat down heavily. She should be poised and composed but she could not stop the trembling that over took her. She was afraid that she might start to shriek.

The woman came and sat down beside her, resting her hand gently on Cassandra's thigh. "Cassie, you banged your head last night. Mrs. Rivers came across you by the mirror at the beginning of the east wing. You could have been lying there for a long time, for all we know. I have phoned the doctor."

Cassandra pushed her hand away. "No! No doctor. I will not be leeched. I will not!" The ferocity and fear in her voice were almost equally matched. She moved across the room and out the door, her voice catching in her throat. "I will see Miss Blythe about this."

The boy, Jonah, was standing at the end of the corridor in the doorway of Miss Blythe's room. When he saw her, he disappeared inside and closed the door firmly. Cassandra paused in her progress and looked around her. The hallway was different, pieces of furniture missing. She moved steadily to the stairs and began to descend. The family portraits were there, as always but some of the faces were different, some she did not recognise. Where was her mother's portrait?

She took the stairs, two at a time, in an ungainly manner until she got to the hallway. Forgetting all of her instructions in propriety she began to scream, yelling at the top of her lungs, calling for Miss Blythe, Cook, her father, anyone who could aid her. The woman appeared at the head of the stairs, her face streaked with panic. "Cassie," she called, concerned.

Cassandra turned and ran towards the kitchen, sure that someone would be there, a maid, the slops girl, someone, anyone. She stumbled down the cool corridor and along the passageway, tears blurring her vision. In the kitchen, the stout preparation table was missing, the copper pots, the hanging foul, the big vats for preparing soup and the scrubbing board, the baskets for bread and eggs; all were missing. Instead, large white boxes with handles lined the walls. There was a woman at the sink, washing dishes, bright yellow gloves stretching to her elbows. She turned and looked at Cassandra, her head slightly cocked to one side.

"I told you not to go to the east wing," she said, in a slow, drawn out voice.

Cassandra tilted her chin a fraction. "And who are you to tell the lady of the house what to do?"

"No one, me lady. I'm no one."

For a fraction of a second Cassandra thought the voice sounded familiar.

Chapter Seven

~ Cassie ~

To list her many discomforts, Cassie would have to start with the corset. According to Molly, and she should know, the awful contraption was called a stays. The thing itself was boned all the way around and when fastened into it, Cassie felt her posture straighten, her waist cinched in. Molly methodically laced the ribbon, pulling the thing tighter and tighter.

"Molly, I can't breathe." Cassie was holding onto the timber post of the bed, as Molly tugged the corset closed.

"Straighten up, Miss. Ya need to straighten up."

Cassie pulled back her shoulders, stretching to her full height. The pressure lessened a little, making it easier for her to suck in a lungful of air.

Next, Molly produced a huge contraption, shaped like a small boat. "Step in," she advised, nodding her head towards the hoop.

Cassie looked at her, unsure. "You want me to get into it?"

"Yes, hurry, please, Miss." The hint of panic in the servant's voice made Cassie move. "I still have to dress yer hair and I am not sure how that is goin' to work unless we cut it."

Cassie's hand flew to her hair, which tumbled loose around her bare shoulders. "No way. You're not cutting my hair." The pink ends stood out against the pale fabric of her stays. "I'll get into that stupid looking hoop thing, but you're not cutting my hair."

Cassie lifted her leg and stepped into the hoop, her undergarments already restricting her movement.

"It is a pannier, Miss"

"A what?"

"A cane and linen hooped petticoat. It gives yer dress the proper shape."

"Proper according to who?" asked Cassie, her patience waning. Molly reached around her small waist and pulled the ribbons tight, securing the hoop. Cassie took a few steps, moving cautiously as the contraption bounced around her, threatening to get in the way of her legs.

"Now, Miss, I shall bring in yer dress."

"More stuff? I already feel totally overloaded."

"Yes, well, ya cannot go around unclothed. I believe people would take note."

The girl smiled the smallest of smiles and Cassie got the impression that she might be enjoying herself. The lady's maid disappeared through a door in the far wall. Cassie had not noticed it before. It was covered in the silk wallpaper and the joins were practically seamless. It appeared as if she had her very own walk in wardrobe.

"Carrie Bradshaw, eat your heart out," she said out loud, as she raised her hands and tilted her head back. The last couple of hours had been totally surreal and it surprised her how calm she was. Okay, so she was stuck in a different century, it might be cooler than having to listen to her mother lecture her.

Two years ago, when she had a really bad cold, Cassie and her mum had watched *Pride and Prejudice*, the BBC version with Colin Firth. Cassie didn't know what the big deal was, had found the programme kind of dull, but her mother was hooked. At the time, Cassie was just glad to be spending time with her mum, regardless of the viewing material. It might be the wrong century but at least Cassie had some idea what to expect.

The rustle of material heralded Molly's return. Cassie turned, pushing thoughts of home to the back of her mind. Her mouth dropped open when she saw the dress. It was a dusky pink colour, with full skirt and bodice. The material was embroidered expertly with coral-toned flowers. Delicate gold roping piped down the front of the bodice, ending at the waist, drawing the eye to the slenderness of the figure. Cassie had to admit, she was impressed.

"Wow! How am I going to get into that?"

"Why do ya think ya have a maid 'specially for helpin' ya dress?"

Cassie smirked; Molly's attitude to her stand-in-mistress was becoming a little lippy. Maybe Molly wasn't such a stick in the mud after all. Cassie let the maid help her into the dress. More tightening of ribbons and strings ensued until eventually Cassie was in, barely able to breathe but in nonetheless.

"Now, yer hair."

Cassie crossed her fingers as they moved towards the dressing table and the large mirror.

"I should be able to do somethin' with it, if I tuck the ends in a plait and then wrap the plait around."

Cassie exhaled loudly sitting down at the table, "Yeah, that sounds good."

"Ya will have to greet the doctor when he arrives and accompany him to yer father's room, then ya and Miss Blythe will retire for breakfast. Whatever ya do, ya must not give any indication that anythin' is amiss We cannot afford to raise suspicions."

Cassie looked at Molly in the mirror, her eyebrows arched. "I think the fact that I look like a rabbit caught in the headlights is proof enough that something is up?"

Molly pulled her hair back tightly winding it into a bun, securing the ends expertly with ribbon and pins. "Ya would pass for me mistress. Ya are perhaps a little taller and yer hair is not as light but ya look well enough alike."

Molly gave her one more critical look before adding, "Besides we do not have much of a choice. Ya must pass yerself as Lady Cassandra or …" She paused, her lip caught in between her teeth. Cassie could see the indecision. Molly was keeping something from her.

"Or what?"

"I do not know if I should say, Miss"

"Say!" demanded Cassie.

"The previous mistress, Lady Augustine…" Molly slipped another pin into Cassie's hair, buying time so she wouldn't have to speak.

Cassie glared at her in the mirror.

"The servants say that she was committed."

"Committed?" Cassie wasn't sure where this was heading.

"It is supposed to be a secret, Miss. Nobody is supposed to know. His Lordship never speaks of it. She went a bit mad you see, towards the end."

"Mad?" Cassie's face was draining of colour, her blood pressure plummeting. "What are you trying to tell me?"

"They say it runs in the family."

"Madness?"

Molly shrugged, unable to look her in the eye. "So ya see, ya have to convince everyone. Or ya are for the sanatorium."

Cassie twisted around in to look at Molly directly. "The sanatorium? You think I'm mad?"

The servant paused for a moment. "No. But I wonder, is it actually myself who has lost her wits for believin' in such a high tale. Only for I knowin' the mistress of this house so well, I would never believe it. One thing is for sure, Lady Cassandra Miller would never behave in the manner that ya do."

Cassie huffed. "Well, stuff Lady Cassandra Miller. I am not going to the loonie bin. I have to keep it together till we figure out the on/off switch on that blasted mirror. Ouch."

Molly jammed a pin tightly into her hair, skimming very close to Cassie's scalp. "Ladies never use profanities, Miss. And anyway," Molly eyed her creation, a large coil of hair on the top of Cassie's head. "maybe ya are here for a reason."

"A reason?" Cassie was sceptical.

"Yes, Miss. If ya did come through this wolf mirror, then maybe there is a reason for it. Maybe ya are supposed to do somethin'."

Cassie was about to argue but decided against it. Molly was still dangerously close to her head with sharp pins. She sat in silence as the girl completed her work, pondering on what the maid had said.

Finally, she was dressed. She looked like an idiot, poofie and pink. Her shoes were slip on, made from soft embroidered material. She was inexpertly trying to figure out how to move herself, her corset, the hoop and dress all in one go when there was a knock on the door.

A stern looking lady walked in without invitation and addressed

Cassie. "Lady Cassandra, you are late in your toilette this morning; no doubt the servant's dallying." She cast a dismissive glance in Molly's direction and sniffed. Cassie looked at the girl for help but she seemed busy gathering up the discarded clothing. Cassie noticed the lady's maid push a pair of trainers under the bed, out of view of Miss Blythe.

The governess was tall and thin, with mousy brown grey hair pulled back from her face. Her eyes were beady and bright with indignation, her nose sharp and pointy, her lips pursed together.

Oh great, thought Cassie, the governess is a totalitarian.

Cassie moved across the room slowly, conscious that it would not be advisable to rush. For a fleeting moment, she had an image of herself, upended in a mass of fabric, skirt, hoop, linen, unable to right herself. She smiled a tight smile and greeted the governess, hoping she sounded like Lady Cassandra.

"Good morning, Miss Blythe. I apologise for my lateness, I decided to change gowns. I wanted something appropriate for meeting Doctor Brown. It's always important to look your best."

Miss Blythe studied her, her beady eyes scrutinising her face. Cassie heard Molly drop a comb on the table behind her. "Tidy up, can't you?" she said dismissively, hoping that her tone was appropriate in addressing a servant. With a cursory glance over her shoulder Cassie swept, or waddled, with as much dignity and poise as she could muster out of the room and down the corridor, her hoop very nearly getting caught in the doorway.

I don't want to end up in a loony bin in 1714, but this is not going to work, she thought as she came to the top of the stairs, swaying in the unsteady heels.

"Lady Cassandra."

The tone of voice made Cassie stop in her tracks, vying for balance. She turned as expertly as she could manage and raised an eyebrow in what she hoped could be interpreted as nonchalance. "Yes?"

Miss Blythe swept beautifully to a stop beside her, regarding her over and down the bridge of her nose. "Doctor Brown is here and in your father's anti-room. Where he always waits to receive you. Have you forgotten?"

"No," snapped Cassie, hoping that her acting was convincing, "I was merely going to go downstairs to see if breakfast was ready." The governess looked at her, disbelief marring her imperfect features. "Never mind, Miss Blythe, let's go see this Doctor Brown." Cassie turned and headed in what she hoped was the right direction. Molly had said that Lord Miller's room was located in the east wing.

"Are you in good spirits this morn, Lady Cassandra?" enquired Miss Blythe as she walked along the corridor beside her.

Flip, thought Cassie, I've blown it already. Cassie took a minute to compose an answer based on what little she had deduced about Miss Blythe's character.

"To be honest, Miss Blythe, I feel a little off this morning. I didn't sleep very well last night and I will need your help today to get through all the stuff I have to do. I know your directions will be the best I could ask for, as you are of course so sensible and wise. If you would be so kind to assist me today, I would be very grateful." Cassie lowered her eyes and did her best to look forlorn.

The governess did not say anything for a minute, but as Cassie hoped, her pride had been tickled. "Why of course Lady Cassandra, you know I will assist in any manner I can."

They entered the east wing. It was strange for Cassie to be able to see all along the corridor, her view unimpeded by renovations. The gold mirror, as tall as a full-grown man hugged the wall. Cassie stared at it as they walked by. The immobile wolves were as she remembered. Perhaps she was imagining it but the air seemed cooler as they passed by.

Cassie noticed that Miss Blythe had slowed down as they approached the middle of the east wing. A large door loomed up ahead. She glanced to either side of the corridor. It was the biggest door in the wing and Cassie deduced that it was the door to Lord Miller's rooms. A mongrel of some sort was lying across the threshold snoring quietly. He stirred in his sleep and rose as they approached. He sniffed the air and began a low growl at the back of his throat, his attention focused solely on Cassie. She held her breath.

"Snap," called the governess, "stop that noise." She shooed him to one side. Cassie gripped the handle of the door, her palms sweaty. She had to get away from the dog before he jumped on her. She pushed the door open, stumbling her way into the room. Once inside she took a breath to steady herself.

It was a distinctly masculine room, tall bookshelves on one side, a large leather chair in front of a fireplace. There was a dark wool rug on the floor and several portraits along the walls. Cassie noticed the picture of a striking woman above the fireplace. She looked strangely familiar and Cassie assumed that this was the first and original Lady of Ludlow Park.

A man sat in a smaller, more understated chair to the other side of the fireplace. He was about forty years old, wearing short pants with white stockings pulled up to just below his knees. His coat had long tails hanging down the side of his chair. He wore it over a white, flouncy shirt. He was small, with deep brown eyes, a flat nose and greying hair, which was receding noticeably at the front. He had pulled it back into a greasy ponytail. Was this the doctor? She shuddered involuntarily.

He rose from his seat when she and Miss Blythe entered the room. When he spoke, his eyes darted from one side of the room to the next, his gaze never once resting on anything.

"Lady Cassandra." The *s* of her name sounding long and laboured. "You honour me with your presence this morning. I am about to attend to your father." He rose to leave the room, his retreating form prompting Cassie to speak out of turn.

"I will go with you," she practically shouted. Miss Blythe inhaled sharply. For a moment, Cassie stalled. Was the governess uneasy about the lack of etiquette or was it something else? A slow curl of apprehension unfolded in her belly. What if Lord Miller's sickness was contagious? It wasn't as if they had a local emergency room you could go to, a 24-hour pharmacy, a reputable doctor.

"Doctor Brown," the governess said as she moved towards the physician, her bony hand slightly outstretched. "Lady Cassandra is a little out of sorts today. Forgive her abruptness." Miss Blythe attempted to smile, but it looked more like a grimace. The doctor nodded sagely and moved to the door into Lord Miller's room. He shut it softly behind him leaving an empty silence in his wake.

Cassie stood still, her mind racing. What exactly was wrong with Lord Miller? What was the doctor doing to him? There was the sound of muffled voices from the interior of the bedroom. If Lord Miller was conscious and capable of conversation, then surely, he might be able to tell her something about his symptoms.

She walked quickly past Miss Blythe, not pausing, even though the governess called her name sharply. With a jolt of energy, she pushed open the heavy door and charged her way in, hooped skirts and all.

The bedroom was dark, similar to the anti-room. Rich tapestries hung on the wall, depicting hunting scenes. The bed at the centre of the room was large and decorated sumptuously. It contained a man, over which Doctor Brown was standing, a bloodied cloth in his hand.

"What are you doing?" she demanded, anger slowly creeping into her voice.

The man in the bed was obviously unwell. He was somewhere in his mid to late fifties, with a fine head of curling, steel-grey hair. His frame was large, but Cassie could tell from where she stood that he was withered. His face was familiar and she recognised it from the painting that hung at the top of the stairs in her own Ludlow Park. So this was Lord Miller. His milky eyes regarded her expectantly, "Cassandra," he rasped, holding out his spare hand towards her.

Doctor Brown held Lord Millers right arm outstretched away from the body. A rubber tie was secured tightly to just above the patient's bicep. At the junction between his forearm and upper arm, Doctor Brown had made an incision into the flesh. A white porcelain bowl was held underneath the arm and into it trickled a steady drip-drip of blood. Cassie stood still, unwilling to move, in case she passed out.

The doctor bent over his patient, applying pressure to the wound, but instead of trying to stop the blood flow, he was actively encouraging it. All of Cassie's first aid training came back to her in an instant and she took a step towards Lord Miller, demanding in a stronger voice, "What are you doing Doctor Brown?"

The doctor refused to answer for a moment as he finished squeezing blood into the bowl. Miss Blythe was behind her, a hand curling around her forearm, trying, unsuccessfully, to remove Cassie.

"Cassandra," her supposed father called her name again, his voice sounding weak. Cassie could not ignore the plea of a sick man and went towards him, taking his bony hand in hers.

"Father," she said, forcing the lie from her mouth, "How are you feeling?"

"Much better my dear, much better, Doctor Brown will see me right, will you not, my friend." He smiled a laboured smile at the doctor, his cheeks completely drained of colour now. The metallic smell of the blood accosted her nostrils and Cassie felt her stomach heave.

The doctor, finished in his task, took the bowl and covering it with a cloth, set it on the side table.

"I only feel the odd ache and pain my child. I have not slipped into any deep sleeps yet these last two days and I feel confident that I am rounding a corner," continued Lord Miller.

Cassie had nothing to say. Instead she smiled down at him and patted his hand reassuringly, the anger she felt inside burning hot. After several seconds, with a great deal of effort she managed to choke out a coherent sentence, "Perhaps Doctor Brown would help settle you in your bed and then come outside to have a word with me." She eyed the doctor with a stony stare. He nodded his head once, to show that he had heard her and began to dry his hands.

She left the room, promising that she would be back to visit Lord Miller soon. As the door clicked closed behind them both, Miss Blythe was upon her in an instant. "Lady Cassandra, you asked for my council earlier on this morning and really I feel it is my duty to advise you that your behaviour is very wanting. To speak in such a tone to Doctor Brown is quite shocking."

Cassie paced up and down the small area in the study, thinking, completely ignoring Miss Blythe. "Doctor Brown is a conscientious and talented surgeon; he has your father's best interests at heart."

"Best interests?" Cassie paused to stare at the governess. "He will bleed that poor man to death with his barbaric medical practices." Maybe that was his intent, to get rid of Lord Miller. The thought caused Cassie to stop dead, right in front of the governess whose cheeks were flushed. Cassie could see the indignation in the other woman's face and for a moment she wondered what kind of relationship Miss Blythe had with Doctor Brown.

Cassie's eyes widened. That was it. That was why the wolf mirror brought her here. Something very bad was happening at Ludlow Park and it was up to her to figure out what. Her job was to save Lord Miller, to save Ludlow Park. But from what or whom?

"Miss Blythe," she began cautiously, "I'm not sure that Doctor Brown's methods are the best. That's all. Lord M... My father has been unwell for some time and nobody seems to be able to pin point the cause or do anything to alleviate his suffering." She glanced at the governess who was watching her intently. "I simply," she emphasised, "wish to discuss his treatment with the doctor."

"Yes, but Lady Cassandra, it is not your place to question the good doctor, he is a learned man and after all, you are merely..." she paused.

"...merely..." coaxed Cassie.

"...merely a woman, my Lady. And a woman's duty is to her father and then to her husband..."

Cassie held up her hand. There was no good pretending to be in charge if you didn't get to act the part every now and then. "Miss Blythe, could you please go down and check that my breakfast is ready. I will follow you shortly."

The governess had been given a direct order by the lady of the house. This was evident. The fact that it had never happened before was also in evidence. A look of outrage clouded Miss Blythe's face. Cassie should probably have been more sensitive to the governess's position but right now she was intent on finding out what exactly, was wrong with Lord Miller. Cassie turned towards the door to her father's room, dismissing her companion by the position of her body.

She did not look around but she could hear the rustle of skirts as the woman exited. Cassie sighed and sagged in to a chair, uncomfortably aware of the restriction of her corset. Molly's words from earlier were ringing in her ears. Perhaps she was here for a reason.

Chapter Eight

~ Cassie ~

Cassie sat down in the chair to the front of the fireplace, bunching her skirts underneath her. The sharp hoop poked her as she shifted her position, trying to get comfortable. She needed to figure out what she was going to say to the doctor, how to demand an explanation without arising suspicion. That Lord Miller was unwell was obvious, but from what? Cassie had absolutely no idea how to help him.

The door to the chamber creaked open and Doctor Brown emerged. He was unrolling his shirt sleeves, bringing them down over his forearms. He did not look at her as he made his way to the seat opposite and sat down.

His expression was not defiant, there was respect in the way he addressed her but Cassie realised that he did not fear her. She tilted her chin a fraction and considered her first sentence carefully. She did not know how comfortable they were with each other or the correct tone to take. His practices seemed barbaric to her, but perhaps Miss Blythe was right, perhaps he was a great surgeon of his time. One thing was certain, if he continued to bleed Lord Miller, the old man would surely die. And if he died on Cassie's watch, she would be in big trouble.

"Doctor Brown," she began, smiling tightly at him, "I'm sorry for bursting in on you like that but I was anxious to see Lord...my father. I didn't think that you would be in the middle of...a procedure."

The doctor nodded his head and continued to avoid her gaze. Cassie bristled, irritation working its way through her.

"Can you please go over again the symptoms that my…father is suffering from and tell me how you hope to treat him?"

Doctor Brown leaned forward in his chair, avoiding her gaze, studying the rug in front of them. "Surely this is not something to concern yourself with, my Lady. The details of Lord Miller's condition might be too harsh for a woman's sensibilities?"

Cassie wanted to slap him. Thankfully she was too far away, her dress impaling her to the chair. "Yeah, well, as everyone keeps telling me, a lady's duty is to have children, which is a messy, bloody business. Wouldn't you agree? So I think that a woman's sensibilities will be able to handle details of diagnosis and treatment. If Lord Miller dies, then I will be head of this house." The threat of her words was evident. "I want to be informed."

There was a slight pause as the doctor hedged his bets. It was obvious that Cassie spoke sense. If Doctor Brown wanted to maintain his position in the neighbourhood it was important that he treat the prominent families. Luckily for Cassie, the most prominent family of all was the Miller family.

"His lordship suffers from lack of appetite, shivers, night sweats, hallucinations and at times has lapsed into coma. I have prescribed a tonic, and weekly blood lettings to help overcome this trial."

Cassie stared at him, her disbelief evident. She felt like giving the doctor a lesson in biology. Whatever was wrong with Lord Miller, cutting him and bleeding a pint of blood into a bowl was not going to fix him. If anything, it was this action that was making him worse. "What's in the tonic you are giving him?" she asked, to distract him while she thought of a plan of action.

The doctor shifted in his seat. "Really, my Lady, I am not accustomed…"

"What's in it?" she repeated, raising her voice a fraction.

"There are complicated ingredients; it is not within a woman's power to…"

"Please answer my question." Cassie could feel the blood rising to her cheeks.

The doctor paused for a moment, then, thinking better of it, continued. "Distilled alcohol, Wormwood for inflammation, Angelica root for digestion, Horseradish to clean the blood and quinine to reduce any fevers."

Cassie nodded, thinking the list of ingredients over. It seemed like the doctor was covering all bases; digestion, fever, inflammation. She looked at him, examining his features, the way his hands were folded on his lap, the ruffle of his socks, pulled up to his knees. His posture was alert but not tense, he seemed relatively at ease. What other kind of procedures was he carrying out in that room, behind closed doors? The thought made her shift in her seat. There was something very bad happening at Ludlow Park.

And it was up to Cassie to stop it.

If only she had the internet, then she could go on DocHelp, discover what happens to the body when you bleed it constantly. Sighing, she brought her attention back to the person sitting in front of her. She found herself caught in the confines of her dress, literally and figuratively. She could not lecture the doctor on anatomy and biology because she was a simple female and not supposed to know anything outside of embroidery and dancing. If she did manage to convince him of her knowledge she would probably be burned as a witch. Cassie wasn't quite sure of her history but the time period concerned her. Did they still do that in 1714?

And would that be worse than the alternative: she would be committed to the asylum, Ludlow Park given to the obnoxious Mr. Huxley, the wolf mirror never to be seen again and Cassie, stuck in the year 1714. She shivered in the coolness of the room. "How often do you give my father the tonic?" she asked, to buy herself time.

"Every seventh day. I am nearly complete with this bottle. I must send a boy to the village to the apothecary for more."

Cassie considered that new piece of information. "I will go." She needed to see what else existed in and around Ludlow Park, to get a feel for the people, to try to figure out if there was any foul play. She might be able to ask a few questions about Doctor Brown. Perhaps the apothecary could tell her something.

Cassie wanted to dismiss the doctor but was unsure how to do it. Taking a chance, she said, "That will be all, Doctor Brown. Thank you for seeing me this morning. I am sure my father will recover under your care." Cassie tried to put some sincerity.

The physician unfolded himself from his chair with ease. He bowed stiffly before disappearing back into Lord Miller's room.

Cassie exhaled a loud sigh. Was Doctor Brown trying to bleed the master of the house to death? "Flip me," she said, sagging into the support of the chair, "this is too much." She took a moment to compose her features, the governess would be waiting for her downstairs. With a huge effort she struggled up from the chair and made her way slowly to the door. She would have to pass the wolf mirror on her way along the corridor. She resolved not to look at it, to keep her eyes trained on the landing and to get through this hideous day as best she could.

Miss Blythe was waiting for her in the breakfast room, her features pinched as if she had just sucked on a lemon. Cassie guessed that her earlier dismissal had not gone down well. She had to resist staring around the room as she made her way across to the breakfast table. The walls were lined in grey-blue wallpaper, with dark mahogany wainscoting. A marble fireplace with huge mantle took up almost an entire wall. The flooring was dark also and a sumptuous rug of mixed burgundies, blues and browns covered the floor. A large table with ten expertly carved chairs took centre stage. Miss Blythe was sitting in one chair away from the top of the table, her plate empty except for a slice of bread.

Cassie's stomach churned, she was starving. The table was covered with a number of dishes. Some of the food she did not recognise. There was a side of ham, a plate of greasy looking eggs, chops from some kind of animal, kippers, the smell reeking, bread and a pot of gruel. Though Cassie's stomach clenched at the prospect of eating anything from the table, she was hungry. Ugh, what she wouldn't give for a bowl of crunchy nut cornflakes right now.

Cassie pulled out the seat at the head of the table and sat down heavily.

This dress is going to be the death of me.

She reached forward towards a pot of tea and began to pour herself a cup.

Miss Blythe was staring at her. Something moved at Cassie's shoulder and she jumped, almost dropping the pot of steaming liquid. A boy, about fourteen stood beside her. His skin was dark, his hands a luscious mahogany colour. He glanced to the floor, his brown eyes downcast.

He nodded his head once, asking silent permission before reaching forward, easing the pot from her grip. He continued to fill her cup until it was almost at the brim. He deposited two spoons of sugar and a dribble of milk into it before stepping gracefully back towards the wall and his position as a live statue. Cassie tried not to stare at him, her mouth slightly open.

She shook her head to focus her thoughts and gazed down at the cup in front of her. She didn't like milk or sugar in her tea but she didn't say anything. It was best not to draw any more attention to herself.

She lifted the china tea cup as daintily as she could manage and risked a glance at Miss Blythe from beneath her dark lashes, hoping that the woman had desisted in staring at her. She had not, instead, her hawk like eyes were following every move that Cassie made.

"Did you enjoy your tête-a-tête with Doctor Brown?" asked Miss Blythe, in a strained voice.

Cassie took a moment to consider her response. "Doctor Brown is very capable." She watched the governess to see if she could glean some information. "I just wanted to reassure myself that everything is being done for...my father's best interests."

Miss Blythe's reaction startled her. "Cassandra, how can you think otherwise? Do you question that the servants in this house wish Lord Miller unwell? We are wholly committed to seeing a full recovery." Miss Blythe sniffed and reached for her cup, taking a loud sip.

The passion in the governess's voice left Cassie in no doubt. She obviously felt some kind of affection for the family. However, Cassie was untrusting by nature. "I have told Doctor Brown that I want to help," offered Cassie. "He needs more tonic for my father. I have volunteered to go into the village to the...apothecary to collect some. Will you come with me?" Cassie wasn't exactly anxious for the company but she did not know the way to the village, would not know where to go and did not have a means of transport. She needed the governess.

"Of course I will accompany you, my Lady. I will call for the carriage." She raised her hand in the air and flicked her wrist twice, with quite a flourish. Cassie heard the soft footfall of feet and the boy who had served her tea tilted his head towards Miss Blythe, waiting for instruction.

Almost an hour later, Cassie was 'handed in' to an open topped carriage. She thought the term should have been 'legged in' rather than handed in. The assistant carriage driver, which Miss Blythe called the liveryman, pulled open a set of folding black stairs and held out his arm. Cassie had to push down firmly in an effort to hoist herself and her skirts up.

The carriage was a rich green colour with cream detail to the timberwork; the back was tall and shaped like an ornate, upside down 'U'. The sides were not as high but equally decorative. A team of chestnut horses completed the set-up. Cassie resisted the urge to crane her neck, to examine in detail the trappings of the carriage. She wanted to lean over to get a look at the horse tack, to peer down at the huge wheels but at that moment the driver clicked his tongue and the horses moved forward. Cassie was forced back in to her seat by the jostle.

Cassie had never been in a carriage before and the movement startled her into gripping the side timber, her knuckles turning white against the wood. Miss Blythe seemed comfortable enough and paid little attention as the horses jogged down the driveway towards the gates of Ludlow Park. The wind picked up and blew into Cassie's face.

She'd had no opportunity to talk to Molly properly, being accompanied by Miss Blythe all morning. Before they left the house, the governess had summoned the maid to bring a shawl. Cassie was wearing it now, a terrible itchy thing. She was also forced to wear the most horrendous floral hat she had ever seen. It was shaped like a fried egg, made from straw, and trimmed with dusky pink ribbon and finished off with sprigs of lace and dried flowers. A bow, tied under her chin, secured the hat in place. It was not very aerodynamic and Cassie wanted to jam her hand on it, in an unladylike manner, in an effort to stop the wind from carrying it away.

She restrained herself, however, and tried to get more settled. Over every lump and bump in the roadway, the carriage bounced, moving her body with it. She cursed the restriction of the corset and hoop silently as she looked out at the passing countryside. Jane Austen movies never showed how horribly uncomfortable carriages were to ride in.

The countryside did look beautiful she had to admit. Everything was so green, so large. Field after field stretched out in all directions. Every now and then the odd farmer's cottage, with wisps of smoke coming from the chimney, would percolate the countryside. They passed a stone church, pretty and well maintained. The day was crisp and clear and Cassie began to relax a little.

The carriage was on an open track way now, with few bumps and pot holes. The horses were maintaining a nice comfortable speed. They passed through a small wooded area, the track way rising up a hillock. As they neared the top, a rider could be seen trotting towards them in the distance. Cassie leaned forward, curious to see who it was. The horse was tall, easily sixteen hands, and shiny, chestnut brown in colour. He was an impressive animal and Cassie guessed that the owner was not short of a few pennies.

As the carriage trundled along the rider came properly into view. It was a man, in his early twenties. He wore polished knee high riding boots and dark pants. A floppy cravat of silk material wound its way around his neck. He had on a striking russet red coat, with grey panelling to the front and dark, polished buttons. His hair was black and long, pulled back in to a small pony tail at the nape of the neck.

She had no idea who this person was and as the carriage drew nearer she realised, with a sinking feeling, that the rider was slowing down and about to turn his horse around, so that he could walk beside them.

Oh crap.

Cassie began to panic, her heart rate increasing. What was she to do? Wave at him, ignore him, say howsitgoing?

He bowed in the saddle. "My lady." His voice was deep and he kept his body angled forward for a few seconds. Miss Blythe cleared her throat, an obvious signal. Cassie realised she needed to say something.

"Sir," she said with as much control as she could muster. She didn't know if he deserved this title, but from the corner of her eye she could not see much of a reaction from Miss Blythe so she felt safe.

"You ladies are out for a drive?"

"Obviously," replied Cassie, before she could control the tone of sarcasm in her voice.

An awkward silence descended on the group, the snuff and shuffle of the horses the only sound.

Cassie had to say something, quickly. "Your horse is very nice." *Doh*, she sounded like such a dunce.

He smiled a small smile and patted the mane of his animal. "Yes, Byron is a fine animal. He is relatively new to the stables. May I enquire after your father, Lady Cassandra?"

"Yes." She wasn't sure what he wanted to enquire, so she thought she had better wait and see.

The man looked at her. Miss Blythe looked at her.

"What is it you want to know?" she asked.

The governess stifled a gasp behind her gloved hand and looked in the opposite direction.

"I am sorry, Madam, I did not mean to offend you. I merely wished to pass my regards to your father. Good day." And with that he bowed, turned his horse around and cantered away. Cassie craned her neck to look after him, flummoxed as to what just happened.

"Lady Cassandra," began Miss Blythe, her voice a high-pitched squeak, "I know your families do not get on very well but your incivility was in very poor taste."

Their families don't get on? Why? Cassie didn't even know who he was. These people, she thought to herself, are seriously stuffy.

Chapter Nine

~ Cassandra ~

"I will not concede to see the doctor," Cassandra said aloud.

If he prescribed leeches, she was sure that she would lose her composure. Whatever happens she must remain calm. There was to be no giving in to one's feelings. It was beneath her.

Cassandra took a step towards the back door, determined to make her escape. The woman at the sink turned around completely, eying her with a cold stare. Cassandra gasped. On the servant's face, there was a long angry mark down her visage.

"I wouldn't do that, Miss, if I were you. Best stay put so you can get looked at."

"What can you mean? I do not need 'looking at'." Cassandra could feel her heart beating fast in her chest. "I am the lady of the house and you will do as you are bid." Cassandra tried to hold on to what poise she could as she exited the kitchen and hurriedly retraced her steps towards the front door.

She could hear the woman's voice upstairs. Words floated down from the landing, *hysterical* and *sedate* caught Cassandra's attention. They would come for her, hold her down, bleed her like they did her father. She was trapped. There was no going out the front door, the silver locks unbreakable. Her resolve weakened, what was she to do? Distract herself, think of something else.

She stood in the hallway for a long time, staring at the open chequered space, the tiles stretching across, drawing the eye to the stairs and bringing a great deal of light into the entranceway.

Mr. Huxley had suggested renovating the front area of the house, in the French style, very fashionable by all accounts.

Cassandra clenched her fists now at the thought of it, the impertinence of the man. Mr. Huxley had not even inherited Ludlow Park yet he was giving orders as to its renovations.

Cassandra turned and moved to the stairs, ignoring the unfamiliar portraits, trying to keep her thoughts together. She must keep her wits about her. She turned right at the head of the stairs, heading towards her bedroom.

Miss Blythe's door was open. Cassandra approached with caution, the sound of voices stoking her curiosity. The woman who had come into her room, claiming to be her mother, was talking to someone. The other voice Cassandra did not recognise.

"Thank you for coming down at such short notice. I appreciate your speed," the woman said.

"Ya." There was a long pause. "What's happened then?" the other voice enquired.

"She won't see Doctor Nevin, went absolutely ballistic when I suggested it, then stormed off. I tried to rationalise with her and she *dismissed* me." The tone of disbelief was evident in the woman's voice.

"Dismissed you?"

"Yes, she ordered me out of her sight."

"Okay. That sounds a bit weird."

"Mrs. Rivers found her in the corridor of the east wing last night after midnight. She was in a daze, mumbling about wolves."

Cassandra flattened herself against the wall and edged closer to try to peak around the door jam, unobserved.

"Then what happened?"

"Well, we put her to bed and then I texted you. Then this morning Jonah comes to tell me Cassie is acting strange. I thought perhaps it was because of last night...because...well, we had a rather heated argument regarding her new... Let's just say, we did not leave things on good terms."

"Okay, so why did you call me? I'm sure I'm not your favourite person at the moment."

"Tallulah, you know Cassie the best. If there is something wrong, then maybe you can talk some sense into her. Get her to tell you what is bothering her. I love my daughter and would do anything to protect her, to help her. If that means inviting you to our home, then I will do that." The woman's voice had turned cooler. "I won't pretend that you were my first choice but you were my only choice. It seems that Cassie is not good at making friends at Winchester College."

"If that's what you think..." The voices faded away as the two people moved further into the room.

Cassandra slumped back against the wall. Who was the woman talking to? Why did she keep mentioning a person called Cassie? Cassandra needed to sit down, to rest, she was becoming light headed. There were no smelling salts in sight and fainting was not an option right now.

Once inside her room, she went to the bed and perched on the edge, thinking over all the things she had heard. It was exhausting. Cassandra lay back and stared at the faded canopy overhead. She closed her eyes and pinched the bridge of her nose, feeling the pin prick of tension there.

The door of her bedroom burst open and Cassandra sat bolt upright.

A witch girl stood in the doorway, her hair aflame. Cassandra screamed and scuttled back across the bedclothes, her long skirt tangling around her legs.

"What is wrong with you?" the girl demanded, closing the door firmly behind her.

Cassandra was speechless, terror pining her to the post of the bed. The girl took a step into the room. "Get away from me, witch!" Cassandra stuttered, fear making her voice shake.

"Who are you calling witch, bitch! What the hell is going on? Did you lose your memory when you hit your head? It's me, Tallulah, your best friend!"

She came across and perched on the edge of the bed, a look of concern in her eyes. Cassandra could go no further, the solid timber post pushing into her back. The girl's hair was huge and streaked with bands of fiery red. The tight curls made it stand on edge like a lion's mane and when she moved her head the red steaks caught the light. Her face and hands were black, as if someone had dipped her in strong coffee.

She was wearing tight black stockings which went all the way up, under pantaloons of blue material, like the ones Cassandra had found in her bag by the tall square clothes trunk. On her torso, she had a bright blue undershirt and a black leather short coat with silver buttons. On her feet she wore red ankle boots.

Dangling from her ears was a cord of white. Cassandra could hear the drone of angry bees coming from the girl's personage, proof that she was a witch.

Slowly the girl, noticing Cassandra's gaze, reached into a pocket of her leather short-coat and drew out a tiny pink flat square, with a white circle on the front of it. She held it up to Cassandra. "Want to listen? I have Usher's new song."

Cassandra did not know what she meant, staring first at the pink square, then at the brown hand covered in silver rings. This was Cassandra's first proper "negro", as Miss Blythe called them. George didn't count, he was Caribbean and he had been with their family for years, an orphan rescued from a travelling circus. The child had been paraded as a spectacle around the towns and villages of the countryside, but when no longer a pleasant baby, the circus manager abandoned him. He waited on table at breakfast.

Cassandra knew that the Percival family of Royston House had an actual negro. They called him Juba Thomas. However, Royston House was several townlands away and Cassandra never had cause to go there.

The cook often told stories of how, when she worked in London, she would see the black people come in on the ships to the docks, starving, badly-clothed and disease ridden. One of the house maids had told her a terrifying story about their magic. The maid had said that a black witch lived in a cottage at the edge of Dalton Forest, in the next county over.

Now, faced with her first proper coloured person, she herself was not entirely composed. After a moment, curiosity overcame her and she reached out her hand. She took the pink box and held it to her ear. The girl began to laugh, curling her hand around the white string that hung from the thin square box. "What are you like, Cassie? You really must have banged your head hard. Here, give it to me, let me show you."

She reached forward and held out two oval buds on the end of the white string. "Put these in your ears."

Cassandra was dubious and for a moment hesitated but she saw that the girl did not mean any harm, so she placed the buds next to her ears, pushing them in a little. The sensation was strange, as if someone had muted the sounds of the morning. The girl was playing with the thin pink box, touching the white circle with her finger, clicking it.

Suddenly a blare of sound filled Cassandra's ears and she was immobilised, stuck between terror and awe. She could not lift her hand to pull the cord away, dislodging the buds from her ears. She was afraid of what would happen if she moved. Instead, she remained, pinned against the bedpost listening to her first hip hop song, whilst staring at her first black person.

Tallulah was laughing at her, bent double over the bed. Eventually, when she had laughed till she almost cried, she pulled the cord, unstopping Cassandra's ears. The music receded to a dull drone. "Your face," the girl said, slapping her thigh, "you would swear that you never listened to an iPod before."

Cassandra looked at her, unmoving.

"So" she asked, "what's the deal?" What's going on? Your mother is freaked out; so freaked out that she called me and asked me to come down for the weekend. Your mother hates me. What happened? And why are you dressed like that?"

Cassandra glanced at her clothing, considering what to say and decided that she was the lady of the house, she was in charge. There would be only one person asking questions. She unfolded herself from the confines of her skirt and slid off the bed, a little unsteady on her legs. She walked to the window and looked out across the lawn, considering, then she turned. "Your name is Tallulah?"

"Duh. Cassie, what's going on?"

Cassandra held up her hand, to signal for silence. "What is the date?"

"The twelfth of October."

"And the year?"

"Are you kidding? 2014. Why are you asking such stupid questions? And when did you dye your hair, the pink is missing?"

Cassandra wasn't listening. Instead her legs gave way and she half sat, half squatted to the floor.

The girl was off the bed and over to her side in an instant, "Cassie you are really scaring me. What is it? What's wrong? You're acting as if you don't even know me. We have been best friends for two years."

"We are friends?" Cassandra's voice sounded shocked.

"What kind of thing is that to say? Of course we're friends, we practically got expelled from school together, thanks to that weasel Becky 'The Troll' Travers and your waster of an ex-boyfriend. It's a pity Dwane can't handle rejection!"

The girl kneeled down and punched Cassandra in the upper arm, not too hard, but enough for her to feel it. "Which was pretty stupid by the way. If you had told them what really happened, then maybe you wouldn't have been in so much trouble!"

Cassandra did the most undignified thing she could think of. She began to cry. Wet, runny tears slid down her cheeks. Where was Miss Blythe when she needed her for guidance? Tallulah sat on the floor beside her, took her hand and waited.

Eventually, Cassandra stopped and sniffed, pulling her hand away with distaste from Tallulah's. "If you punch me again, I will have you whipped," she said, half-heartedly. No servant had ever touched her in that manner before. If Miss Blythe was here she would have the girl removed and handed over to the housekeeper for punishment.

Tallulah frowned and pushed away from her. "Okay, miss high and mighty, just because your family owns a big house in the countryside and I'm a council brat. If your mum heard you say that, she would kill you."

"She is not my mother." Cassandra pushed herself up from the floor, wiping her skirt free of invisible dirt.

Tallulah looked up at her from the ground, her eyebrow raised in an unspoken question.

"She is not my mother," continued Cassandra. "I am not this person Cassie who you all think I am. My name is Lady Cassandra Miller, I am the daughter of Lord Henry Miller and when I last enquired, the year was 1714." She looked down at Tallulah, silently daring her to challenge the statement.

"Well," the girl said slowly, "the last time I checked we both got tattoos at Georgie's in town." The girl jumped up and with speed belaying her size, she grabbed Cassandra, pinning her arms to her side, turning her around with one good push. The girl pulled at Cassandra's clothing, revealing the base of her spine. Cassandra was so shocked she froze.

"Ha Ha!" Tallulah said delightedly, the sound slowly dying on her lips. "Where is it?" She struggled to complete her sentence, bending down to peer at Cassandra's exposed lower back.

Regaining her composure, Cassandra wriggled free from the grip around her and turned quickly to glare at the negro. "Desist in touching me, or I swear on my mother's grave, you will suffer the consequences." Both girls stared at each other, silence descending.

"What's a tattoo?" asked Cassandra as she straightened out her top, determined to restore some kind of order.

"A tattoo..." began the other girl, ignoring Cassandra's previous threat, "we both got one together last week. You got a tribal design and I got..." Tallulah pulled up the jacket and undershirt, exposing her midriff and turned her back to Cassandra. At the base of her spine was an elaborate floral pattern, intertwining vines and a bright red rose. It was beautiful.

Cassandra stepped forward and peered at the design before gingerly touching the skin with only the tip of her index finger. The picture was inked in, embedded in the flesh. Never before had she seen such delicate work. "Are you a sailor?" she asked, stepping back.

Tallulah turned around. "What?"

"Are you a sailor?" repeated Cassandra. "They are the only ones I know of who get marked like that."

"No, I'm not a sailor, don't be stupid."

"Yes, well, I think we have proof who is stupid in this instance. A true Lady of Ludlow would never be foolish enough to get a sailor's mark." Cassandra decreed her judgement with a flick of her hand, as if dismissing her small, singular audience.

Tallulah stared at her, her mouth hanging open. Several emotions flitted across her features but all she said was "Holy crap!", before lagging against the bed, the energy sucked from her by an invisible vacuum.

Chapter Ten

~ Cassie ~

The rest of the carriage journey to the village was pretty boring. Cassie frowned for most of it. The meeting with the rider had irritated her. Who the hell was he anyway, the arrogant ass? She had expected the governess to chastise her for her behaviour, for her insult to the gentleman. But Miss Blythe spent most of the journey fidgeting with her skirt, folding and unfolding her hands. Cassie sighed in exasperation.

Determined to glean some information, she turned to Miss Blythe and said, "That was a really nice horse the man was riding…" She let the sentence hang there, hoping that Miss Blythe would take the bait.

"Hmm."

Frustrated, she tried again. "Do you think that he was offended by my comments?"

The governess sniffed. "I think your conduct was beyond rude. I do not know what has come over you, Lady Cassandra. It reflects on me too. Have a care for that, as you go blundering into exchanging insults with a man like Charles Stafford."

Charles Stafford. A name was a good start. Cassie wanted to know more. She looked at Miss Blythe expectantly but the scolding was over, the governess silenced. "Miss Blythe, I'm trying to be more honest." Cassie wasn't sure where this was going but she continued on, regardless. "I want to be more open with people and I wish to express myself in a more free and honest way."

The governess blushed. "You wish to be free with yourself?"

Cassie deduced that she had said something inappropriate. "No, Miss Blythe, I didn't mean it in that way. I would like to repair any damage done between my family and Mr....Stafford." Cassie held her breath, hoping that the introduction to the topic would be enough to rally the governess to give one of her lectures.

As expected, the governess could not resist the high moral ground and began to recount how a lady should behave, even in the most troublesome of situations. Cassie had to restrain herself from yawning. Lord Miller and Mr. Stafford Senior had fallen out over a piece of land, or so Miss Blythe said.

"Do you not remember the altercation between the two landowners, Lady Cassandra?" asked the governess, eying her suspiciously.

"Of course I remember." Cassie picked at a piece of lint from her tumbling skirts.

"I should think you remember it well enough, given you had cause to punch Charles Stafford in the nose after you found him stealing apples from your orchard."

Cassie gasped in disbelief. Lady Cassandra had done that?

"You were, of course, quite wild back then, before I came to Ludlow Park." The governess nodded her head, convincing herself that she was right in all things.

"I had forgotten," remarked Cassie, trying to sound suitably appalled.

"Yes, I would imagine you have forgotten. You were both very young, perhaps ten or so. You gave him a black eye." The governess smiled, an unusual sight, the ends of her lips turned upwards.

Cassie looked out across the countryside, deep in thought. So the prim and proper Lady Cassandra had punched a boy for stealing apples. Maybe she wasn't such a boring sap after all. The thought made Cassie feel a little better.

The carriage passed along a dirt track onto a wider, brick paved roadway. The houses on either side went from ramshackle cottages to rickety shop fronts. The elevations were not straight, the upper storey poised to topple over on to the street.

A woman walked along the side of the road, carrying a woven

basket. There was a dress shop on the street, with ribbons and white linen in the window, a cobbler's, a butcher and a candle shop. As the carriage progressed along the street they came into a large village green.

It was the smell of rotting flesh that assaulted Cassie first. She felt the gagging reflex at the back of her throat. A cart with every imaginable carcass of animal polluted the clean air with an odour so disgusting. She deduced a pig's head, animal hooves, several purple coloured tongues and a number of suspended chickens, dangling from their recently twisted necks.

The carriage came to an abrupt stop, literally knocking her from her contemplative state. The driver came around and opened the carriage door, unfolding the steps. He stood dutifully to the side, helping the ladies disembark. Cassie thanked him and heard a little squeak of surprise emanate from the servant. She glanced up. His face was smooth and impassive, his gaze staring at nothing somewhere in the middle distance. He was holding his breath, trying to take back the sound that he had made.

Cassie frowned, clearly talking to the other servants wasn't something that Lady Cassandra did either.

A blush of pink rose to the man's cheeks but he remained silent as the governess exited the timber carriage. Cassie nodded once at the servant and moved across the square. She was trying really hard not to stare about her like a newbie. She stepped gingerly over animal dung and other unidentifiable substances as she moved away from the carriage. She did not want to get any dirt on the hem of her impressive dress so she hefted up her skirts an inch or two. Before she knew it Miss Blythe was beside her huffing and puffing as if she had run a marathon. "Lady Cassandra, are you determined to ridicule your family name? Lower your skirts this instant. The men across the square can see your ankles!"

Cassie glanced up, taking her attention away from the missiles on the ground. Sure enough across the square a group of men were gawking at her. She looked at Miss Blythe expectantly. "But if I lower my skirts, they will get all dirty."

"Yes, well, that is why you have over a hundred gowns, my Lady, so you never need wear a dirty one. Once you are home Molly can change you."

A hundred gowns, thought Cassie, where the hell do they keep them? She followed after her governess's retreating form, suitably chastised. They crossed the square and turned down one of the side streets, taking them out of the light and warmth of the sun. Miss Blythe was moving fast for a woman of such poise, her shoulders were plunged forward, her head bent, her body intent on reaching its destination. Cassie was surprised at the buzz of energy from the otherwise stoic woman. They proceeded to move up the rise of the street, bending into the gentle climb of the hill.

The governess stopped outside a brown façade and fixed the pleating of her skirt, tugging down the cuffs of her sleeves. She smoothed her hair and drew herself up to her full height before pushing open the door. A bell rang overhead as they moved into the shop.

Cassie blinked in the dimness, her eyes adjusting to the dark interior. A long, painted countertop stretched across one side of the shop. Covering a vast majority of the counter were bottles and jugs, jars and pill boxes, cork stoppers and sprigs of unusual looking plants. Along the back wall of the shop were several shelves with large vats of oily contents. Cassie gazed around her in awe.

Behind the counter was a single archway, leading into the back room.

"Mr. Evins?" Miss Blythe stood at one side of the counter, her voice sounding strange, her hands clasped together, the knuckles white.

Cassie observed her carefully and was shocked to discover that Miss Blythe was shaking. What was going on?

A rustling noise from the rear of the shop, the clinking of glass and a man appeared. He was short, with a ruddy face, ginger tinged hair with long unkempt sideburns. He greeted Miss Blythe with a bow but little more, his attention instantaneously shifting to Cassie.

He was drying his hands in his shirt, the material rolled up over thick muscles on his forearms.

"Lady Cassandra," he muttered, "It is not often you condescend to visit me." Cassie could hear the sneer in his voice. She stiffened, her senses on high alert.

"I am on a very important job today, Mr. Evins," she said, as calmly as possible. "I thought it best if I came to see you myself. Doctor Brown recommends only *your* services." There now, she thought, that would do, nothing like a bit of ego boosting to get what you want.

Mr. Evins remained impassive and a veil of silence descended between them. He continued to stare at her for a moment before saying, "Doctor Brown requests the usual tonic for Lord Miller?"

"Yes," Cassie and Miss Blythe answered in unison.

"I will prepare something directly. If you ladies wish to take a turn about town..."

"Oh no," answered Miss Blythe, before Cassie could get a word in, "We will wait here. We do not mind."

Cassie frowned. Then Miss Blythe turned around, giving Cassie a full view of her face. Her cheeks were flushed and her eyes bright.

She fancies him, realised Cassie, as she moved over to the window, turning her back on the governess. She could not let Miss Blythe see her smiling. She fought to control the chuckle that threatened to bubble up within her. They would look ridiculous together, Miss Blythe towering and thin, Mr. Evins squat and robust. Still, thought Cassie, there is no accounting for taste. She spied a little girl with bonnet and shawl scurry past the front of the shop, a half empty jug of water clasped to her chest.

Mr. Evins had gone in to the back room. Cassie could hear the grating together of a pestle and mortar. She wandered over to the shelves of potions and lotions, examining their contents. Some looked totally gross, others claimed healing properties Cassie knew to be impossible. Thank God for modern medicine, she thought to herself as she skimmed her fingers along the glass bottles.

The apothecary came back to the counter and Miss Blythe immediately engaged him in conversation. Cassie began to fidget. The multitude of vials containing frogs' spawn, bulls' testicles, snake eyes and all the other quack medicines were giving her the heebee jeebies. She wandered over to the window again and looked out in to the street. All was quiet.

She turned and noticed a large green plant poking out at the side of the archway that led to the rear of the shop. She vaguely recognised it and moved towards it, touching its leaves with her fingers. She lifted a leaf towards her nose and sniffed. Her eyes widened as she recognised the smell. It was a giant cannabis plant. Glancing over her shoulder to make sure the apothecary wasn't looking she moved quietly into the back room. What else did he have hidden here?

The rear of the shop was even darker. Two dirt-encrusted windows leaked grey light into the basement. One of them was open, the briefest of breezes into the workshop space. She could see that the window opened up onto ground level, the building having been built into the side of a gentle hill. The smells from the various vials and plants was momentarily overbearing. Cassie scrunched up her nose, giving her senses time to adjust. She scanned the room. Shelves lined two walls where jugs, jars, bottles and vials took up residence. Some of the items were so caked in years and years of dust that labels were indecipherable.

Cassie reached for the nearest of these bottles. She chose the least dirty, least dusty one, rationalising that it was the most utilised. The label was yellow and peeling. "A...R...S...E...N..." Cassie was reading the letters out softly, but she did not finish. Instead she hastily put the bottle back on the shelf, rubbing her hands vigorously in the material of her dress, getting rid of any and all dust.

Arsenic. What was an apothecary doing with arsenic in his store? She moved around the room to the far bench, next to the window. There was evidence that whatever Mr. Evins had been making for her father was still in the base of the biggest mortar bowl. She bent near it and sniffed. It smelled vile.

Next to the pestle and mortar there was a timber bowl covered with a cloth. Cassie couldn't resist. Catching the corner of the cloth in between her thumb and her forefinger she lifted it. Inside was the root of a plant, gnarled and hideous, like a shrivelled, naked man, bulbous at the top where its head should have been. It appeared to have wreathing, intertwined limbs striking out from the main part of the body. The roots were like tentacles, wriggling, and one of them had recently been cut.

Engrossed by the knotty bulb, Cassie didn't notice Mr. Evins until his hand was on her wrist. He dragged it firmly away from the cloth. Cassie exclaimed in alarm, struggling to pull her hand free but his grip was tight.

"A lady should not snoop." His brown eyes were cold and hard.

Cassie swallowed loudly.

"You do not know what kind of danger you might confront here," he said. Cassie stared at him and nodded, unable to speak. Mr. Evins did not need to say anything else. Cassie knew how to read between the lines. *Touch anything in here and I will chop off your hand.*

Cassie tried to remain calm, pulling herself free from his grip. She moved from the workshop back into the relative brightness of the store. She stopped next to the governess. "I am going for a walk, Miss Blythe. I'll meet you at the carriage." Miss Blythe cracked a smile, delighted to be left in Mr. Evins' presence. Cassie had to restrain herself from running from the premises. She could not get the image of Mr. Evins' cold, brown eyes from her head, nor the knowledge of what was in the bowl.

Mandrake root; the most poisonous of all plants.

The apothecary worked with some very powerful poisons.

Chapter Eleven

~ Cassie ~

"Molly," Cassie shouted as soon as she entered the room. The servant was nowhere to be seen. A small fire was burning in the grate and the curtains had been tied back, letting the bright autumn light slant in through the window. Cassie's mind was racing. She needed to find out about Miss Blythe and the seriousness of her infatuation with the apothecary. What if the two of them were working together to poison Lord Miller? That would explain his strange symptoms.

The ribs of the corset were digging into her skin, the folds of the heavy skirt pulling her down. She stopped where she was and sank to her knees, crumpling the skirts and hoop. She didn't care, the relief was instant, the restriction lessening. She swung her legs around in front of her and lay back on the floor, her body half on the rug, half on the floor boards, her neatly arranged hair squashing under the weight of her head.

The exhaustion of the last twenty-four hours weighed heavily on her. She was desperate for a cigarette, the craving gnawing on her like an eager parasite. Despite the fact that her mind was brimming with questions, she felt her eyes drooping closed, her head lolling to one side.

She could have been asleep five minutes or an hour but the next thing she knew, Molly was beside her, shaking her roughly. When Cassie blinked her eyes open, Molly sat back on her heels and sighed heavily. "Oh, Miss, ya gave me an awful fright. I thought ya had swooned."

Cassie struggled up to a seated position, her neck stiff.

"I am going to order ya some tea, Miss." Molly went and pulled the cord beside the bed. "It is unusual for Lady Cassandra to take tea in her room but I can say this mornin's trip into town tired ya out."

The mention of town reminded her of the apothecary and she shivered involuntarily. "Molly," she asked, as she moved towards the bed, "Mr. Evins, what do you know about him?"

The lady's maid was standing still, her hands folded neatly in front of her. She glanced anxiously at the door.

"What is it?" asked Cassie.

"Nothin', Miss. It is just, I do not usually stand around talkin' to the mistress. I normally have work to do and…"

Cassie shook her head. "Don't be silly, Molly. I have much more important things to discuss than what dress to wear later. I need you to help me figure out what that creep, Mr Evins, is up to."

Molly huffed at her language choice, her lips pressing together in disapproval. "Miss Cassie!"

Cassie wasn't listening. "It's definitely something dodgy. And I'm not even sure if Miss Blythe is involved or not…" There was a knock on the door and both girls turned guiltily towards it, hoping that it was not the governess.

Molly was the first to move. "It must be the tea. Here," she added, as she pushed Cassie back on to the bed, her skirt flying up, "Yer hair has fallen down, I can see the colour at the ends, ya need to lie down. Move yer feet." Molly pushed her roughly across the cover of the bed into an uncomfortable position before hurrying to answer the door. She spoke to the person for a moment, took the tray and closed the door firmly.

"Help!" called Cassie quietly, her arms held up in the air, her body unable to manoeuvre itself into a sitting position. Molly deposited the tray on the writing desk and clambered onto the bed. She knelt over Cassie, grabbed her hands and heaved her upwards. Cassie's legs were caught in the confines of her skirts and she was unable to kick them out to act as any sort of momentum or leverage. She was relying solely on the pulling power of the servant. Cassie began to giggle, her corset nipping her, causing her to want to laugh even more.

"What is so amusin', Miss?" asked Molly, her voice straining with the effort.

"Nothing. I can't, can't…" Cassie gave one final heave and was righted into a proper sitting position. She was flushed in the face, her breathing raspy. "This dress is a health and safety hazard." She took a moment to catch her breath and said with solid conviction, "I'd kill for a cup of tea."

Molly moved quickly. "Of course, Miss." She placed the china cup and saucer on the table and began to arrange the milk and tea pot, ready to serve.

"No," said Cassie, swinging her legs over and off the bed. "I'll do it." Cassie suddenly realised how pale Molly was, her hands shook ever so slightly as she arranged the tea things. The servant had been working all day, probably very hard, and had gotten as little sleep as Cassie.

Molly stared at her, the tongs for the sugar lump in her hand, her expression unreadable.

"I'll make *you* a cup of tea," repeated Cassie. "You look like you need it." The servant stood very still for a moment and Cassie was worried that the girl was about to cry.

Cassie moved to the writing desk and shooed Molly back towards the bed. Her conundrum was immediately evident. So much for trying to do something spontaneous. There was only one cup. Cassie sighed and thought for a second before dumping out the sugar lumps on to the silver tray.

"Oh, Miss," began Molly, a tone of reproach.

"Sit!" Cassie pointed to the bed. "I need to find out information about Mr. Evins and you are going to tell me everything you know about him." Cassie poured milk into one cup and added the liquid brown tea, a pretty stream of steam forming. Next, she played it safe, adding a splash of milk to the emptied sugar bowl, so the china would not split and poured a measure of tea for herself. Cassie took the cup and saucer and dropped an awkward curtsy before Molly. "Would Madame like her tea?" she asked, in her best posh accent.

Molly laughed and accepted the cup with an exaggerated gesture. Cassie took the sugar bowl in her hands and dropped to her knees on the rug beside the bed.

"Right," she began, a tone of quiet determination in her voice.

"Let's figure this out."

"Ya met Mr. Evins then?" Molly eyed her over the rim of her cup, her expression shaded.

"Yes. He is, well, never mind what I think. I want you to tell me what you know about him."

Molly shrugged her shoulders. "Very little. He came to the village about five year ago, to apprentice to Mr. Whiggs, our old apothecary. Mr Evins is very precise, very methodical…"

"Very creepy," cut in Cassie.

Molly smiled knowingly.

Cassie shivered. "Does he have any connection with Ludlow Park?"

"No, not that I know of. He is Doctor Brown's apothecary. He makes up any tonics, pills, or ointments that the doctor might need for his patients. Doctor Brown will not use anyone else. But then…" She paused.

"But then what?"

"Oh, I do not know. Village rumours."

"Go on," coached Cassie.

"It is said about the village that the reason Doctor Brown will not use any other apothecary is that Mr. Evins knows somethin'."

"Knows something?"

"Yes, Miss."

"Like what?" asked Cassie, bending forward, anxious to hear the big secret.

Molly shrugged her shoulders. "Some people say that Doctor Brown had a lady associate, an unmarried lady associate. And Mr. Evins discovered this."

"So you're saying he had a girlfriend?"

Molly looked at her, a blank expression on her face.

Cassie sighed. "Never mind, go on."

"Mr. Evins threatened the doctor with exposure if he did not make him his business partner. If the village fishmonger needs a salve for a cut on his finger, Doctor Brown will recommend Mr Evins. And only Mr. Evins." Molly took a sip from her cup. "In the space of three years, Whiggs' Apothecary had changed to Evins' Apothecary. The old man died sudden in his sleep one night. It was a bit of a mystery. All told, since then Mr. Evins' business has been goin' from strength to strength."

Cassie considered the information, weighing up the facts. Perhaps it was not Mr. Evins and the governess, perhaps it was Mr. Evins and the doctor plotting against the Miller family. The apothecary was obviously ambitious, and had no compulsion towards ethics or morals. But as far as she could tell, he had done nothing to her, Lady Cassandra or the Miller family.

Cassie leaned her head forward on to her forearms. She remembered the feel of Evins's hand gripping her wrist. It was very hot. She could feel the beginnings of a tension headache right at the bridge of her nose. She would need a Panadol soon. "Ugh," she moaned in to her sleeves.

"Miss?" asked Molly.

"I just realised that there are no twenty-four-hour pharmacies anywhere nearby." Cassie lifted her head. "I'm getting a headache and I don't have any Panadol."

Molly shook her head.

"Panadol, it's like pain relief for headaches," offered Cassie

"I can make ya some herbal tea. Cook has feverfew leaves in the pantry."

Cassie didn't know what feverfew was and she didn't really want to find out. She was happy enough to suffer the oncoming headache. Then a thought struck her. What if she got sick? Like really sick. She scanned through her memories. Had she gotten her vaccinations when she was a child? Weren't things like smallpox, whopping cough and flu the type of thing that killed people in the eighteenth century? There were no emergency services, no on-call doctors. Well, of course, there was Doctor Brown.

Cassie felt her head spin. She needed to sit down. She *was* sitting down. Molly was beside her, her hand on her arm. "Miss Cassie, are you well?"

"Ugh, it's very hot. I can't breathe properly." She began to claw at the bodice of her dress, saying, "I can't breathe, I need to…need to get…" Cassie could feel the waves of panic rolling over her.

Molly was behind her, something metal in her hand. She pushed Cassie's upper body forward, leaning on her shoulder, forcing her face towards the ground. In three deft movements Molly wedged whatever she had in her hand under the ribbons of Cassie's bodice, snipped and pulled. The feeling of relief was instantaneous. Floods of air filled Cassie's lungs, the bodice spreading from around her thin frame, alleviating the pressure on her lungs, her ribs, her back, her vital organs.

Molly came around to kneel in front of her, a pair of silver scissors in her hand. "Are you quite well?"

"Yeah," panted Cassie, "thanks".

"It is not a good idea to sit on the floor too long. The bonin' in the corset squeezes tight. Come along." Molly helped her up into a standing position. "I will have to see if I can find ya somethin' less restrictin' to wear. I cannot have ya faintin'. It does not do well for appearances."

Cassie let Molly help her out of her heavy skirts, delighted to be free from the weight of them. With a lot more willingness than that morning she shrugged into the long linen night gown and crawled under the covers of the bed. The light of the day was only just beginning to fade and Cassie guessed that it was somewhere around five o'clock. She would have to go down to dinner later but until then, she was not going to wrap herself up in any more restraints.

"Molly?" she asked sleepily, as the girl folded the skirts of her dress neatly.

"Yes miss?"

"I met a rider on the way to town this afternoon."

"Oh," she said uninterested.

"A Mr. Charles Stafford."

The maid stopped what she was doing instantly, her expression shocked. "Did he speak to ya, Miss?"

"Well..." Cassie squirmed under her scrutiny, the sleep sensation leaving her. "You could say that."

"Oh, Miss, what did ya say to him?" the panic in the servant's tone evident.

"Nothing. Nothing. You're as bad as Miss Blythe. He asked me a question and all I said was..." She paused. "Well, all I said was... I can't actually remember what I said, but Miss Blythe seemed to think that I insulted him."

"Miss! Ya must try to remember."

"Why? It's not like Lady Cassandra even likes him...is it? She doesn't fancy him? Does she?" Cassie propped herself up onto her elbow, scrutinising Molly's face.

"Are ya suggestin' Lady Miller and Charles Stafford? Well, I do declare. No, Miss, that is highly unlikely given that the two of them are sworn enemies since childhood and rarely a civil word passes between them but up until recently." The servant seemed rather insulted.

"What do you mean...until recently," asked Cassie, ignoring the wounded look the other girl cast in her direction.

"There is some bad blood between the older Mr. Stafford and Lord Miller. Somethin' to do with land and cattle but really, everyone know it is because...but nobody ever speaks it aloud...it is..."

"A woman," volunteered Cassie. She was not as stupid as Miss Blythe obviously thought Lady Cassandra was. No two grown up, educated men would seriously fall out over just some cattle. It was obvious that a woman was involved, and that woman was probably Cassandra's mother. Cassie had seen her portrait hanging above the stairs on the landing, and another in the room off Lord Miller's bed chamber. She was a very striking woman and reminded Cassie a little of her own mother.

Her hand involuntarily went to her cheek. She thought of her mum and wondered what she was doing, if she was working on some case files, if she had even noticed that her daughter was missing. She probably preferred having the real Lady Cassandra as a daughter, much more convenient than having to deal with Cassie and all the trouble she brought with her.

Molly was watching her.

"So," she said, shaking the thoughts of her mother from her mind, "they had an argument over a woman...Lady Cassandra's mother. And Cassandra and Charles are sworn enemies since birth."

"Well not quite. They are not enemies, they have just been raised to keep their distance and of course stories grow legs sometimes and things get exaggerated. Though Lady Cassandra did..."

"Hmm, well, I think I put a spanner in that works today when he came and tried to talk to me."

"Was he civil to ya?"

"If you mean was he polite, then yes, I suppose he was, even when I inadvertently insulted him."

"Oh Miss All the good work they have been doin'."

"Who?"

Molly looked at her hands. "My mistress and Mr. Stafford have been tryin' to bring their fathers together this last year. The young people had cause, once Cassandra came out and was old enough to attend balls and assemblies, to meet each other."

Cassie raised her eyebrow. "Meet each other? Are you sure they are not an item?"

Molly looked to her hand and began to rub at a spec of imaginary dirt. "I am certain they are not lovers."

Cassie frowned. She had a feeling that Molly was not telling her everything.

"Okay," continued Cassie cautiously, "so they saw each other at parties and got talking…and…"

"Yes, they tried to overcome the feud and reconcile. The gentlemen used to be great friends, a long time ago."

"So how had they planned on bringing their parents together then?"

"They each were tryin' to convince their fathers to meet but then Lord Miller fell ill."

Cassie considered this. How convenient. Just as the two houses were due to reconcile, Lord Miller becomes unwell. Perhaps that was why Charles Stafford was so eager to enquire after her father's health. She remembered the shift in the colour of his eyes. Maybe Lord Miller's death was the news he had been waiting for.

Chapter Twelve

~ Cassandra ~

Tallulah must be a sailor, rationalised Cassandra. She had the worst language Cassandra had ever heard.

"Holy crap!" The girl was pacing the room, her hands in her hair, pulling it out to even wider proportions. Abruptly she stopped and turned. "But I saw you get the tattoo, I was there, next to you. We got it done together." She lifted her top again to reveal her lower back complete with entwined flowers. She rubbed it vigorously, "This does not come off!"

Cassandra was concerned for the other girl. It would not do for either or both of them to become hysterical. They must remain steadfast, must maintain poise. Cassandra's eyes darted about the room, reaffirming that the door was an easy distance away. Maybe she was having a terrible nightmare; perhaps she had inhaled foul air. She had not let her mind wonder about the strange situation. She knew if she thought about it too much she would begin to lose her composure. And if that were to happen, lord only knows where it would lead to. Miss Blythe had spent the last six years schooling Cassandra in the art of calm. She was not going to let this half-crazed heathen break her resolve.

Tallulah was now mumbling to herself, biting her nails, an unsightly, disgusting habit. The girl's speech was becoming more and more erratic, her hands flying in exaggerated gestures. Clearly, she needed a few moments to compose herself. It was very unbecoming to display such extremes of emotion, especially in front of superior company such as Cassandra's.

Cassandra frowned; perhaps she should be the one who was showing signs of distress. It was her, after all, stuck in a strange place, three hundred years later than she should be. Was it normal to be so calm? Miss Blythe had always commended her on her steadfast temperament, had always been there to tell her how to behave, to moderate any excessive displays of feelings. She should not be exposed to this type of spontaneity. Her wild nature would resurface and Cassandra had a duty, she could not afford to deviate from what was expected of her. She must put her own wants to one side.

"I have to get home," she said out loud. Briskly she addressed the servant, "You must help me find a way back into the wolf mirror."

"The what?" asked Tallulah, her mumbling rant interrupted.

"The mirror. One minute I was standing in front of it, the next I was lying in this uncomfortably hard bed." Cassandra motioned to the mattress. "The mirror is the last thing I remember. And the cook spoke of the east wing."

"The cook?" asked Tallulah.

"Yes, the woman in the kitchen, with the scar."

"Creepy Mrs. Rivers? She is half off her head. Cassie is always telling me weird stories about her. Judge Miller must have a soft spot for the ol' doll."

"Judge Miller? A magistrate?" Cassandra stood bolt upright, a ripple of excitement running through her. "I must speak with him at once. He will be a learned man. He will know what to do as regards my current situation."

Tallulah looked at her, a flicker of amusement playing across her features. "She."

"She whom?" asked Cassandra.

"Judge Miller."

"Yes, I must see him, this instant. Don't stand around gawking at me." Cassandra flicked her hand in the servant's direction, indicating that some action was required. "Go and fetch him this instant, Negro, or I shall call the housekeeper to have you punished for your insolence."

Tallulah stopped, her features and body growing very still. Without warning, she sprang forward pushing Cassandra against the hard timber of the window frame, the back of her legs pressed against the wallpapered wall, her torso against the slick glass.

Cassandra whimpered in an unladylike manner as Tallulah towered over her, her big hair adding extra emphasis to her stance. "Now you listen to me, Miss High-and-mighty. You aren't in your cushy century any more. This is the twenty first century. There are no servants, there are no slaves. You don't get to order me about. Ever! Understood?" She lifted her hand and pointed her index finger at Cassandra.

"Desist in your handling of me," Cassandra said, her voice quaking. A finger of fear spread through her and she disliked how it made her feel. She was weak, dependent, exposed. "Desist," she pleaded, louder this time.

"Don't be such a baby." Tallulah's body was relaxing a little, the tension lessening.

Cassandra's control and calm was wavering. If Miss Blythe had been present to witness what she did next, the governess would have withered on the spot. However, to be spoken to by someone who was so obviously inferior was intolerable and would not stand.

"Help!" shouted Cassandra, as if she was a common shop girl instead of the lady of the house. The sound echoed off the walls of the room. Tallulah looked as if she had been slapped in the face.

She stepped back, releasing Cassandra from her hold. "Get a grip would you? Stop whaling like a brat."

"I am not whaling. How dare you insult me further. To think, you have the audacity to suppose that you, a servant, can…"

"Oh, here we go again with this crap. We don't keep servants. Get with the programme, Lady Muck.

"I am not…" Cassandra's voice was rising to a high-pitched squeak. She swallowed and tried to regain composure.

The door burst open and Judge Miller barrelled into the room. "Girls…" She was panting, her breath coming in short bursts. She had obviously come running from somewhere, hearing the raucous from their recent tussle. "Cassie. Tallulah. What is going on?" She looked from one to the other, clearly expecting an explanation.

Both girls replied at once, "Nothing."

Tallulah stepped forward. "Cassie fell off the window ledge."

Judge Miller turned towards Cassandra, a look of concern marring her features. "Are you okay?"

She took a step forward and instinctively Cassandra moved back. "Yes, thank you, I am well." The coolness was not personal, it was simply the way that Cassandra had been taught to behave with a new acquaintance.

The woman stopped, her features pained. She nodded and turned to leave. "Okay, we're making dinner. Lasagna. I have Doctor Nevin on standby, so if you experience any dizziness, nausea, confusion..." Tallulah snorted, then tried to hide the noise behind a string of coughing. "...I will call him immediately. I'm hoping that you are responsible enough to let me know if your health is in danger, instead of holding on to a childish fear of needles. Doctor Nevin is a very capable doctor and I trust him implicitly." She looked at both girls, a weight of implication in her words.

They both nodded dutifully.

Shaking her head, she turned and left the room, muttering something as she went.

"She," remarked Tallulah tiredly, as she flopped to the floor.

"She what?" enquired Cassandra, rubbing her wrist where Tallulah had pinned her. Cassandra was eying the space on the floor beside Tallulah, wondering if it would be a good idea or bad idea to go sit on it.

"Judge Miller is a she."

The disbelief momentarily overcame Cassandra's caution and she sat down heavily, "A female justice. But that is impossible. Women cannot be judges."

"Yeah, well, there are lots of things about this place that you don't know."

Cassandra tried to think of something intelligent to say as a retort but nothing came to mind. She had to admit that the girl was right. Cassandra did not know enough about this strange place.

"I know, a bit of a head melt, isn't it?" offered Tallulah.

Cassandra felt like crying. Instead she sniffed back the threatening tears and said, "You do not understand. This is all wrong. None of this...you...her..." She jerked her head in the direction of the bedroom

95

door, "where I come from, this would not be happening."

"Yeah, but it is happening, isn't it? You're here, Cassie is God knows where. And you have to fix it. You have to figure out how to fix it."

Cassandra groaned loudly into her hands. "But I do not know how."

"I'll help you. We will figure it out together."

Cassandra looked expectantly at the other girl.

"Assuming you don't try any of that servant master B.S.," Tallulah added, before smiling.

Cassandra straightened up. "Yes, I apologise for my behaviour. It was extremely out of character. I would never…"

"What? Order a beating. Yes, you would. You would if you thought that it was the right thing to do. If you thought it was your duty. You would do whatever you are told."

Cassandra was silent, the sting in Tallulah's words echoing in her mind. Was that true? Would Cassandra do what she was told, even if she disagreed with the instruction? Surely not. Miss Blythe only ever offered good advice.

Cassandra frowned. The logic she was trying to utilise seemed slippery, untenable; she was unable to hold on to it, unable to convince herself that she was in the right.

If she had been in Ludlow, the real Ludlow, she would have been expected to deal with Tallulah in an appropriate manner, to hand her over to the housekeeper for punishment, regardless of Cassandra's personal feelings on the matter. Even if she felt that it was wrong.

She wondered what Cassie would do, her substitute, the person who was living her life in 1714. Would she have had the servant whipped as was required? As was her duty?

Cassandra considered for a moment, she wondered what her great great great great great granddaughter was actually like. The thought stopped her breath for a minute. She was her great grandmother many times over. That meant that she had been married, had given birth to children. The revelation cramped her insides. She had a husband. She shifted uncomfortably, unwilling to follow that train of internal enquiry any more. She had to find a way back there, had to get back to her life, her responsibilities.

Cassandra sat up straight. "Mrs. Rivers mentioned something about the east wing. That she told me, Cassie, not to go there. What do you think she meant?"

"Mrs. Rivers is half cracked," volunteered Tallulah, picking some dirt from beneath her fingernails. "Cassie says that Mrs. Rivers creeps around the place, saying hardly anything, watching, all the time watching with those beady eyes."

Cassandra shivered. "Do you think she means well or no?"

Tallulah shrugged. "How should I know? This is my first time here. Judge Miller doesn't approve."

"Does not approve of what?" asked Cassandra.

"Of me!" Tallulah turned her head and glanced out the window, "She thinks I'm a bad influence. Ever since Cassie moved schools she had been getting into trouble. Her mum thinks it's because of me."

"And is it?" Cassandra asked.

The girl was quiet for a few seconds. "Maybe it is. How should I know? Come on."

Tallulah pulled Cassandra to her feet.

"What are you doing?" asked Cassandra, as they moved out of the room and along the corridor.

"If everyone thinks we are such trouble makers, then maybe we should start stirring it up."

The sound of voices from the kitchen floated to their ears. Tallulah put her finger to her lips and crept along the hallway, down the stairs towards Judge Miller's office. She eased the door open quietly and grabbing Cassandra's hand, pulled her in.

"What are you…"

"Shh. Look for her iPad."

"Her what?"

"Ugh," groaned Tallulah. "Never mind. Keep an eye on the door. This communications lock down imposed on you…on Cassie, meant no mobile, no internet. In here is the only place we can get a proper signal." Tallulah moved around the desk, pulling open the drawers, searching the stacks of paper that had already begun to pile up on the desk. "So much for a family holiday," muttered Tallulah as she looked in the box of folders.

"What do you mean?" whispered Cassandra from her position by the half-closed door.

"They were supposed to be up here for some bonding time, mother-daughter stuff. Cassie and Judge Miller aren't exactly on speaking terms at the best of times. Not since…well, not since Cassie's dad left."

"Oh," was all that Cassandra could manage. She was momentarily jealous of Cassie. To think, that she had a mother who was alive, who obviously loved and cared for her. Cassandra would have given anything to have her mother back. She stifled the feeling of sadness that was brewing within her and peeked out the door and down the hallway. She would not cry. She would not cry.

"Ah ha!" Tallulah held up a skinny book, covered in purple leather.

"What is that?" asked Cassandra, abandoning her post.

"An iPad."

Cassandra shook her head.

Sighing, Tallulah began to explain. "It's for accessing the internet. Like a big electronic library on line, you can ask it anything and it will give you loads of answers."

"Very well," Cassandra said tentatively, "so what are you going to ask it?"

"I don't know, I thought you would be able to help me with that?"

Cassandra shook her head. "Ask it how I got here? Ask it if my father is well?"

"No, it doesn't work in specifics like that. Hang on, what is your father's name?"

"Lord Miller."

Tallulah rolled her eyes. "Ya I know but there were probably loads of Lord Millers. What is his first name and do you know when he was born?"

Cassandra told her and watched as Tallulah typed something onto the shiny surface of the book. When Tallulah touched it, letters and numbers appeared. All of a sudden, a list of entries flooded the screen.

"Look, there are a few details about him, here." Tallulah pointed to an entry and went to select it but the screen went fuzzy, the words disjointed. Tallulah cursed under her breath and typed in another name, Cassandra's. A similar list appeared and as soon as Tallulah selected it, the list jumbled up. An error message appeared on the shiny book.

"Search Results Not Determined. What is the meaning of this?" asked Cassandra.

"The search is incomplete. The results are changing. You're not in the database anymore."

Cassandra looked at her. "I am no longer in it?"

"You were in the records, evidence that you were alive, details about your father, your family and now, the computer can't find anything. It's as if...as if you have disappeared. Wiped from existence."

She tapped the keys again, a different name, Cassandra leaned over. "Justice Eve Miller," she read out loud. The results blipped on the page and crackled to random numbers and letters, nothing decipherable. "She doesn't exist either," whispered Cassandra.

The two of them stared at the screen, reading the message which flashed there. "*Search Results Not Determined.*"

"You don't exist in the eighteenth century. If you don't exist, Judge Miller doesn't exist, Cassie doesn't exist."

"Girls?" The sound of someone calling them made them jump. They turned and stared at the door. "Dinner is ready." They could hear Cassie's mother moving across the hallway, back towards the kitchen.

"Come on," whispered Tallulah, "we better go eat before they come looking for us."

Cassandra let herself be led across the hallway, towards the kitchen, her mind racing.

Chapter Thirteen

~ Cassie ~

Cassie was dying for a cigarette. She couldn't take being cooped up in the house for much longer. Miss Blythe had been dogged in her insistence that a decision be made regarding the alterations to the front drawing room. What did Cassie know about renovations? What did she know about anything that was going on? Miss Blythe brought up the topic of the clerk of works at the breakfast table.

"Surely, Lady Cassandra, you see that a decision must be made. The master builder has finished his commission in the next county and will be leaving to go back to London soon. If you want him to renovate then you must see him." Miss Blythe picked up several letters from her side plate and waved them at Cassie. "These go unanswered. If you do not want to bring the matter in front of your father, then…"

"I am not going to bother a sick man with the whims of a…what do you call them…fop from London, who wants his house renovated into the latest style. What happens next year if they decide that they like polka-dots and want to paint the outside of Ludlow Park pink?"

Miss Blythe clearly did not know what Cassie was talking about, her expression unchanging. "Never mind, Miss Blythe." Cassie pushed the piece of brown mutton around her plate. She had eaten a morsel of it to alleviate the suspicious glances that the governess was sending her way, but the smell was putting her right off her breakfast.

"I think you…"

"Yes, Miss Blythe, you have told me what you think, several times. And I disagree," snapped Cassie, regretting her outburst almost instantaneously.

"Well," sniffed the governess, "if her ladyship does not wish for my council then I shall not give it. I hope your father agrees with your decision. Assuming you have spoken to him. Good morning, ma'am." And with that Miss Blythe pushed herself up from the table and left the room, the sound of her skirt dragging mournfully along behind her.

"Flip," exclaimed Cassie, banging her hand on the table. That was all she needed. Miss Blythe running to Lord Miller, telling him that his daughter was incapable of making the right decision. Then he would surely marry her to the first yokel he could get his hands on. And Ludlow Park would be doomed.

Cassie got the impression that the governess was used to having her advice followed, at all times. And now Cassie had annoyed her only ally. Stupid big mouth, she thought to herself. Stupid, stupid, big mouth. The prospect of being committed to the local asylum did not appeal to her. She didn't think Miss Blythe was a threat, but then again, you never know. It's always the person you least expect. Should she go apologise? "Ugh." She pushed her chair back by bumping her bum and hoop into it. It shifted beneath her, but didn't move any further.

She needed to get out of here, to find someplace to think, to figure stuff out. Her mum was great in a crisis, always the voice of sense.

She was stuck half up, half down, wedged between the edge of the table and the unsteady chair. She tried to move her hooped skirts out the way, tugging them but they would not budge. She could not sit down again as the chair was at an awkward angle.

"Argh," she shouted, her frustration getting the better of her. She yanked the material up, exposing her ankles and half of her shins. She heard the immobile serving boy inhale sharply. He was standing by the wall this whole time, unmoving. Her legs were covered in stockings anyway, and Cassie didn't see what the big deal was. Kicking back with her foot Cassie toppled over the heavy chair, its clatter echoing in the otherwise silent dining room. The servant boy remained still, keeping to his position, never deviating from his duty. "This bloody place," cursed Cassie as she half dragged, half pushed the skirts of her dress out the door, the chair upended and abandoned by the dining table, her half-eaten breakfast left on her plate.

She moved through the reception area, heading for the front door. She had to have a cigarette. Her second last fag and her lighter were rolled in a slip of material, tucked in the fold of her waist band. All she needed was a few quiet minutes to herself to figure out what the hell she was going to do.

The butler was standing half way up the stairs, addressing a footman when he turned at the sound of her skirts. Cassie did not stop, did not greet him, instead she barrelled forward towards the door, towards freedom. "My lady, your bonnet," called the butler.

"I don't need a bonnet," replied Cassie pushing out the front door. "I'm going for a walk, not going to meet the queen of England." She did not wait to hear his response.

Cassie walked briskly down the driveway and across the lawn. Molly had been kind enough to root out some sturdy footwear for her. She wore boots of soft leather, finely crafted, laced up to the base of her ankles. They gave her ample support as she strode purposefully across the grass, ignoring the creeping wetness. The ends of her skirts would be soaked soon but she didn't care. If Lady Cassandra had over a hundred gowns then surely Molly could find her something to change into when she got back.

The pins in her hair bit into her scalp. She longed to shake it out, to put on a pair of jeans, to slob around in her trainers. She felt a wave of panic flow over her. What if she never got home? What if she couldn't help Lord Miller? She would be stuck here. Never to see Tallulah again, Jonah, her mum. The thought of her mother brought a fresh feeling of discomfort. She was convinced that Cassie was a degenerate, a trouble maker. Maybe her banishment to 1714 was the wolf mirror's way of punishing her. *She's glad you're gone. She doesn't love you anyway. You're just a nuisance.* The loathsome inner voice rattled around her head, poisoning her resolve.

Mr. Cassie pushed her way through a copse of trees. She stumbled forward, a treacherous sob escaping her lips. She wanted to put as much distance as was possible between herself and Ludlow Park.

She bullied her way further into the thicket, her anger and confusion giving her extra strength. She could hear her dress snag in the undergrowth. She would ruin it, but she didn't care. A few more minutes and she pushed her way out of the thick forest onto a pathway. It was steep and wound its way through a collection of tall trees, oak and chestnut, ash and beech. The pathway was soft with fresh, fallen leaves, the morning air sharp. Cassie breathed out a sigh of relief.

She moved freely now, the leaves on the path rustling beneath her feet. She came to the top of a sharp rise and the trees lessened, opening out onto a circular area of meadow grass. The view from the little platform was surprising. Cassie could see the fields, hills and dales, the green patchwork of farms stretching for miles. She stopped short, her willow stick in her hand, gazing at the sight. "Wow," she whispered.

It was so beautiful. How had she not noticed this before? Why had she never explored the grounds of Ludlow? Because she was always so busy being mad at everyone. Withdrawing her cigarette from the pocket sewn into the waist of her dress, she stared at it reverently. She should really quit.

If she didn't find a way home she would have no choice but to quit. Sighing, she sparked up, inhaling long and deep, savouring the tobacco smell and taste that burned the back of her throat. She gazed across the landscape, trying not to think. For a moment, time ceased to exist and she was just happy to be.

The jingle of a horse's tack startled her and she glanced behind her.

"Oh no!" she groaned, dropping the half-smoked cigarette, grinding it out with the toe of her boot. She tried to subtly fan the smoke away without him noticing.

Charles Stafford reined his horse in close to her and bowed in his seat. "Lady Cassandra."

Cassie bobbed in what she hoped was an acceptable curtsy, but remained silent. She was not sure what she should say. She hoped he would move on and leave her alone. She was not in the mood to make polite conversation.

She was forced to tilt her head back, looking up, just to maintain eye contact. Her hands hung loosely by her sides, but she knew if he continued to look down at her in that infuriating way, an aura of superiority about him, she would punch him.

He glanced around the clearing, concerned. "You are alone?"

"Obviously," snapped Cassie, moving away from his horse, conscious of her delicate toes and the beast's stomping hooves. She crossed her arms in front of her and waited for whatever he was about to say.

"Your companion is not with you?"

Cassie frowned. "Companion? What do you mean?"

"Your governess, a lady's maid, someone to…"

She cut him off rudely, "Babysit me? I think I'm capable of walking around a green field and amongst some trees unaided. I do have two legs of my own you know."

Charles Stafford swung himself down from the saddle, landing expertly only a few feet from her. He straightened up and flipped the reins over the horse's head. The animal lowered its muzzle to the ground and began to graze, ignoring the humans. Charles moved towards Cassie and she took a step back. He was much bigger out of the saddle, well over six foot, his coat stretched across his broad shoulders, his polished boots and riding gear making him seem even taller.

Cassie swallowed loudly, anxiety spiking through her. Why had he asked if she was alone? Cassie trawled through her memory, searching for evidence in support of her suspicions that he was a potential threat. There was nothing conclusive, so she stood still and waited, her fingers curled into a fist ready to punch if he came too close.

He stopped a pace in front of her and bowed slowly once more before straightening up. He looked directly into her eyes. "Have I done something new to offend you, Madame?"

Cassie stared at him, her ability for speech momentarily rendered useless. He had the most piercing blue eyes.

"I think," he continued, "perhaps there is some kind of misunderstanding between us. We had been getting on so well…"

I knew it, thought Cassie. Lady Cassandra and Charles Stafford *were* an item. Oh crap, what if he tries to kiss me? She took a step back, holding up her hand.

"Okay, buddy, I don't know what you think is happening here, but let's get a few things straight…we are not," she moved her index finger to point between the man in front of her and herself, "you and I are not…"

He was watching her intently, his inquisitive eyes unnerving her.

"Ugh," sighed Cassie, throwing her head back, "I have no idea what is going on."

Charles took a small step towards her, closing the distance. "Lady Cassandra, I am concerned for you. I think I should escort you home. If someone were to notice that you had left the house on your own, the rumours would be…"

"What?" bristled Cassie. "What exactly are you saying?"

"Lady Cassandra," he began again, taking her by the elbow to intensify his point.

"Will you stop calling me that." She tried to shake her arm free, but he would not let go.

"I insist on escorting you back to Ludlow Park. I fear you are unwell."

Cassie pushed him away. "You can stick your insistence where the sun don't shine," she half shouted. "I'm not going back into that house till I am good and ready. To think, I can't even take a walk in my own front garden without some rumours. This bloody place!" She turned her back and stalked over to the nearest felled tree and sat down heavily, bunching her skirts underneath her.

He came to stand next to her, his eyes scanning the clearing. After a few moments silence, he flicked his coat tails behind him and sat down. "Would you care to discuss your…plight with me? Is it about your father? His health?"

Cassie eyed him suspiciously. "Why are you asking about my father?" Her corset was pinching her again, the weight of the hoop dragging her down. She half stood and gripped the base of her skirts, lifting them up so she could sit properly on the log.

Charles jumped up and turned his back instantly.

"What?" asked Cassie, scanning the clearing to see if something incredibly fierce was coming at them. "What?" she repeated, when she couldn't see anything.

He half turned, indicating her skirts. "Your deportment, Madam."

"Oh, for the love of God." Cassie pushed off from the felled tree and gripped her skirts once more, pulling them up to her knees.

"Lady Cassandra," he choked, "Please, do not expose yourself in such a way."

Cassie was ignoring him, doing a little jig in front of the fallen log, her petticoats showing, the cream of her horrendous itchy stockings exposed for all to see, but not an inch of flesh was on display.

He grabbed her, shaking her roughly, causing her to drop her skirts, "Show some poise. What would your mother think of you...?"

Cassie stopped dancing and looked at him. His cheeks were flushed, his temper rising. "My mother hates me," she whispered. He stared down at her. In an instant, she realised what she had said. If she told him her secret, he would surely think she was crazy. "I'm sorry. It's just, it's just..." She brushed her skirts, keeping her gaze lowered, afraid that if they locked eyes again she would blurt out something terrible. Cassie realised how close he was to her. The masculine smell of sweat and horse mingling together, tickled her nose. As if he read her mind, he stiffened and released her arm, brushing his hands together in a business-like manner.

They both stepped apart, silence descending between them.

"I..." she began.

"I will lead you back to the house," he interrupted, turning towards his horse, and retrieving the reins. They moved down the main path, cutting across the lawn, keeping a respectable distance between them.

At the front door, a flustered Miss Blythe greeted them.

"Oh," she exclaimed, "Lady Cassandra, where have you been? We were so worried about you. What with gypsies in the woods, you could have been set upon."

Cassie didn't say anything, she just wanted to go inside, to crawl into bed and forget everything.

"Thank you, Mr. Stafford, thank you for seeing her home safely. I do not know what has gotten in to her. It is her father you understand. His illness has quite shaken her." The governess bundled her up the steps.

Cassie glanced over her shoulder at the door. Charles was standing there, a frown of concentration on his fine features. He was watching her. She smiled meekly and raised her hand to salute him, hoping that he would interpret it as an apology. He remained still as stone, not a muscle out of place. She felt a momentary pang of regret that she could not have been his friend. But it was impossible, a man like that followed every rule and respected protocol.

The main door closed firmly behind her and she was escorted back to her room.

Chapter Fourteen

~ Cassie ~

Cassie desperately wanted a shower, a peanut butter sandwich and an episode of *Once Upon a Time*. She was exhausted, and had the beginnings of a tummy ache. Her outburst in the forest was not exactly in fitting with the character she was supposed to be portraying. What must he think of me, she wondered? A mental image overtook her, crazy dancing around the clearing, her skirts pulled up. She cringed at the memory.

Miss Blythe, on reaching the bedroom directed them both inside, closing the door firmly. "Lady Cassandra," she began, straining to remain calm, "I am aware that you are distressed over the illness under which your father is suffering."

Oh no, thought Cassie, the governess is about to give me a lecture.

"But I want to say that nothing, nothing is an excuse for your behaviour. You must always…"

"Do your duty," interrupted Cassie, moving towards the bed, leaning against it.

"Precisely, my Lady." Miss Blythe attempted a bright smile but did not succeed. "Now, if I may suggest that you take a tonic for your nerves and get some rest, you look altogether washed out." Miss Blythe rang the bell and a few minutes later a serving girl appeared at the door, bearing a silver tray. On the tray was a goblet filled with steaming liquid. It smelled like Christmas time.

"What is that?" Cassie asked as she moved closer and sniffed.

"A simple tonic that Mr. Evins made, to calm the nerves. Camomile, basil leaf and clove I think. It will calm you after your…exercise earlier."

There was another knock on the door and Molly entered. "There you are, girl," exclaimed Miss Blythe impatiently, "get a move on. Help Lady Cassandra from her dress, the hem of which is ruined."

Molly bobbed a curtsy and scurried to help Cassie out of her damp and dirty skirts.

"See that Lady Cassandra drinks all of her tonic, Molly," and with that the governess swept from the room, banging the door behind her.

"Was she always like this?" asked Cassie as she wriggled out of the soiled material.

Molly did not answer for a moment, her lip bitten between her teeth, a look of concentration on her face. "Who?" asked the girl, glancing at Cassie.

"Miss Blythe, was she always so…so…I don't know, unhappy with everything?"

Molly shrugged her shoulders. "I cannot say, ma'am…" Her tone was tight.

Cassie craned her neck around to get a better look, as Molly bent forward to undo the ribbons at the back of her skirt. "Is something wrong?" Cassie asked.

"No." The girl pulled the ribbons tight, fighting with a knot, causing the bones of the corset to dig into Cassie's flesh.

"Ouch!" She pulled away from the lady's maid and turned to look at her. "Okay, there is obviously something wrong, so why don't you just tell me, instead of trying to kill me by stabbing me with this damn corset."

Molly looked at her, remaining tight lipped.

Cassie, mirroring her stance, tried to stare her down.

"If you insist, Miss Cassie," the lady's maid squeaked with restrained emotion, "Ya decide to take yerself off out for a walk and the whole house becomes undone. Miss Blythe down in the kitchen shoutin' at Cook, upstairs in the hallway, shoutin' at Mr. Genkins. If ya do somethin' unthinkin' then it is usually us who pay the price."

Cassie frowned. "I didn't know. I only went for a walk. I didn't think that it wasn't allowed."

Molly came and turned her around, fiddling with the ribbons again. "*You*...Lady Cassandra... is the most eligible woman in the neighbourhood, her father is a very rich man. If someone had come upon ya who was up to no good, I dread to think what could have happened."

Cassie understood what Molly was trying to tell her. The difference between them and us, servant and master, rich and poor was very evident.

Cassie suddenly felt very tired.

"I need to sit down, Molly. Help me out of this thing, please." The final ribbon was undone and Cassie stepped less than gracefully out of the heavy dress before padding on bare feet to the bed and slipping under the covers. She was cold, the actions of the day weighing heavily on her.

"Here." Molly handed her the tonic which had stopped steaming, "drink this, it will help ya feel better."

Cassie sipped the brew, expecting it to be vile, but surprisingly, it tasted alright, like a funky herbal tea. She buried a little deeper under the covers, snug in the dip of the horsehair mattress. "Sorry," she murmured over the rim of the silver goblet as Molly bent to pick up the soiled dress. "I didn't realise what would happen."

Molly nodded. There was silence for a minute, save the rustle of fabric as Molly wound all the ribbons together, gathering the dress material. "Ya asked about Miss Blythe," she began, not looking up from her task.

"Mmmm," muttered Cassie, the heat of the tonic working its magic.

"She was not always so...severe."

Cassie perked up slightly. "Go on."

"When she came to the house first, I do not remember it, but Cook can tell the story, Miss Blythe was young, and though not beautiful she had a plain kind of prettiness about her."

Cassie couldn't quite imagine that.

"She taught Lady Cassandra and her sister, Elizabeth. My mistress came on quite well, havin' run wild in her mother's *absence*." The girl tripped over the final word in the sentence. Cassie wondered what it had been like, how Lord Miller could commit his own wife to the asylum.

These were definitely strange times.

"Well, she was getting' on very nice but then…there was a man…"

"Typical," interrupted Cassie, rolling her eyes.

Molly smiled. "A young curate named Gibbs. She was madly in love with him, him too by all accounts. Except the curate's mother was wicked, with desires on a fortune for her and her son."

Molly paused for dramatic effect. "She persuaded him that Miss Blythe was not good enough and put him in the path of a rich merchant's daughter in a parish nearer to London. He moved there within a month and Miss Blythe never heard from or saw him again."

"What was he like?" asked Cassie, hanging on every word.

"Whom? The curate? Not very handsome, according to Cook." Molly gathered the last of the dress in her arms, the material overflowing around her. "She said he was short and ruddy with ginger hair, but the best of temperament. He was supposed to have been a very nice man."

Cassie considered the description and was struck by a thought: the curate and Mr. Evins were similar in appearance. She remembered the way Miss Blythe fawned over the apothecary, her eyes never leaving his reddened face.

"I will leave ya now, Miss, I must get this dress to the laundry before the stains dry in."

Cassie yawned, leaving the tonic to one side. "Okay, Molly, I think I am going to just have a snooze. I'm very tired. Thanks," she murmured as she settled back onto the pillows.

The girl had barely left the room before Cassie was asleep, a haze of exhaustion washing over her. A knock on the door a few hours later woke her. She ground her fists into her eyes, wiping the sleep away. "Yes," she croaked.

The door opened and a small serving girl entered. "Miss Blythe sent up another tonic for ya, me lady." The serving girl, barely twelve years old, bobbed a curtsy and left the tray on the writing desk. Cassie struggled into a seated position and looked around her.

Her head felt fuzzy and there was an uncomfortable sensation in her gut, like somebody pressing fingers into her intestines, applying too much pressure. She took in a deep lungful of air and tried to resettle herself against the pillow. She exhaled long and deep. Maybe she should drink something. She pushed back the covers and swung her legs out of the bed before standing up and padding across the room towards the desk and the steaming drink. She made it half way before a sharp pain stabbed her in the belly, causing her to double over. "Oh." She hobbled to the tonic, hoping that the warmth of the soothing liquid would help the pain in her stomach.

She glanced down at the silver goblet, the steam rising from it in wisps. She reached out her hand, ready to take the cup to her lips and then stopped, her gaze fixed on the steaming contents. The pulsing pain in her stomach seemed to match the beat of her heart. Mr. Evins had prepared the tonic. The words ricocheted through her head. Had he used all the ingredients in his workshop? Were Miss Blythe and Mr. Evins working together, the doctor too, all with the aim of killing off the Miller family?

She opened the window and flung the steaming contents outside. It all made perfect sense. Lord Miller was being poisoned by the apothecary. But was he acting alone? And what was his motive?

Cassie gripped her stomach as it rumbled. She limped back to the bed and pulled the corded bell, the echo of it ringing along the hallway. She needed some water, needed to see Molly.

After a few minutes a gentle knock, followed by Molly's reassuring presence, "Ya rang, me lady?" She closed the door behind her and moved across to the bedside, her eyes narrowing, "Ya do not look well, Miss."

"Ugh, I have a terrible pain in my tummy. Like I've been poisoned."

The lady's maid turned pale and moved to the bed. "Do not say such a thing, Miss." She took Cassie's hand and held it gently. Her eyes were searching Cassie's, an undertone of fear in them.

"It's okay, Molly. I've probably just eaten something bad." Cassie didn't want to alarm the girl any further. There would be no more drinking of tonic as far as she was concerned. Ever!

"About his Lordship..." she began, addressing the lady's maid, momentarily pushing the feeling of discomfort to the back of her mind.

Molly nodded, letting go of Cassie's hand, remembering her station. She stood up abruptly. Cassie rolled her eyes heavenward and reached across, ignoring the pain, to pull the servant girl back to the bed.

"Sit down, can't you? Take the weight off. I think you and the other servants were right about Lord Miller. His illness is odd because he is not really sick. Mr. Evins is using mandrake root in the tonic. Doctor Brown, knowingly or otherwise, is giving Lord Miller a poison each time he administers the medicine."

Molly's brow puckered.

"Come on, Molly, think about it. How else is Lord Miller momentarily recovering then slumping back into ill health? He gets better, then takes another tonic, his symptoms return, even worse than before. It has to be Evins…it is the only answer."

"Mandrake," asked Molly, her eyes large and round, "What's that?"

"It's a root, a very poisonous plant, looks like a naked twisted man when it's pulled from the ground. Believed to scream if it is dug up, Harry Potter, Mandrake root? No?" Visions of botany lessons at Greystone's school floated to Cassie's mind's eye.

Molly shook her head. "I have no knowledge of such a thing."

Cassie sighed. "Yes, I know, you don't have Harry Potter here yet, do you?" She cursed under her breath. "If only we had the internet, I could check up the symptoms of mandrake poisoning. I bet you any money that they are what Lord Miller is experiencing." The dinner gong rang from downstairs. "I have to go down to dinner."

"But I thought you were being poisoned by your food?" asked Molly, rolling off the bed.

"Yes, yes, but I need to be downstairs, I want to talk to Miss Blythe, to question Doctor Brown about his tonic. I need to be sure." Cassie scanned the room. "Molly, quick, you will have to help me dress, and my hair is a mess. I wish I could just throw it up in a bun, hide the ends."

Molly stood up and moved across the room towards the walk in wardrobe. "What colour would ya like, Miss"

"Colour?" Cassie asked impatiently, "I don't care about colour. I just want to figure out what is happening to Lord Miller, and then when I set things right maybe I can go home. Give me cream," she shouted into the annex, "it makes me look skinny."

It took the girls a great deal of effort, pulling and pushing, primping and preening to get into the large contraption of a dress and to do up Cassie's hair so it resembled some kind of style.

Molly left her at the door of the bedroom and wished her good luck, squeezing her hand reassuringly, "I'll wait for ya here after I've finished my chores."

Cassie nodded and made her way slowly downstairs, ignoring the pain in her gut, which had eased somewhat in the last half hour.

At the door to the dining room she steadied herself and moved with as much grace as was possible into the room, watching the reaction of Miss Blythe and the doctor, keen to note any flicker of disappointment that she seemed alive and well.

Both parties were seated at the table, waiting for her and both seemed genuinely pleased to see her.

The starters arrived, three courses of them. Cassie pushed her food around her plate, rearranging it from one side to the next, making it look like she was eating. As the meal progressed, Miss Blythe and Doctor Brown were making polite conversation about some neighbour or another who had recently gotten married and the expected arrival of the new wife to the area. Cassie was only half listening, her brain ticking away, rotating over and over again. "Doctor Brown," she interrupted.

He glanced up, his food on his fork raised halfway to his lips.

"Sorry, I have a question regarding my father."

Cassie thought she heard the governess sigh loudly. Doctor Brown lowered his fork and looked just beyond her, his gaze never settling.

"His medicine, the tonic you give him, how often do you prescribe it?"

If the doctor seemed surprised by her question, he didn't show it. "Lady Cassandra, your father receives a high dose tonic once a week. The ingredients are quite rare and strong and it is recommended that they be administered once every five to seven days. I am in fact meeting with Mr. Evins this evening to collect a new tonic for your father."

Miss Blythe cleared her throat and Cassie glanced at her, noting the heightened pinkness to her cheeks. "You collect the tonic from him yourself?" Cassie asked.

"Normally I send someone to town for the supplies, but in special cases I like to deal with him directly. Mr. Evins is kind enough to meet me out of hours if there is anything urgent I need. He concedes to meet me at the Horse and Hound tavern in the village."

Cassie took up her fork and chewed a roast potato methodically, thinking on what Doctor Brown had said. She looked up at Miss Blythe innocently and conversed on mundane topics for the rest of the evening before feigning tiredness and excusing herself.

Chapter Fifteen

~ Cassandra ~

Search results not determined. Search results not determined. Search results not determined.

"Pass the peas please, Cassie?"

The woman was talking to her. Cassandra was too busy thinking about the words on the moving book. *Search results not determined.* She did not exist in this time. She wondered if she even existed in her own time? If her father, sister, Miss Blythe, if they were safe in 1714.

"Cassie, are you alright? You're not eating your lasagna," remarked the woman. "It's your favourite. Mrs. Rivers made it especially."

Cassandra looked across the table. The housekeeper was staring at her, piercing green eyes watching her every move. Cassandra pushed the half-eaten plate of food away. "I am not hungry." She detected the half rise of the housekeeper's shoulders, a slight shrug, but apart from that the woman said nothing. What did the housekeeper know about the mirror, wondered Cassandra?

This *In Her Net* seemed to be a type of information book, a very advanced encyclopaedia. Cassandra wondered if the *In Her Net* would have any information on Mrs. Rivers.

The boy, Jonah, was staring across the table at her, his mouth half full of food. "When did you dye your hair, Cassie?" he asked, cheekily. Cassandra looked at Tallulah, who shook her head.

Cassandra searched frantically for an answer and then it came to her.

"Shut your…" She was trying to think of some of the common language she had heard the lower servants use, "…trap, it ain't none of yer business."

"Cassie, don't be rude to your brother. Jonah, finish your dinner. We are going to the autumn fair after this. We're overdue some quality family time." Judge Miller was staring pointedly at Cassandra.

"Can I be excused?" asked Jonah, pushing his seat back from the table, his legs already out from underneath him, ready to sprint from the room. Mrs. River's rose stiffly from her seat and gathered what empty dishes she could. She moved to the door and disappeared down the corridor towards the kitchen. Cassandra relaxed a little when the serving woman left.

Judge Miller was reading through a document that she had brought to the dining table, barely glancing up as her son bolted. Cassandra frowned. How rude she thought, to be reading at the dinner table when there are other people to converse with. It showed a terrible kind of disregard. Miss Blythe would not approve.

Forgetting herself, Cassandra said, "Must you read at the table?"

The woman looked up, "Excuse me?"

"Do you always read at the …" Tallulah kicked her sharply on the shin. Cassandra gasped in pain. "Nothing," she muttered, "Excuse me." She rose slowly, glared at Tallulah and moved out of the room, limping slightly on her sore leg.

She would search the study, look for some paper traces of her family. If the *In Her Net* was faulty, then surely paper records could not be changed. She pushed open the study door, her breath hitching in her throat; to snoop was scandalously unladylike. Cassandra felt a thrill through her body. At a deeper level, she was shocked to realise, she liked breaking the rules.

"This is completely necessary for the greater good," she said to herself, appalled at her own brazenness.

"Hey!" Tallulah's hand came around the door, stopping Cassandra from closing it fully.

"What are you doing?" hissed Cassandra, the blood draining from her face in fright.

"I can't let you take all the blame when you get caught. Anyway, two pairs of eyes are better than one. What are *we* doing?"

The girl clicked the door quietly shut behind them.

"The family records…" Cassandra said the words slowly, uncomfortable with complete disclosure.

"Oh, yeah, that big book. Cassie showed it to me once." Tallulah stopped in front of one of the large bookshelves and traced her finger along the spine of the dusty books.

Cassandra highly doubted that a person of Tallulah's ilk would have been allowed access to a book of such import.

"Look on that shelf over there and see if you can find anything." Tallulah waved her hand in the direction of the large bookshelf on the opposite side of the room.

With slow, precise movements Cassandra walked to the bookshelf, annoyed that Tallulah was telling her what to do. Who gave her the authority, she grumbled silently to herself? She craned her neck to the side and began to walk alongside the bookshelf, reading the titles as she went, unwilling to touch any of the dirty, dusty books. One shelf up, at the end, was a book with a large brown spine. Unlike the other books, it had no title on it. Cassandra stood on her tip toes and reached upwards, edging the book loose of the tight shelf. A shower of dust drizzled to her face, causing her to sneeze. "Tallulah, I think I have found it."

Cassandra carried the book to the mahogany desk and dropped it unceremoniously in the middle of Judge Miller's paper.

"Careful," chastised Tallulah. Cassandra remained tight-lipped, biting back a reproach.

They opened the brown leather cover. It was stiff and cracked with age, its corners curled. Inside the first page was an etching of the façade of Ludlow Park, beneath it a date, 1852.

"Wow," murmured Tallulah, impressed with the statuesque nature of the building.

Cassandra turned the page and read the inscription, "Ludlow Park domain history and heritage, Richard Henry Miller…" The book contained cuttings, information on the family, abstract information, nothing detailed, nothing specific.

They flicked through the first few pages, nothing of importance, a newspaper article detailing the extensive renovations to the rear of the house in 1865, a copy of marriage licences, births, deaths, local news.

Then, in the midst of all that Cassandra saw something, an article about a storm knocking over some of the oldest trees on the estate, next to the Stafford's land. She had told her father that those trees would grow to be an inconvenience, but would he listen?

There had been a very great storm, roofs of the labourers' cottages had been pulled off in the torrential winds, four large trees felled, the windows of the church broken. As long as the text did not mention any Miller family member directly it appeared to stay put, stuck to the paper. Then, on the following page Cassandra saw a clipping from the same year, the same month. A girl, one of the servant girls from the big house had gone missing. The men investigating her disappearance had asked for any help in finding her. They believed that she may have been caught in the storm.

Cassandra remembered the howl of the wind the night in the east wing, the shriek of it hammering at the windows. "There," she said, pointing her finger to the heading.

"What?"

"The storm, a missing girl. What if...what if," she couldn't finish the sentence.

"What if the girl came through the mirror?" offered Tallulah.

Cassandra nodded her head mutely, flicking through the rest of the book, slowly at first, then more quickly, pulling the pages apart till she came to the end. "There is no mention of her again. No article saying what happened to her, if they found her or not."

"Maybe she ran away, or was simply hiding and when they found her, they didn't bother putting it in the local paper."

"No," said Cassandra, shaking her head, "They never found her. She came through the wolf mirror to some time, to some strange place and could not get back. They never found her." Cassandra's hands were shaking.

Tallulah quickly closed the heavy cover and lifted the book back to the shelf, slotting it in where they had taken it from.

"Come on," suggested Tallulah changing the subject, "we should get ready for the fair. Do you need clean clothes?" asked Tallulah, scanning Cassandra's outfit.

Cassandra raised her eyebrow, "Are you suggesting that there is something wrong with my attire?"

"No, no," insisted Tallulah, "You look lovely."

Chapter Sixteen

~ Cassie ~

"Molly," Cassie jumped up from the bed as the servant entered, "Your brother works in the stables, right?"

"Miss Blythe sent me to help ya undress," replied Molly, ignoring the question. She came and began to untie the ribbons of the dress.

"Does he have access to the horses?" continued Cassie.

The maid stopped in her task and looked up, her eyes narrowing, "A horse? What for?"

"I need to go to the village. To the Horse and Hound."

Molly dropped her hands by her side and stood still, her mouth slightly ajar. "You want to go to a tavern?" she asked in disbelief.

Cassie rolled her eyes, "Come on, don't dismiss the idea before you have even heard the plan. Doctor Brown is meeting the apothecary at the Horse and Hound tonight. He collects his weekly supplies there and I just want to go along…"

"As Doctor Brown's guest?"

"No! Of course not. That's why I need the horse. I'm a bit rusty but I'm sure it's like riding a bike."

Molly stared at her.

"Okay, so you don't know what a bike is, anyway, I need a horse and I need some clothes, I can't go like this." She indicated her large gown. "So, I need you to help me."

Molly shook her head. "I do not think this is a good idea. If ya are caught, if ya fall from the horse, if Doctor Brown sees ya... No miss, I cannot."

"If. If. If! Come on, Molly, I have to try. I just know there is something going on and Evins is involved. You can keep the coast clear here. All I need is a horse?" She smiled persuasively. "Please?"

The girl was silent, thinking it over, her teeth chewing on her bottom lip. After a few moments, she said, "I do not think..."

"Molly, you have to. I can't help Lord Miller without you."

The servant looked torn between propriety and loyalty. Cassie held her breath.

"Very well," the servant whispered reluctantly, "I will help ya."

"Yes!" Cassie punched the air and did a little dance, excited to be finally doing something other than primping and preening herself. "I'll finish undoing all these ribbons and catches myself. Can you go get me something more suitable to wear?" The servant disappeared from the room and Cassie fumbled with the remainder of the stays, almost toppling over in her eagerness to get out of the dress.

A short time later Molly returned, carrying a linen sack. She plopped it on the bed. "This is the best I can do."

Cassie eagerly opened it. Inside was a pair of coarse tweed pants, a dull brown shirt and a loose-fitting hunting jacket, with suede patches to the elbow. She shrugged into the clothes and found that they fitted nicely though the trousers itched a little. She pulled on her brown ankle boots. "Okay, I'm ready," Cassie said triumphantly.

"Wait." Molly reached into the linen sack and drew out a floppy cap. The maid arranged it on Cassie's head, stuffing stray strands of hair up under the rim. It fitted Cassie perfectly and if drawn down at a slant over her eyes you would barely recognise her.

"Am I okay?"

"Yes," replied Molly, "I think ya are O...K. I will take ya to the servants' entrance and out the yard, across to the stables. Keep yer head down and do not say a word to anyone."

Cassie followed Molly with obedience to the end of the corridor, through a hidden door that looked like a regular wall panel. Cassie had not noticed it before. Once through the door she found herself in a corridor. It was bleak and cold with bare unpainted floor boards, patches of damp on the walls. The corridor stretched a long distance. Cassie had to watch her step, the floor worn uneven by the passing of so many servants throughout the years.

She felt a shiver of cold, a gust of wind coming from somewhere, no fires to keep these corridors warm, no carpets, tapestries or candle holders to chase away the gloom. At the end of the corridor they descended two flights of steps and emerged into the pit of the house, the kitchens. There was a flurry of activity in the room. The plates and dishes from the meal they had just eaten in the dining room had been brought back for scouring.

Behind a large slab of timber stood a woman, ruddy cheeks, rounded body, hair sticky with condensation. She was shouting orders to two serving girls who were ferrying plates of mutton, dishes of salmon, pans of eggs back from the main table. Cassie barely had time to take in the scene as Molly led her quickly through the mire of food, bodies and steam, out into the cool air. They picked their way across the yard in the dying evening light. The gate opened out onto the herb garden and a narrow-cobbled path wound its way to the stable block.

"My brother George is waitin' for ya at the corner of the stables. He has a horse. Do not tell him anythin', just say I sent ya. Stick to the main road all the way to the town." She glanced to the sky. "It is not very cloudy so when the moon comes out, ya should have enough light to get by. Good luck," she said and squeezed her hand. "Be careful." And with that she turned and retraced her steps across the yard.

Cassie was nervous, could feel her heart beating rapidly in her chest. She pulled the cap down a little further over her eyes, checking that her hair was tucked under and made her way resolutely through the herb garden.

At the wall to the stables she paused and scanned the yard. The stable grooms had bedded down the horses for the night, the gates and sheds firmly locked. There were tools and feeding buckets stacked neatly in the corner of the swept yard. In the fading light, Cassie moved as silently as possible to the corner of the stable block, pausing in the shadow. She was only there for a moment before a boy appeared, about fourteen years of age, tall and thin, with a cap, similar to Cassie's, pulled down over his eyes. He nodded to her, saying nothing and led her across the yard to the rear gate. They slipped through silently. He motioned her towards a collection of trees that offered some shelter. In the middle of them, a saddled grey mare stood patiently, her breath coming out in puffs in the cool of the almost night.

"She's a steady one, but prone to fits of spirit," the boy said, his voice deep, on the verge of manhood. "Molly says ya can ride?"

Cassie nodded.

"Up you get so." He bent down and cupped his hands, ready to give her a leg up.

Cassie swallowed any doubts and gripped the reins and front of the saddle, hefting herself up. She dipped her feet into the stirrups and settled back in the seat, squeezing her thighs together. She could smell the leather, the scent of the horse, the aroma of sweet hay, "Just like riding a bike," she muttered to herself.

"I be waitin' here, will whistle for ya." The boy nodded his head towards the stone wall of the stable block.

Cassie kicked the horse in the ribs, clicking her tongue, encouraging the animal to move along. They trotted down the forest trail until they reached the dirt track road that led to the village. Cassie managed to keep her seat with relative ease and she felt confident enough to let the mare have more reins. She spurred the animal to a canter and then into a gallop. The wind rushed past her and Cassie could feel the exhilaration of the ride take hold. By the time they reached the edge of the main green the new moon was rising in the sky.

She pulled the mare up to a walk, ambling across the grassy space. She had rehearsed her story in her head, in case someone stopped her. She was a boy from Ludlow Park, sent by the mistress to retrieve medicine for the master of the house.

There was a horizontal wooden post by the edge of the green, to which Cassie secured the mare. She dismounted and tried to walk with as much manliness as she could muster, jamming her hands into her pockets, pushing her hips forward, strutting with intent, across the green towards the tavern.

The Horse and Hound was the only drinking establishment in the village. It was a watering hole for the locals, an eating place, as well as a pit stop for travellers on the passing coach. The noise emanating from the premise was suggestive of a party of some sorts. She pushed her way in through the main entrance and stood for a moment, letting her eyes adjust to the dimness. It was full almost to the brim. Cassie was glad that the tavern was busy. The more people there, the less notice she would attract.

She squeezed in and stood by the wall, trying to look inconspicuous, her gaze scanning the crowd. There were several tables around the edge of the room. Most of them were occupied by weary travellers, dusty from their journey. Plates of mutton, bread and cheese, as well as tankards of foaming ale filled the tables. Cassie noticed a few well-to-do people, a lady in a fine travelling dress and bonnet sitting with two companions by the fireplace.

The proprietor was standing behind the counter, bellowing at a serving girl. He was large and stout, with a balding head of hair and an oversized moustache on his face. He had a fine sheen of sweat on his forehead and paused every now and then to wipe the back of his hand across it. Orders for jugs of ale were coming fast and furious. His shirt was stained brown and Cassie baulked, she hoped the stains were from spilt ale.

She scanned the room. There was a stairwell to the back of the tavern, a heavy curtain covering the opening. Cassie noticed one of the serving girls disappearing up the stairs with a tray of food. A few tables away from the stairwell was Mr. Evins. She recognised his solid bulk. There was a tankard of ale on the bench in front of him, but surprisingly, he was alone. His back was to her so she decided to move a little closer. She skirted around the edge of the room and slipped behind the curtain at the stairwell, pulling the material closed behind her.

Cassie peeped out. She had a full view of the apothecary now. Where was Doctor Brown? Surely, she hadn't missed him? The noise in the tavern seemed to be getting louder, the punters more raucous. Cassie was beginning to feel uncomfortable. Maybe this hadn't been such a good idea after all.

The apothecary sat at the table drinking the last of his ale. The crowd seemed to heave together as one. A man shouted something obscene at the other end of the bar, followed by the sound of shattering glass. Cassie pressed herself against the side of the stairwell, her heart hammering in her chest.

"I better get out of here," she whispered, peeping around the edge of the curtain. She was just planning her exit when she noticed a man walking towards Mr. Evins' table. He had his back to her. He was tall, wearing a black top hat and a long, knee length coat. He addressed the apothecary and sat down in the seat. He placed his walking cane across his knee. It was gold topped, in the shape of a lion's head. Mr. Evins was leaning in towards his guest, his eyes hungry, his hand gesticulating rapidly.

Who is that, wondered Cassie, edging a fraction closer, straining to hear, to get a glimpse of the stranger's face. The man slipped a letter, sealed with red wax across the table. Mr. Evins took it quickly, placing it securely into his pocket. "Damn it!" Cassie took a small step to the bottom stair her boots peeping out from under the curtain.

They were talking about something important, she heard the words *money*, *blackjack*, *gamble* and then there it was, the words she was listening for; *Ludlow Park*. They were talking about the estate. Cassie squeezed forward another fraction of an inch. They were talking about Reginald Huxley. Cassie heard his name clearly over the din of the patrons.

"You! What ya doin' there, boy?"

Cassie jumped in fright, her heart leaping in her chest.

The serving girl was standing at the top of the stairs, an empty tray in her hand. "What ya doin', I said?"

Cassie shook her head.

"Pick pocketin' are we?" She moved down the stairs towards Cassie. "Wait till I tell the master." She opened her mouth to shout out to the tavern owner. Cassie did not wait around to hear her. Darting out from behind the curtain, Cassie streaked through the crowded room, pushing roughly past the customers.

"Stop!" came a shout from behind her, "You there, stop! Thief."

That was the magic word. Half the punters in the tavern ceased what they were doing and looked around wondering what the ruckus was all about. Cassie was almost at the front door before anybody knew what was going on. She was inches away from freedom when something snagged her coat, pulling her to an abrupt halt. Her arms and legs flayed, trying to move forward. "Got ya!"

Cassie glanced around, a small man, with no front teeth, dirt engrained face and smelling of manure had the tail of her coat gripped firmly in his shovel like hands. Inch by inch he was pulling her towards him, a wicked grin on his face. Cassie whimpered. With fumbling fingers, she started to undo the buttons of her coat. She shrugged out of the sleeves, thankful that the coat was too big for her. It slipped from her slim frame. She ran, fear spurring her on.

She could hear the shouts of her pursuers as she streaked across the village green. She ducked down a side alley, running to the end before doubling back on herself. Cassie hoped that she would circle around the tavern, ending up back by the horses, avoiding anyone following her.

She was about to make a run for the green, when a hand grabbed her from behind, pulling her backwards. Strong arms wrapped around her body, pinning her wrists to her sides. She tried to scream but the pressure around her middle was cutting off the supply of air to her lungs. She aimed a well-placed kick at the man's shins. He grunted in pain but would not let her go, half pulling, half pushing her down another pathway into the darkness.

Cassie struggled, wriggled, kicked and bit, trying desperately to get free. Her cap had come down over her eyes, plunging her into total darkness. Her assailant pushed her roughly against the wall of a building, its timber panelling digging into her back. She tried to push the cap out of her face. He batted her hands away and pinned her to the timber, sandwiching her body. Cassie could hear the shouts and calls of men, running somewhere along the main street. She filled her lungs full of air, ready to scream for help.

"Keep still would you. Or you will get us both caught!"

Cassie stopped moving and sagged against the wall. The noise of the mob was coming closer. She squeezed herself into as small a shape as she could manage. She could feel the heat from the person in front of her as he leaned tight against the façade of the building, his breathing loud near her ear. Cassie wanted to push the hat out of her eyes, regain what little night vision she could but she had bigger problems to think about.

The mob passed close making its way towards the horses. She would have been caught for sure if she had continued on her intended route. Cassie held her breath, listening to the angry shouts.

After a moment or two the noise moved off and she began to breathe again. When she was sure they were gone, she stamped her boot down with as much force as she could, landing a clean blow. He cursed loudly and loosened his hold on her. She pushed him away, her free hands rolling the cap up from her eyes, brushing her hair out of her face.

"You!" she accused.

"You broke my blasted foot!" he complained.

"Well, you almost crushed my ribs. Who do you think you are grabbing me like that, pushing me down a dark..." Cassie looked about her, unsure how to describe the pathway "anyway, where do you get off, pushing me about!"

"I saved your neck. In case you had not noticed, madam, there was a mob of angry men chasing you!"

"I can take care of myself," sniffed Cassie.

"Evidently. Dressing in boys' clothes and stealing from a tavern. What. Is. Going. On? Tell me Lady Cassandra or so help me, I will deliver you personally to that mob myself."

"Mind your own business, Charles Stafford. It has nothing to do with you."

He grabbed her arm roughly. "It does concern me when I am in the tavern with my steward and I recognise the marriageable daughter of one of the most respected families in the county. What if someone had seen you?" He shook her. "Do you think I want to see Ludlow go to that London cad, Huxley? Do you? Do you think I want my estate adjacent to a man whose notion of countryside is eating a plumped pheasant!"

Cassie stared at him in the dim light, "I...I..."

"My family has struggled for years to gain the foothold that we have now. I will not see it jeopardised by a silly girl like you, frolicking around in these..." he indicated her shirt and trousers... "garments. You are supposed to be looking to secure your estate and its future."

"It's not as simple as that," Cassie tried to explain. "It's never as simple as that."

"I do not want to hear it. You are nothing but trouble! I am taking you home." He pulled her along the pathway and out into the village square, towards the green.

Cassie shivered, unsure if it was from the cold of the evening or Charles Stafford's indifference.

Chapter Seventeen

~ Cassie ~

Cassie stuck close to Charles's side as they advanced towards the horses.

He glanced at her, noticing her attire. "Here." He shrugged out of his coat and put it over her shoulders. "This will maintain your modesty." His tone was serious, the set of his jaw tight.

Cassie assumed he was still angry at her. They came near the grey and Charles clicked his tongue, reassuring the animal. He bent down, his hands interlocked, ready to give Cassie a leg up into the saddle. She gripped the reins and the pommel, about to hoist herself up, when he moved, dropping his hands. Cassie stumbled forward, hitting her shin off the metal stirrup. The horse grunted and shifted its weight.

"What the…?" Cassie glanced around, looking for potential danger.

"Do you intend to ride like that? Cross saddle?" hissed Charles, his face turning a pale shade of puce in the light of the moon. "Have you taken leave of your senses?" he asked.

Cassie stared at him. What was the big deal? She was wearing pants for God's sake.

"I mean to say," he continued, "Lady Cassandra does not, has not ever ridden…" His words trickled to silence and he stared at her, his earnest gaze making her feel uncomfortable.

A shout from across the green drew their attention.

"Can we talk about this somewhere else?" implored Cassie. "Let's get out of here. I will explain everything. And stop calling me Lady Cassandra." She pulled herself less than gracefully up into the saddle. "My name is Cassie."

"Fine," he retorted, sounding unconvinced, "If you insist on riding in that way I will ride slowly so you can keep up."

Cassie wanted to scream. As her reluctant companion pulled himself up into the saddle she kicked her horse forward into a quick trot. Before she knew it she had crossed the open space and was moving steadily out of the village. She urged the mare into a gallop and streaked into the moonlit darkness. The wind tugged off her hat, but she didn't care. She just wanted to ride, to speed her horse on, to get as far away from the village as possible.

The horse lengthened its stride and Cassie felt the pins in her hair loosen, the wind whipping it free from its restraint. She rode hard and fast, the exhilaration making her heart beat, rat-tat-tat.

After a few minutes, she rounded the brow of the hill and reigned in her mare, wheeling the animal around, it's breath coming cold into the night air. Cassie's legs were shaking, as much from excitement as from relief at having made it out of the village in one piece. She slipped her feet from the stirrups and flinging her leg over the back of the saddle, slid to the ground.

Charles drew his horse beside hers as she flicked the reins over the mare's head. His cheeks were flushed. Cassie, smiling tightly, as she looked upwards, said, "I thought I had better slow down. I wanted to make sure you could keep up!" She turned in the direction of home and tugged the reins, leading her horse.

"Are you going to explain?" he asked, dismounting quickly.

Cassie shrugged her shoulders. "You're not going to believe me even if I do tell you..."

He took hold of the reins of her horse and pulled the animal to a halt. "I insist, Lady Cassandra."

"Okay, so for the hundredth time, stop calling me Cassandra. My name is Cassie." She folded her arms tightly. "There was a storm. The electricity went out. The Wolf Mirror. Next thing I know I'm waking up and it's frigging 1714! I should be in the twenty first century, not the eighteenth!" She was rambling, her words coming fast and free, her right foot tapping a quick rhythm against the sod. It felt good to unburden herself to someone else, even if he was going to have her committed.

They made their way to a copse of oak. Charles took his mount and tied the reins loosely to the branch of one of the trees, before doing the same to Cassie's mare. Slowly, he turned to her. "You are expecting me to believe the tale that you are not Lady Cassandra, but someone else from the year 2014?"

Cassie threw her hands in the air. "I told you, you wouldn't believe me."

"I did not say I doubted you." He reached into his jacket and pulled out a crumpled sliver of paper. Cassie took a step forward, peering in the darkness at the palm of his outstretched hand.

"Where did you get that?" she asked, a hint of annoyance in her voice.

"The clearing, the other day, after I saw you safely back to the house."

"You went back for it?"

Charles nodded, watching her expectantly.

"It's the stub from my cigarette."

He gestured to the loose strands of her hair. "And this?"

Instantly Cassie's hand flew to the bedraggled mane, streaming loose around her shoulders. She had forgotten about the slight inconsistencies in her hair colour.

She shrugged her shoulders. "It's all the rage where I come from. So," in an effort at indifference, she tucked a strand of hair behind her ear, "are you going to send me to the asylum?"

"I do not know."

"Oh, come on!" whaled Cassie in frustration. "I'm telling the truth. I may not be Lady Cassandra Miller, but I am her descendant and that means that you should extend some manner of courtesy. I am confiding a secret to you and if you were a gentleman," she paused for effect, "you would help me. It's not like I want to be here. This place has so many rules! Ankles…I mean, ankles are considered on a par with flashing your boobs!"

She leaned against the trunk of a tree, exhausted by her outburst and the events of the night. "I just want to go home," she whispered, dejected.

Charles was silent for a moment. "I apologise," he said. "I believe you…are not from this time, this place…because Lady Cassandra would never carry on in the…"

Cassie raised her head and glared at him.

"…Lady Cassandra would behave differently," he added, unwilling to offend her. "However, if you do not manage to get home soon, your antics, if they are noticed by too many people, will do irrevocable damage to Lady Cassandra and the future of Ludlow Park, which I admit is linked with the Stafford family. So you see, Lady…so you see, Cassie, I too want you to return home."

Cassie shrugged. "Yeah, but I can't until I figure out how to help Lord Miller. If I could do that, then maybe the mirror will let me go home."

"And that is why you were in the tavern?"

"Yes. I think that Evins is up to something. The man he was meeting, with the cane, he mentioned Huxley's name." She slapped her thigh with her hand in irritation. "If only I had gotten closer, I would have been able to hear their conversation."

"Yes," mused Charles, "but you would have been recognised. And then…"

"Let me guess…ruined?"

He smiled in the light of the moon, his teeth eerily bright. "What do you intend on doing now?"

"Right now, I need to get home." She pushed herself away from the tree and brushed the seat of her pants.

"I will accompany you," offered Charles. "It is getting late."

"You seem to make a habit of seeing me home, Charles…"

He stopped in his tracks, his hand on the neck of his horse, his body rigid.

"What?" she asked, sure she had done something wrong again. "What?"

"Nothing, it is just…"

"Oh for God's sake, spit it out."

"You are very familiar. You should not call me Charles, it is too, too…"

"But it's your name! What am I supposed to call you…Block Head?"

He frowned. "I am not familiar with that expression, but I imagine you have just insulted me."

Cassie laughed, the tension melting from her. "Yes, Mr. Stafford, I have just insulted you."

Charles began to lead the horse back onto the track way. "It is best to keep it formal. That way there is no room for mistakes. I do not want to think what would happen if you were found out. It would kill Lord Miller. Huxley would be only too happy to claim Ludlow Park as his own, considering the heir to the family fortune has gone missing and the only living Miller family member is currently indisposed."

"I want to go to London," she said abruptly.

"Pardon me?"

"You heard me. I want to go to London. I want to meet this Huxley person, find out what he is at."

"What he is at?" asked Charles, unconvinced.

"Look," began Cassie, "Evins is connected to Huxley. And that man this evening…"

Charles shook his head. "Stay clear of Mr. Evins."

"What do you mean?" Cassie stopped in the roadway, her horse's nose nudging her forward, "Do you know something?"

"No, of course not. If I did, I would inform you." He moved on, leading his horse. "Come along, we must return home. It is late."

Cassie jogged to catch up with him. "Wait," she called, "tell me what you meant about Mr. Evins."

"It is nothing. I do not want to alarm you."

"Alarm me?" Cassie laughed. "The guy has a mandrake root and arsenic in his workshop and he is blackmailing Dr Brown."

Charles frowned. "Where did you hear that?"

"Nowhere." Cassie shrugged and added, "Look, I know he is crooked. He is definitely involved in some way. I'm just not sure how and Huxley is the key. I need to find out about him."

"Yes, well, you cannot just take yourself off to London, with no invitations, no chaperones, no social outings to attend."

"Can I not just stay in a hotel? Say I want to go shopping or something?"

"Lady Cassandra detests town. Her father has cultivated a kind of distaste for city living in his children. She would never voluntarily go there, least of all to shop."

"You will have to go for me, then!"

They had come to the edge of Ludlow Park, the moon illuminating the woods around the boundary of the Miller lands.

"I do not quite understand you, madam."

"You will have to go to London, find out about Huxley," continued Cassie.

Charles did not look convinced.

"If I am so restricted that I can't even go to the city then I'm of no use. I will be too conspicuous. You are a man! This is the only way we will get to know..."

"We?" he interrupted.

"Yes, Charles, I mean Mr. Stafford. We. I can't do this on my own." She was tired, her voice sounding unsure. "I just want to get home. You *have* to help me."

He stood still for a moment, his head tilted to one side and considered. "Yes, I suppose you do need my assistance. But my sister Jane, she has returned from her wedding tour with her new husband. They are due to arrive tomorrow."

Cassie nodded, unsure what this had to do with his trip to the city.

"There is a ball at the Assembly rooms in three days. You will have to go to it, you and Jane..." He paused.

"Me and Jane what?"

"You moved in the same circles," he added cautiously.

Cassie recognised that look. "You mean we don't get on?"

"No, I would not put it in such a way. You are both very...strong willed and perhaps are a little abrasive towards each other. However, she will want you at her homecoming ball."

"Why would she want me at the ball if she hates me?"

"I did not say she hated you. In fact, if there was not this insipid social competition to outdo one another, I think you would both get along quite well."

Cassie made up her mind instantly that Jane Stafford was probably a

135

total cow. "Okay, I'll go to the stupid ball, if it keeps you happy, but what has that got to do with Huxley."

"He has been invited."

"Oh." Cassie was suddenly very tired, the ground looked comfortable, like it would be alright to lie on it, snuggle into the dried leaves, lay her head down and sleep through the awfulness that was her life.

Charles took her arm, steadying her as she swayed. "Cassie? Are you well?"

"Yeah, sorry. I am just tired. It has been a long night. Do you think Reginald Huxley will come to Jane's ball?"

"No," began Charles, "no, of course he will not come. He receives an invitation as a matter of courtesy but never concedes to leave London. Do not concern yourself."

They had reached the wall that encircled the garden and stable area of the big house. Charles handed her the reins of her horse. "I need to go to London on some business for my father. I can go early. Tomorrow perhaps, to make enquiries, see if anyone knows about Huxley. I will be back the evening of the ball."

"Thank you," Cassie said quietly, touched by his kindness. She heard a whistle from inside the wall. "I have to go."

"Wait."

She turned towards Charles.

"You will be on your own Cassie, with my sister, my family, the other leading families of the neighbourhood. Mr. Wrix will be there…"

Another shrill whistle floated over the wall to her ears, and she decided she had better get a move on. She hurriedly reassured him "Yeah, yeah, I will be on my best behaviour, I promise. I may even decide to wear a dress. These trousers are not the best." She smiled in the darkness and moved away, leaving Charles alone. At the wall, she turned and waved once before disappearing into the paddock next to the stable block.

George was waiting for her at the corner. He took the reins without saying a word. If he heard her conversation with Charles Stafford, or noticed her change of attire, her arms getting lost in the big coat that she wore, he did not say anything.

They slipped as quietly as was possible across the stables. "I will take her from here, miss, she needs a rub down and feed." He nodded to her hair, "Ya best see to that before ya go to the big house."

Cassie touched her head gingerly. It had almost come completely undone, the pink exposed. She tied the raggedy ends into a hasty knot and picked her way across the lawn.

She moved through the herb garden, crossing the yard to the kitchen door, trying the lock. It opened smoothly under a little pressure. She grabbed a dry hunk of bread from beneath a linen cloth on the table and eased her feet out of her boots before treading her way across the kitchen to the stairway. She remembered the way back along the servants' passage and pushed the heavy door open at the end, coming out into the well decorated and designed hallway just by her bedroom.

The door of her room creaked in protest as she pushed it open. A candle was burning on the mantle and a large puddle of clothing lay on top of her bed. Cassie frowned and took a step forward.

Molly. The girl was asleep, exhausted from her day. Cassie shoved some bread into her mouth and pulled off her trousers, shrugged off the jacket and slipped her cold toes, legs, torso and finally her arms under the covers.

As she drifted to sleep, she remembered what Charles had said. Who exactly was Mr. Wrix?

Chapter Eighteen

~ Cassandra ~

Cassandra was terrified, the type of fear that takes a hold of you and blocks out all your other senses, squeezing you into a terrible panic. She gripped the edge of the padded chair, trying to keep herself from screaming. Judge Miller sat beside her, a large wheel gripped in her hand, supposedly controlling the speed and direction of the horseless carriage. Tallulah and Jonah were in the rear seat, completely oblivious to Cassandra's terror.

Every bend and curve in the road caused a bubble of panic to well in her throat. There were high stone walls, with blocks of limestone packed tightly together. Bronzed hedges, turning colour in the autumn light. Every now and then a gate of tall, spiked metal would loom at the edge of the roadway. Cassandra was convinced they were going to die, impaled on one of the many hazards that whizzed past them.

She tried to distract herself by looking at the semi-familiar countryside. She noticed a great many changes. A number of trees had been felled, buildings erected on her family's land.

She stared in a mixture of awe and horror as they entered the village. Houses, blocks and blocks of houses, rows lining the street, the market square reduced to half its size.

They did not stop in the square. Instead they took a sharp turn to the right and drove along a street, till they came to a plot of land and Cassandra, despite her upbringing, could not help but open her mouth

138

and stare.

The largest wheel she had ever seen, like a mill wheel only bigger, took centre stage. It was lit up brightly with dazzling white, blue and green lights. Beside it were a number of other brightly coloured arenas. Music blared and the sound of excited screams bounced off of the nearby buildings, echoing back to Cassandra's ears.

There were a great many people milling about. To one side of the lot there were colourful amusements, to the other side there were carts and stalls, booths and buggies full of all sorts of different produce.

Cassandra saw a hog roasting on a spit behind a glass case in a large horseless carriage with see-through windows. There was a small cart and a man twirling what looked like pink wool onto sticks for grabbing children. There was a woman selling baked goods, cakes, buns, slices of tart. Several stalls were selling knitted ware, scarves, gloves, hats, some timber carvings, shining jewellery.

Cassandra was desperate to explore.

The wheel moved slowly and Cassandra noticed that you could get into a box and go to the very top, with a view over the surrounding countryside. Her heart skipped a beat and she was not sure if it was because of the rush of excitement or fear.

They parked the horseless carriage beside a row of other horseless carriages and made their way slowly into the crowd. Jonah took his mother's hand, squeezing it in excitement. Cassandra wanted someone to take her hand to squeeze in reassurance but she straightened her spine, refusing to portray any weakness.

"Are you alright?" whispered Tallulah, stepping closer to her.

Cassandra nodded, her gaze shifting from left to right, taking it all in.

"Mum, Mum," Jonah squealed, "can we have a go on the bumper cars? Please?"

They were slowing down next to a corral full of tiny horseless carriages with fat rubber underbellies. People were sitting in them, driving at each other with yells of delight. Cassandra had never seen anything like it. Children and grown men and women clambered into the carriages and when a loud bell sounded the carriages moved with speed towards each other, crashing with thunderous noise.

Jonah was hanging from his mother's arm, adamant and impatient, "Please, mum, please."

Judge Miller nodded after a few seconds. "Okay, get four tickets, we will all have a go."

"Certainly not," blurted Cassandra, outraged at the suggestion. How was she going to clamber into the horseless carriage? It would involve rolling up her skirts, compromising her position as a lady? It was too much for her to take in.

Judge Miller looked at her sternly. "Cassie, the least you could do is partake, for your brother Jonah. Look," she stepped towards Cassandra, placing a cool hand on her arm, "I'm sorry about the other evening but I want us to try to be a family. I know that I have to learn to leave my work in the office and…"

Cassandra took a step back, uncomfortable with Judge Miller's touch. It reminded her of the absence of her own mother.

Judge Miller stopped talking and took her hand away, slowly. "Cassie, I want to fix this, but you have to meet me half way."

Cassandra did not know what to say. The best thing to do was to remain silent. Jonah bounded back to them brandishing four tickets. "Come on," he called, gripping his mum by the hand and pulling her in the direction of the carriages. "They're about to start."

Tallulah glanced at Cassandra and nodded in the direction of the cars. Cassandra shook her head. She watched as the three of them disappeared behind the barrier.

As the bell sounded and the horseless carts began to pummel into each other, Cassandra turned and walked away into the crowd.

She did not recognise anybody, did not know a single soul, and the thought lodged like a heavy stone in her belly. She moved slowly through the groups of people, looking from left to right. The smell of spiced wine and freshly toasted macaroons filled the air. She tried not to think of her situation, instead enjoy the newness all around her.

She put her hands in the pockets of her coat, or hoodie as Tallulah called it, surprised at her audacity. The girl had implored Cassandra to change. Even suggesting that she wear an item of clothing called a jean. However light, and at times cold, her long skirt was, Cassandra was not ready to embrace men's clothing.

The notion made her think of Miss Blythe. If her governess were to see her now, hands in pockets, like a boy, she would be shocked. But Miss Blythe is not here, Cassandra rationalised, and I will be damned if I am letting my hands get any colder.

She caught the glimpse of a person in the crowd, the profile of his face and she stopped dead in her tracks. *Him!* The man moved on, ducking into an enormous canvas tent, with coloured light dripping from the awning. Cassandra was sure it was him, the tilt of his chin, the slightly crooked nose. "Charles Stafford. But how?" she hurried forward, towards the opening of the tent, determined to follow.

A heavy-set man, dressed from head to toe in black stepped in front of her, a gloved hand blocking her way. "I.D. please?"

"Pardon me?" she asked, in her most dignified voice.

"I.D. please, love. No I.D., no pub." He nodded his head in the direction of the tent. Cassandra noticed the chalk board, displaying a sign, "Two For One On All Bottles". There was some bunting hanging from the rim of the tent, advertising an ale or beer of some kind.

A tavern? Cassandra was confused, why would Charles Stafford want to go in there?

The man looked at her, waiting for her to produce whatever this I.D. item was. She had no idea, had nothing on her possession, no coin to pay him with. "I do not know what you mean, sir, I simply wish to go in there to see if I can find an acquaintance of mine." She inclined her head in the direction of the tent.

It was frowned upon for women to frequent such establishments, but Cassandra threw caution to the wind. If Charles Stafford were here, then perhaps he knew a way for her to return to her home. She was determined.

"Love, if I had a pound for every time someone said that. No I.D., no in. Simple!" He stood back and looked over her head, dismissing her with his indifference.

"Cassie, what are you doing?" Judge Miller was behind her, a hand on her arm.

"I am attempting to gain entrance to this place," Cassandra nodded at the tent.

"Cassie, are you seriously telling me that you came to the fair to go to the pub, despite the fact that you are underage?" She pulled Cassandra away from the tent and stopped next to a stall selling toffee apples. "Are you out of your mind?" she hissed. "We are here, with Jonah, spending family time together, and you are brazen, or stupid enough to try to get into the drinks tent." Her voice had risen to a dangerously inappropriate level. "Are you deliberately trying to provoke me, is that what this is?" Judge Miller threw her hands in the air. "I don't know what to do with you. I really don't. You are impossible."

Cassandra had never been spoken to in that manner before. The woman was angry, practically shouting. Something inside Cassandra rose its ugly head. She wanted to shout back, to yell, to scream, to stamp her foot, to release all the pent-up emotions from her three years of duty, restraint and poise. Her face was heating up, blotches of colour marring her features. She compressed her lips and turned on her heels, marching off into the crowd, her fists balled tightly by her side. She needed some distance or else she would lose her cool.

"The gall of that woman!" she said aloud, her voice raspy with suppressed anger.

To speak to her as if she were a degenerate!

"Hey." A young man, about eighteen, jogged towards her, a smile lighting his features. He was sallow skinned, with dark hair and chocolate coloured eyes. Cassandra couldn't help but stare. He was extremely agreeable looking.

"I know, I know," he said, holding up his hands in mock surrender, "I'm the last person you'd expect to see here." He grinned a lopsided grin, a single dimple forming on his cheek. "I had to see you." He stepped forward, closing the distance between them, his hand snaking around her waist.

Cassandra was mesmerised by his audacity, frozen in suspense, the outrage from earlier forgotten. He was manhandling her and for some reason she was letting him. He was so close she could see flecks of amber in the iris of his eyes.

"I'm sorry about the other day," he murmured, his lips dangerously close to her earlobe. "I didn't get a chance to tell her that I want to break it off. Something came up, you know how it is?"

No, she didn't know. She had no idea who this person was, but he clearly knew her.

He leaned in, his body pressing against her. Cassandra could feel the heat of him through the light material of her clothing. A blush of shame uncurled from her belly, making its way up to her cheeks.

"Becky overreacted, that's all."

Becky! That name was like a dagger of frozen ice plunged into her stomach.

"Dwane?" Cassandra asked slowly, her lips forming around the word as if around barbed wire. He grinned, his face moving in to steal a kiss. Cassandra's composure couldn't take any more. She slapped him full force across the face, decorum forgotten.

She spun on her heels and marched into the crowd, ignoring the boy who called after her.

Cassandra blindly stomped in between stalls and along pathways, trying to put as much distance between Dwane and herself. Why was this place so difficult to understand? The men and women mixed together in very familiar ways, there was no distinction between peoples, no class separation. At least where she came from, there were rules to follow. And she knew those rules, inside out. Here, she was totally undone.

"Cassie," someone called and Cassandra turned around automatically, expecting it to be Tallulah or Judge Miller. She was done with the fair. She wanted to go home.

A group of girls, three in total, were leaning against a fence which ran around the outside of the fair ground. Cassandra was indecisive for a moment. These people obviously knew Cassie. It would be important to keep up appearances, to be polite. Cassandra moved across the space towards them.

The girl in the middle was tall and striking, with long flaxen hair and a pretty almond shaped face. Her lips were pressed tight together. She was wearing jeans, over black boots and a tight, brown leather jacket. The two girls on either side also wore similar pants and coloured footwear, with hoodies like Cassandra's.

"Good evening," she greeted them, smiling pleasantly.

"Where's your monkey?" one of the girls asked, snorting in amusement.

"My monkey?" asked Cassandra.

"Your little pet, Tallulah."

Cassandra's eyes narrowed. "Pardon me?"

"Are you especially thick today or something, Cassie?" The two girls on either side sniggered together. "Well done on getting suspended, by the way. It's such a pity you don't have better…family connections." The girl pushed herself away from the fence and leaned towards Cassandra. "We have unfinished business, slag. Nobody tries it on with my boyfriend and gets away with it!"

Becky.

Her breath smelled of something rancid, like gone off meat, Cassandra took a step back. The girl grinned. "Still afraid of me I see."

Cassandra arched her eye brow and said nothing.

"Cassandra," Tallulah was behind her.

"There she is, Tal oh oh lah!" the girls made a funny sound, pretending to scratch their arm pits, hopping from one foot to the other. "I didn't hear you whistle, but I suppose your monkey knows when to heel."

Cassandra bristled and made to take a step forward but Tallulah grabbed her elbow. "Come on Cassie. Your mother is waiting for us." She emphasised her name and that made Cassandra stop. This was not her fight. What was wrong with her? She was Lady Cassandra Miller of Ludlow House, not some brawling scullery maid.

She turned on her heels and moved back into the crowd, trying to ignore the sound of laughter behind her. After a moment, Cassandra cleared her throat, regaining her sense of aloofness. She tried to ignore the boil of emotions churning in her stomach. *Decorum. Poise. Elegance. Duty.* The words tumbled around her brain. She must hang onto those words as if they were her saviour. She would not succumb to the evils of this place.

"Are you well?" she asked Tallulah, trying to engage in a normal conversation, glossing over the fact that she had almost instigated an argument with a complete stranger.

"Yeah. I just want to smash that girl in the mouth, so bad." Cassandra choked on an inhale of breath, covering it over with a series of short, sharp coughs. Tallulah had just voiced the very action that Cassandra wanted to give into. "But I know if I touched her she would have me expelled before you could say *"my aunt's the vice principal"*! Or worse, she would beat the crap out of us. She's crazy." Tallulah kicked an empty plastic bottle across the walkway, "It's so not fair. Becky has actively been trying to get me expelled since I got into Winchester. She doesn't think it's right to have her precious Grammar school tainted..."

"Tainted?" asked Cassandra.

"Yeah, you know, because I'm black." The girl looked down at her feet.

On impulse, Cassandra reached forward and took Tallulah's arm, linking hers through it in a show of companionship. "She will get what's coming to her, Tallulah, never fear," offered Cassandra.

But for some reason she didn't quite believe her own advice.

Chapter Nineteen

~ Cassie ~

The three days following Charles Stafford's departure were the dullest Cassie had ever spent. The weather broke on the first day and continued to pour. Loud rain spattered against the thin window panes.

The governess had taken it upon herself to shadow Cassie at all times and barely left her side. This made it impossible to talk to Molly about the night in the Horse and Hound, to question her about Mr. Evins.

Cassie's only reprieve from the constant surveillance was when she was alone with Lord Miller. The gentleman was asleep now, his hands resting on the covers. They were clean hands with long fingers and short, clipped nails; hands unused to manual labour. His face was lined and weathered, sunken at the cheeks. She worried he might die any day.

It seemed like he was improving for a while but then a fever took hold and Cassie had no idea how to help.

She considered refusing to allow the doctor to treat his patient. But what if she were wrong? What if the tonic was the only thing keeping him alive? If she insisted that the doctor stop administering the formula, Lord Miller could die. You couldn't gamble with someone's life like that. She needed to be sure that he was being poisoned.

She sat upright in her chair, an idea forming in her head. Biology and chemistry mixed together, snippets of long, drawn out lessons muddled together in her brain. "Crap," she cursed, "if only I had the internet!"

Lord Miller stirred in his sleep and moaned loudly.

I have to do something, she thought, as she eased herself out of the chair. She slipped into the study room and out the door, breathing a sigh of relief, inhaling the clean air of the hallway.

"Lady Cassandra?"

Cassie jumped at the sound of her name and turned to see Miss Blythe advancing towards her. Cassie wanted to roll her eyes to heaven and say a very bad word, but instead she smiled tightly. "Miss Blythe. You were looking for me?"

"Yes. There are visitors in the drawing room downstairs. They request an audience."

"Who is it?" she asked politely.

"Perhaps you should go see for yourself, ma'am." Miss Blythe was being annoyingly vague.

Cassie turned towards the stairs and gingerly made her way down them. At the base of the steps, she smoothed out the skirt of her dress and tucked a strand of hair behind her ear before pushing open the heavy doors to the drawing room. The fire had been lit in an attempt to chase away the gloom of the rainy autumn day. This room, Lady Augustine's favourite, was also Cassie's. The walls were painted a bright vibrant lapis lazuli blue. The furniture was mostly cream. There was a large ornate writing desk by the window with a gold painted chair. A divan was positioned in front of the fireplace of black marble, which was topped with a gold mantle.

Standing by the fireplace was Charles Stafford. He turned towards her when she entered. She smiled at him, a genuine smile of pleasure. She crossed the room in a few steps, half carrying, half dragging the weight of her skirts. She was about to blurt out a greeting when his stance and tone stopped her in her tracks.

"Lady Cassandra, how good of you to see me on such short notice. I am sure you are busy attending your father." His voice was strained.

Cassie frowned. "What..." she began. A flick of his eyes made her turn around. There, standing by the window in the dull grey light of the fading day was another man. He cleared his throat and advanced towards her, offering his hand. She took it automatically, unsure what else to do.

He bowed formally before her, "Lady Cassandra," he said nasally,

"How charmed."

Cassie glanced at Charles, desperate for some kind of clue. "I hope you do not mind, Lady Cassandra," Charles seemed to emphasize her name for good measure, reminding her who she was supposed to be. "I met with Mr. Huxley in London and he expressed a wish to visit his cousin. I am here to formally introduce him."

Cassie stared at the man in front of her. He was short and balding, his hair covered in some kind of black lacquer. He had a round face, small mole like eyes and cheeks as red as the best apples Cassie had ever seen. His clothing seemed expensive, and well-tailored, but she noticed a food stain on his lapel and the bottom button of his jacket was close to popping open of its own accord. He smiled winningly at her, his face brightening. She couldn't help but smile back at him. "Welcome to Ludlow Park, Mr. Huxley."

Cassie wanted to shake off her visitor's clammy hand but did not know how to do it without causing offence. This person in front of her could prove to be very important.

Oh god, thought Cassie, as she looked down at him. Lady Cassandra's troubles would be over if she would decide to marry this person. The thought made her stomach heave. The idea of anyone marrying Mr. Huxley seemed preposterous.

"Tea," said Cassie loudly, aware that this might be a way of extracting herself from his grip. He was looking at her with something akin to awe. Cassie needed to get away from him for a minute to compose herself. She tugged her hand free and walked to the mantelpiece to ring the bell. She glared at Charles, who stood quietly in front of the fire. He shrugged his shoulders the slightest bit as she passed, indicating that he was not in a position to do anything.

"Please, sit down gentlemen." Cassie went to the hard, straight backed chair across the room, easing into it, ensuring that she had a good view of both men, as they sat, one gracefully, one with the girt of an elephant, onto the divan. Cassie wanted to giggle at the sight of them. Charles looked so composed, so straight-laced, his features stern, while Reginald Huxley gaped around the room, his mouth slightly open, the tip of his pink tongue protruding.

"What a lovely room, Lady Cassandra. I heard you have been

thinking of opening it up, changing it to the French style. Lady Mellicent Buxton from London has recently converted her drawing room into an open reception area. It has done wonders for her social standing. She can accommodate easily an extra ten people to any of her little evening card games. Not that they are little of course. Lady Buxton is quite wealthy and moves amongst the best of the best of London society. Have you ever been to London, Lady Cassandra? I am sure you would adore it. Such a beauty as yourself would embellish any ball or gathering. Your father? Has he improved any? I was hoping to speak with his doctor, a Doctor Brown…"

Reginald Huxley could certainly talk, thought Cassie, losing interest in his prattling. She wanted to speak with Charles alone. She had not realised how much she had missed him while he was away. How on earth had he gotten Huxley, a man who never left London, to travel all the way to Ludlow?

"…wouldn't you say so, Lady Cassandra?"

Cassie was shaken out of her musings by the question. "What?" she blurted. Mr. Huxley stopped immediately and looked affronted, his eyes staring. "Sorry, Mr. Huxley, I meant pardon me, I didn't catch the question."

"Oh, yes, yes, quite. I was asking when Doctor Brown would be calling?"

Cassie frowned, unsure how this was relevant to Huxley. "He will be with Lord…my father in another half an hour I think."

"Excellent. Excellent. I will need a word with him."

"Why?"

Charles looked at her sharply, signalling silently for her to watch her manners.

"Well. Well…" bumbled Huxley, his cheeks firing a deeper red than they already were, "I mean to discuss some important matters of …business with him. I wish to get acquainted with what's what, if you understand me."

Oh I understand you alright. Instead, she nodded screnely and remained silent. The arrival of the tea tray saved her from bellowing at this new visitor. She poured the tea and offered slices of cake and all the time her brain was working, thinking, thinking. What does he want to say to Doctor Brown? What could he be asking of him? Could he be the one who is orchestrating the tonics for Lord Miller? She glanced at Huxley from beneath her lashes; he was mouthing off to Charles about the merits of porter cake over fruit cake, neither of which Cassie had ever tasted nor wanted to taste by the sounds of their description. Why had he come?

"Mr. Huxley," she began, "you will be staying here at Ludlow Park for your visit?"

Huxley was trying to cram the last of his cake into his mouth, chewing hastily, a steady stream of crumbs falling onto his lap. "Yes," he spluttered, taking a slurp of tea, "yes, if you would be so gracious as to have me, I would be delighted. I have always wished to see my...I mean your estate."

He smiled brightly at her, and Cassie wanted to slap his stupid face. She twisted the napkin in her lap tightly. It began to cut off the blood supply to her fingers.

A servant arrived with fresh water for the tea, and Cassie turned to her, asking her to find Miss Blythe. No sooner had the servant left than Miss Blythe entered the room, moving with upright rigidness. How she got the skirts of her heavy dress so perfect, Cassie would never know. The governess must have been loitering down the hallway somewhere. "Miss Blythe," Cassie said, unable to keep the hint of suspicion from her voice, "you came very quickly."

The governess nodded, her cold eyes calm, giving nothing away.

"You have met Mr. Huxley and Mr. Stafford already. Mr. Huxley is going to be staying with us for a night," Cassie looked at her guest, "two nights..." She left the question open hoping that he would fill in the blanks for her.

"Oh, yes, yes, I was hoping, I was hoping quite a great deal to be able to trespass on your kindness for a week or two..."

A week or two? Cassie wanted to yell at him, don't be ridiculous.

"...I do so wish to acquaint myself with this part of the country and I hear that the card games are quite..." he stopped and looked from Miss Blythe to Cassandra, "...of course I have come to inquire after the health of Lord Miller, also. That has been my primary concern."

Yeah, right, thought Cassie. "Can you show Mr. Huxley to a guest room please, Miss Blythe?"

The governess bristled, obviously, this sort of task was not in her job description but Cassie didn't care, she wanted both of them gone from her sight. She needed to talk with Charles.

Ever an example of good manners, Miss Blythe sniffed her disdain and gestured to the rotund man to follow her out of the room.

"Much obliged Miss Blythe, much obliged Lady Cassandra," Huxley bowed and bumped his way out of the drawing room, trailing along obediently in the wake of the governess.

Cassie took a sip of tea and waited for the door to close firmly behind the two before putting her cup down quietly. Then she glanced over her shoulder and rose with as much speed as she could, reaching for Charles and pulling him from his seat. She marched them both over to the window, far away from the door and any potential eavesdroppers.

His coat was covered in dust from the ride, his hands the same. Cassie looked at his boots, normally polished to a shine and they too were dulled by road dirt. "Mr. Stafford," she uttered urgently, "what is going on? I sent you to London to find out information about Huxley, not to bring him back with you. Did you see him looking around, probably making plans for more renovations." Cassie slumped against the window frame, dejected.

Charles took a step towards her, his hand outstretched as if to touch her, then he thought better of it and folded his arms. "I did not have a choice. I went to London as you asked and put in some requests at a club I know Huxley frequents. Before I knew it, I was being introduced and asked the particulars of my visit."

He glanced out the window at the sound of a barking dog. "It did not take him long to establish that I was a neighbour and the rest you can imagine."

Cassie shook her head, "You could have told him that you didn't like porter cake. That would have ruined your chances of friendship in one fell swoop."

Charles smiled a small smile, a rare occurrence and Cassie found herself staring at him. He had never been this close to her before. She could feel the heat of him.

There was a knock on the door and Charles stepped away, putting an appropriate amount of distance between them.

Molly peeped into the room before stepping hastily inside, "Apologies, ma'am, I thought that ya were alone and needed the tray things cleared." She scurried to the tea tray and began to gather them up.

Cassie crossed the room quickly and closed the door. "Will you stop that nonsense," she hissed, causing the girl to pause. "Get over there." Cassie gestured to the window.

Molly straightened up and moved haltingly to the window, her eyes lowered.

"Charles," began Cassie with emphasis, "This is my friend Molly. Molly, this is Mr. Charles Stafford."

The two looked at each other then back to Cassie, who had folded her arms across her chest and tilted her chin out slightly, daring either of them to refuse her. Molly looked as if she might faint.

Charles extended his hand and took Molly's petite, pot scrubbing hand in his, squeezing it gently. "How do you do, Miss Molly." Molly blushed and Cassie couldn't help but smile.

"Right, we have a problem." Cassie looked at them both. "Huxley is here."

Molly emitted a little squeak of surprise.

"I have an idea about Lord Miller," Cassie said tentatively, unwilling to share it completely. "Molly, you know the bread that they serve with breakfast in the morning, the white, crusty bread?"

The girl nodded.

"I need you to steal a loaf of that and some cheese. The soft cheese. Wrap both of them in a clean linen cloth and put it the warmest place you can find in the house."

"But Miss, they will go bad, start smellin'."

"Yes," added Cassie, "that is exactly what I want. Smelly bread with big chunks of blue mould." She was going to make her own penicillin, assuming she could remember how. She wondered if she would be brave enough to take the chance on her theory when the time was right.

If she was mistaken she would risk the future of her entire family.

Chapter Twenty

~ Cassie ~

Cassie couldn't convince Charles to stay. He claimed he was tired after his long journey and had business with his steward. It was evident that he did not want to spend any more time in her company. The annoying voice at the back of her head flared as he was about to leave.

He doesn't like you, doesn't want to be anywhere near you. Just like your Dad. Cassie shook her head, as if she could physically rattle the thoughts from her brain.

"I need a smoke!" Cassie crossed the room in a few steps, flinging her napkin down on the tea tray.

When she pushed open the door to her room, Molly was busying herself with ribbons on the bodice of a dress. It was a pale yellow contraption with eons of taffeta, lace and some other unidentifiable fabric flowing from it. The servant did not look up as Cassie entered.

"Molly," began Cassie, "I'm going to look like a stuffed chicken in that thing. Is there not something a little less...less..." The servant did not acknowledge Cassie's presence; instead she kept her head bowed.

"Molly, are you alright?" asked Cassie.

"Ay, Miss, I am fine. Just a tad...a little...well, Miss, if ya do not mind me sayin', I am somewhat shaken up by what happened earlier. Mr. Charles Stafford should not be takin' my hand in his, nor t'other way round. It ain't right." She dropped the dress on the bed and frowned at Cassie.

"But Molly, he is my friend. You are my friend. We all want to fix this mess. I don't see why there has to be..."

"There just is, Miss. That is the way things are. And I do not need you givin' me notions. Notions I could be doin' without!"

"Alright, Molly," Cassie felt thoroughly chastised. She'd never witnessed Molly so impassioned. The irony that Molly would demand to be treated less equally was not lost on Cassie. She kept her opinions to herself. Instead, she held the pins while Molly did the ends of her hair up in an elaborate, braided nest. By the time the bell rang to signal dinner, Cassie looked every inch the lady of the house. "Don't forget the loaf of bread or the cheese, Molly. I want them wrapped tight and put someplace warm."

The girl nodded and held the door open for Cassie as she moved out into the corridor, "Good luck, Miss," she called softly.

Cassie made it down the stairs and to the dining room without any trips, a feat that she was quite proud of. At the dining room door, she paused and touched the side of her hair briefly, reassuring herself that it was all in place. Taking a deep breath, she pushed her way through into the dining room, her skirts rustling as she went.

Miss Blythe was already seated while Doctor Brown and Mr. Huxley stood at the big bay window overlooking the lawns.

"Ah, there you are, Lady Cassandra," remarked Mr. Huxley, his nasal tone carrying loud across the room. "I've just been admiring the view, such splendid plantations!"

Cassie smiled and nodded, moving towards the table. Both gentlemen turned from the window and made their way to their seats. Huxley reached the table at the same time as Cassie. Both moved to take the top chair and then paused, their fingertips touching the timber uprights. Cassie considered for a moment letting him, the rightful successor to Ludlow Park, sit at the head of the table. But her stubbornness would not allow it. Smiling with effort, she pulled the chair from beneath his fingertips and eased herself in a less than graceful manner into the seat.

Miss Blythe cleared her throat and began to talk to the doctor about the weather.

Cassie flicked her napkin across her lap and turned to address her guest, "So, Mr. Huxley, is your room comfortable?"

"Oh yes, quite. I...um..." A servant laid a platter of poached eel heads on the table. Cassie tried not to barf. Oh, for a bruschetta starter and side salad.

"I," continued Huxley, "must enquire as to the health of your father? Doctor Brown," he leaned towards her, anxious that the doctor would not overhear his conversation, "has not been very forthcoming."

Cassie glanced across the table at Doctor Brown, wondering if she underestimated his loyalties. Maybe he was genuine in his commitment to Lord Miller. She turned her attention back to Mr. Huxley and chose her words carefully.

"My father's health fluctuates but he is in good hands. Doctor Brown has told me that there is a great chance that he will make a full recovery." Cassie watched Mr. Huxley closely. He let out a deep breath and his shoulders relaxed. The news about Lord Miller seemed to come as a relief to him. Cassie frowned, turning her attention to the hideous contents of her plate. Why was Huxley so relieved? Surely it would be to his advantage to have Lord Miller in declining health. "Did you mean to check out the house Mr. Huxley?" she asked, brazenly. "In case my father did not survive for very much longer?"

Doctor Brown and Miss Blythe's conversation had suddenly stopped. Cassie was looking at Huxley intently. A band of red slowly grew from his collar all the way to the height of his forehead. He dabbed his temples with the corner of his white napkin.

"Lady Cassandra, I assure you, I am doing nothing of the sort. I have every wish to see your father make a full recovery. I am painfully aware that it is my duty to take over the running of Ludlow Park if you are still unmarried by the time of your father's passing but I have no inclination, no inclination whatsoever..." He was unable to finish the sentence.

"You must excuse Lady Cassandra, Mr. Huxley, her father's illness is..." the governess could not articulate a full sentence either. Instead, the occupants of the table looked intently at the contents of their plates and continued to eat slowly and with dedication.

Cassie could not help but smile a little at the awkwardness of it all. So, thought Cassie, as she pushed the eel's head around her plate, unwilling to even attempt to taste it, if Huxley does not wish Lord Miller harm, then who does? Cassie had ruled out Doctor Brown. He seemed genuinely concerned for his patient.

Miss Blythe, though overbearing at times had been nothing but attentive and caring towards Lord Miller. Cassie couldn't see any reason why the governess would be involved in a plot to murder the Lord of Ludlow.

Mr. Evins, on the other hand, was obviously problematic. He was blackmailing the doctor to ensure that all the local business went his direction. Did his schemes stretch as far as attempted murder? He had the means. His apothecary was full of rare poisons and he had access to Lord Miller's medicines on a regular basis. But why? What would he gain? Cassie couldn't see what he could possibly want from her family.

The meal passed off without too much trouble. Cassie was selective in what she ate, and kept an eye on the other diners. She responded when spoken to and smiled at all the right times. Her mind though, was elsewhere. It flitted between Lord Miller's health problems and Charles Stafford's piercing blue eyes.

Dinner mercifully came to an end. As the hour was very late, Miss Blythe requested that Doctor Brown stay the night. He tried to say no but the governess could be very insistent. He was to be installed in the rooms adjacent to Lord Miller's. Miss Blythe stood to go and see about preparations for the doctor's stay, pausing at Cassie's seat as she left. She dipped her head and whispered, "You must lead the gentlemen to the drawing room. They will want to smoke and have a brandy after dinner."

Cassie shrugged her shoulders. "I'm not really a fan of brandy."

"Lady Cassandra," hissed the governess, "You, of course, will not be joining them."

"Oh," added Cassie, rising from her seat, catching the drift of the conversation. After dinner, the men hung around smoking and drinking. Cassie guessed that all that awaited her was embroidery and piano playing. She smiled at her guests and indicated the door, "Gentlemen," she said, smoothly, "I am to lead you to the smoking room."

She led the way across the hall and pushed open the heavy door. One of the servants, she assumed, had put down a log fire. It blazed comfortingly in the grate. The curtains were closed and the room had a nice cosiness to it. A tray lay on the ornate coffee table with two glasses and a flute of amber liquid, next to two large, fat cigars. "Ew," Cassie wrinkled her nose at the thoughts of cigar smoke.

Huxley and Doctor Brown had been talking quietly between themselves. When Cassie turned to indicate that they should enter the smoking room, their conversation halted. She got the distinct impression that they had been speaking about her.

In a flash of inspiration, she addressed her guests, "Gentlemen, if you would excuse me. I am pretty tired this evening. Help yourselves to some brandy. I am going to bed." She curtsied in a clumsy bob and turned, kicking the heavy skirts out with her foot. As she progressed up the stairs, a servant girl scurried down the corridor, fresh unlit candles in her hand.

"Excuse me," Cassie stopped her. "Could you tell Miss Blythe that the doctor and Mr. Huxley are in the drawing room and that I am going to bed early. Also, do you know where Molly is? Can you send her to my room?" The girl was trying to look everywhere but at Cassie, staring at the floor, her shoes, her hands, the unlit candles, she nodded and mumbled something inarticulate before stumbling down the hallway out of sight.

Cassie shook her head and dragged her heavy load to the bedroom. She did not have much time, and she wanted to hear what the men were saying in the drawing room but she couldn't just walk in. Eavesdropping at the door was no good either; Miss Blythe would surely catch her. She needed access to the drawing room and there was only one way to do that—the servants' corridor. Molly arrived just as Cassie was beginning to pace in frustration. She almost pounced on the girl as soon as she entered the room.

"Molly! I need to get down the servants' corridor. I need to get to the smoking room." Cassie was expecting the servant to stall, to refuse to take her, to put up some kind of argument.

Molly turned pale.

Cassie gripped Molly's hand. "Come on, Mols. I need to hear what they are saying. They were talking about Lord Miller, I am sure of it."

The girl was silent for a split second. "The servants are havin' their tea. There will be no one about for at least the next half hour."

Cassie was surprised at the speed of the decision, impressed by the new tone of confidence in the Molly's voice. She followed the other girl out of the room towards the door to the servant's corridor. The corridor was as dark and dreary as before, spits of candle light illuminated the way as the two girls hurried along. Molly walked to the front pausing at certain junctions in the corridor, checking around corners. She beckoned Cassie forward and after several heart-stopping moments, they came to a short off-shoot corridor and nipped into it. They lagged against the cold stone wall. The sound of Cassie's heart beating in her chest seemed to echo off the brick work.

Molly nodded her head in the direction of a plain timber door. "There 'tis Miss," she whispered. "The smokin' room. I will wait here at the end of the corridor and keep watch. Take this."

Cassie took one of the candles that Molly offered her and tip-toed down the corridor. At the end, she snuffed out her candle, plunging herself into darkness. It would not be a good thing to have the light shining under the concealed doorway. She edged forward, her hands outstretched in front of her. After what seemed like an age her fingertips touched the cool of the timber. She pressed her ear to the wood and listened.

"...yes, but Doctor Brown, I am asking for some kind of assurance..." Cassie heard Mr. Huxley say. His speech sounded a little slurred. How much of that brandy have they had to drink, she wondered?

"Now, Huxley," the doctor replied, "you know I cannot give you a guarantee. There is no accounting for the human body. You are anxious that I pronounce his Lordship cured, but I cannot do that."

Cassie heard a pause in the conversation, the crackle of wood in the fireplace. "Hmm, very well, Brown, I will take your word that you will do your best, your damned best, to make sure he survives."

Cassie frowned.

"Yes, yes. I have told you as much. Now, I really must get to bed. I have had many late nights recently. I will take my leave of you, sir." Cassie heard the creaking of the furniture and a steady tread towards the door. Then silence descended. She waited for a few minutes, in the deepening darkness of the cold servants' corridor. She heard it then, a loud snoring sound from the opposite side of the door. She blindly patted the door, looking for a handle but there was none. She considered for a moment then put her shoulder to the timber and pushed. The door gave way easily, opening silently. All the servants' corridor doors were oiled so the noise of the staff coming and going would not disturb the family.

Cassie peeped into the room that was empty except for the snoring figure of Huxley, asleep in a large armchair next to the fire, an empty brandy glass on the table in front of him. His head was thrown back, his mouth gaping open, his tongue lolling to one side. He moaned in his sleep, his hand coming up to rub the tip of his nose. He shifted a little and settled even deeper into the folds of the chair. Cassie stood very still, half in the room, half in the corridor. He mumbled something to himself. Cassie took a step, listening intently. She thought that he had said something in his sleep. She edged a little closer.

"No." he cried out in terror. "No!" Huxley's hand gripped the arm of the chair, his fingers digging into the covering, his eyes closed. Cassie was paralysed to the spot, her heart hammering, afraid to move a single muscle in case he woke up.

Slowly, ever so slowly she took a step backwards, her hand reaching behind her, searching for the door. She did not want to risk taking her eyes off him, in case they would flutter open and she would be discovered.

"No, Harcourt. No!" shouted Huxley his eyes closed, his eyelids twitching in dream-sleep. "You shall not have it!"

Cassie stumbled into the cool darkness of the corridor, closing the door behind her, uncaring if she woke him. A slow creeping dread settled over her as she quickly retraced her steps. Who was Harcourt and what exactly did they want?

Chapter Twenty-One

~ Cassandra ~

Cassandra woke with a jolt. A loud noise, like someone shouting, had permeated her dreams. She pushed herself up onto her elbow and looked warily around the bedroom. She was being fanciful, tiredness making her imagine things. Her encounter with Becky the previous evening had kept her awake into the early morning.

Judge Miller had informed them, as they drove home, that the Travers family owned property in the nearby countryside and were visiting for the weekend.

Cassandra stretched in her bed, contemplating getting up. She touched the gold locket, reassured by its familiar weight. She guessed that it was late in the morning. The light coming under her curtains was bright and insistent. She pushed back the heavy covers and eased herself from under their weight. It was time, she thought, as she padded on bare feet to the upstanding dress trunk. Opening the doors, she looked doubtful as she scanned the hangers. She would need something warm, something practical. Men's trousers it is, she thought.

When she went downstairs, the house was quiet. Glancing out the porch windows she noticed that the car was missing. Judge Miller had gone out. A strange noise was coming from the front of the house, high pitched voices, several of them. Cassandra moved across the hallway, the sensation of her legs encased in tight material strange. This was the way the locals dressed, so Cassandra would have to conform to their tastes.

She pushed open the door to what once was a large drawing room. Tallulah was lounging on a couch, staring at a box. Cassandra moved silently into the room, mesmerized by the unimaginable. Several people, the size of her finger, were having a conversation whilst sitting in some kind of eating house. She was dumbfounded. "How," she began after a moment, startling Tallulah.

"Holy crap!" The girl pushed herself half off the couch in fright. "Cassandra," she breathed a sigh of relief, "you scared me. What are you doing creeping around? T.V. signal is working."

Cassandra had not taken her eyes off the black box. "What," she pointed, "is that?"

Tallulah smiled. "It's a T.V. Sorry, is it creeping you out? I'll turn it off." She pushed a button on some kind of pointer and the screen faded to black, the people disappearing.

"Hey, I like your jeans," commented Tallulah, "They look good on you."

Cassandra nodded slowly, her thoughts flicking back to the large black box. She needed to get out of the house. Surprising herself she made a simple request. "I would like to go for a walk. Would you accompany me?"

Tallulah hesitated. "Sure."

Cassandra had decided to make an effort to become better acquainted with Tallulah, probably to Miss Blythe's disdain.

As soon as they were free of the house, out in the open, Cassandra felt better. The girls decided to walk to the edge of the park, along the old boundary of the Stafford lands. Cassandra studied the changes with interest. The Stafford house, which normally nestled in amongst the trees, barely visible, was on full view now, the woodland around it felled. "Do you know who lives there?" asked Cassandra as they walked past.

"Yes," answered Tallulah, "That is the Stansons or Stevensons, I think. The Millers don't really get on very well with the locals. Something about an estate inheritance, neighbourly feud, you know, the usual."

Cassandra gasped. "They do not like us?"

Laughing, Tallulah continued, "These kinds of places, a grudge can last hundreds of years, I don't think it's anything personal. Hey, maybe it was something your lot did back in the 1700's?" Tallulah was obviously in jest as she was smiling but Cassandra did not find it amusing.

The thought of a feud between neighbours lasting for such a long time seemed ridiculous. Yes, to be sure, her father and Mr. Stafford had not been on speaking terms, but that was with good cause. Her relations with Charles Stafford were amicable, a little restrained perhaps but then, the offspring had to start somewhere in their efforts at repairing the deeds of their fathers. And Cassandra prided herself on being the one who had offered the olive branch of peace.

Charles Stafford was an overbearing, morose sort of person, given to fits of deep thinking and philosophising. Cassandra did not see the use of these pursuits but she could not fault his conduct towards her. She had of course, since her coming out two years ago, had cause to be in the same social circle as him, though he was four years her senior. They had been civil to one another and addressed the issue of their fathers only once. It had been quite delicate, neither wishing to betray their parent or lessen the supposed grievance. Sighing, Cassandra tried not to think of home.

The girls went to the end of the driveway and turned right, walking in the middle of the small country road. The day was fine, the autumnal sun shining with a watery brightness. Tallulah prattled on, telling Cassandra details about people Cassie would know, the adventures she had gotten up to in the last six months, endless information about something called college. Cassandra deduced that here, girls were allowed to attend school, rather than study at home with their governess. Girls were permitted to learn the same as boys if they so wished. The idea fascinated Cassandra.

She did enjoy playing the piano, her French was excellent, her needlework could do with a little attention and her dancing was tolerable, but to think of all the other things she could learn. She could take lessons in agricultural management; learn about new ways of farming, new machinery, new sowing techniques for the benefit of Ludlow Park.

She had asked her father about it many times but he would not indulge her thirst for knowledge, saying that she had no need to fill her head with such learning. She had argued that if she were to run Ludlow Park as an estate she needed to know these things.

Her father had patted her on her hand and told her, "That is what you will have a husband for, my dear."

Cassandra had nodded, dutifully.

She was lost in thought and did not notice the girl stopping.

"Oh crap," uttered Tallulah, her hand gripping Cassandra's arm. Cassandra looked up and saw three figures approaching. There were two girls and a boy. She recognised the flaxen, waist-length hair of one girls and the tall dark hair of the boy.

"It's Becky. Should we turn back?" asked Tallulah, sounding worried.

"Certainly not," replied Cassandra. "Surely the girl has more manners than to ignore us if we pass her."

Tallulah began to laugh, a hysterical kind of sound, "She won't ignore us, Cassandra. She will kick the crap out of us! She has a call out on you since last time?"

"A call out? What is a call out?"

"She never got a chance to finish the job in school…"

"She wishes to fight? But whatever for?"

Tallulah shrugged her shoulders. "Why do you think?"

"Dwane?"

Tallulah nodded.

"What happened?"

"He has been trying to get in Cassie's pants for weeks. She wasn't having any of it, unless he dumped Becky. Kept promising of course, telling her that he needed the right moment. Blah, blah. Spineless weasel."

They squinted in the direction of the group, Cassandra shaking her head. "A boy," she muttered to herself, disbelieving.

"Becky found out and went ballobas. She blamed it all on Cassie. Pushed her around in the hallway that day. It was total self-defense."

Cassandra continued to walk in the direction of the group. They had stopped a few meters ahead, leaning against the entrance pillars of a rather grand house. The gates were large and imposing, erected to keep all manner of people out of the property. The girl said something and Dwane laughed.

Surely if Cassandra could talk some sense they would be able to put the matter behind them. Cassandra walked slowly, unsure how she was going to resolve the predicament. Tallulah trailed along behind her.

"Well, look what we have here. Have you come to apologise, Cassie, for being a total slag?" The girl beside Becky tittered.

"Apologise to an insincere wench like you? Hardly." Cassandra sounded rude, impudent and she liked it.

Dwane wouldn't look at her, his gaze concerned with the ground.

So much for the chivalry of men.

Cassandra licked her lips, trying to regain her composure, thinking of all the instruction Miss Blythe had given her.

Becky's face was blotchy red, her temper making it difficult for her to articulate words. Eventually, she spat out, "You're a lippy little slut, aren't you, Cassie Miller?" Becky pushed herself away from the gate pillar and took a step towards her. "You didn't get enough of a beating in school, you want some more."

Cassandra shook her head, holding her hands up, sure that she could negotiate some kind of truce. "No, indeed. I do not wish for you to..." She glanced at Tallulah, "call me out. I simply wanted to tell you what I thought of you and reassure you that your opinion is inconsequential. You, Becky Travers, mean absolutely nothing to me. You are a nobody." That was not exactly the wording that she had been hoping for. Somehow her brain and her mouth were not collaborating.

Decorum, poise, duty. The three words should be at the forefront of her mind. They were Miss Blythe's mantra, the things that were of utmost importance to a lady.

Instead, she was thinking of smacking Becky's mouth with the heel of her hand. Cassandra could feel Tallulah stiffen beside her. "And it was your boyfriend who imposed himself on me. So, if anyone is a slut, it is he." Cassandra clamped her lips shut, pressing them tight together, afraid that she would say something else to worsen the situation.

"I am going to grind your face into the dirt!" bellowed Becky, her cheeks aflame.

"You're a hack, Becky 'The Troll' Travers." Tallulah groaned loudly beside her. "And I take my leave of you." Cassandra could not control her words any longer. She needed to leave before things got totally out of hand. Turning around, with as much poise as she could muster, she walked away.

Tallulah jogged along beside her, unable to articulate actual words. Instead she was sputtering something incomprehensible "That was... That was. Well, that was probably about the stupidest thing..." She didn't get to finish her sentence as she was pushed from behind, stumbling forward.

Becky was upon them like a flash of white rage, her eyes dilated, her whole body emitting a kind of angry glow. Cassandra turned around, shock registering on her face. The girl was about to explode out of her skin, her rage evident.

"Now," began Cassandra, trying to defuse the situation. She stepped in front of Becky, her hands raised in a gesture of peace. But before she could say anything Becky lashed out. Cassandra dodged at the very last minute, the punch catching the side of her head. A stinging pain flashed into her ear and along her jaw bone.

"You little..." Nobody had ever struck her in her life. Cassandra's indignation flooded through her veins, heating her skin, making her vision cloud. Becky was about to punch her again. Cassandra ducked out of the way, her breath catching in her throat. None of Miss Blythe's wisdom would defuse this situation.

Cassandra swallowed nervously and made her decision. Lady or not, she needed to look to her own best interests. She needed to defend herself, protect what was important to her. And right now, that meant deflecting the advances of a crazed Becky. She spread the weight equally between her two feet and lowered her centre of gravity, bunching her fists and placing them an inch or two away from her face. The stance felt familiar, she remembered it well. The voice of her teacher came back to her, the memory of him giving her some confidence. She dodged another two blows that Becky was trying to land near or on her face then struck, upwards, fast and sure.

Her knuckles connected with the skin, bone and cartilage of Becky's nose. A sickening crack could be heard, followed by the howl of Becky as she doubled over, blood streaming from her nose. Tallulah gripped Cassandra's arm and dragged her away. "Let's go. We've gotta get out of here."

In between sobs and curses, Becky was howling at them, "I will get you for this, Cassie Miller. I'm going to tell my father that you assaulted me!"

Turning around Tallulah pointed to the trees which sentinelled the entranceway to a large farm. To the top branch of the nearest tree was a camera. "You can tell whoever you like Becky but they won't believe you when they see the security camera footage. You started it." Tallulah grabbed Cassandra by the arm and pulled her along the roadway, back the direction they had come.

"What was that?" asked Tallulah, as she hurried along.

Cassandra was panting, adrenaline coursing through her, her fists still balled tight. It took her a moment to regain her composure. "Pardon?"

"You just broke Becky's nose. I thought you were supposed to be a lady."

"I am a lady," replied Cassandra, slightly insulted at Tallulah's insinuations.

"Yeah, so where the hell did you learn to do that?"

"Well, I..." Cassandra felt uncomfortable, her cheeks reddening slightly, her heart rate slowing down. What had just happened? She felt energy zinging throughout her body, from the tip of her hair right through to the balls of her feet. It was exhilarating. She wanted to throw her arms wide, to spin around, to unpin her hair and shake it out like a wet dog. She began to laugh, a slow trickle building to a jubilant thrill.

"Did you see her face?" Cassandra's eyes were tearing up.

"Yeah." Tallulah grinned. "It was epic! Where did you learn to do that?" Tallulah did a fast-footed dance, her shoes causing a tiny puddle of dust to rise from the ground. "You were like a ninja!"

Cassandra giggled, something she had not done in an age.

"So?" continued Tallulah, "Spill. I can smell a juicy story."

Cassandra sighed, some of her adrenaline evaporating. "My steward taught us."

"Us? You and Elizabeth? Your steward taught you how to box?"

"No, not Elizabeth. Nicholas and I." Cassandra was getting very warm. It must be delayed shock from the altercation.

"Who's Nicholas?" asked Tallulah.

"Nicholas is the steward's son. We grew up together, used to play

166

together as children. As a little boy, his father wished to teach him how to fight. I wanted to learn too. My mother was quite amused by the suggestion. I was only eight." Cassandra smiled fondly. "She thought I would tire after a few days but I stuck it out for the whole summer. Of course, they never really hurt me. I mean I never got to do any actual fighting. Apart from hitting Charles Stafford that time, I've never actually hit anyone."

"Well, you did a pretty good job of punching Becky right in the nose. She deserved it though, so I wouldn't worry about it."

"Do you think she will tell her father?"

"Maybe, if she is smart enough to figure out that those cameras are not actually hooked up to anything, then maybe. But I wouldn't worry about it. She is probably currently more concerned about her swollen face!"

Cassandra smiled and flexed her hand. It would hurt terribly by tomorrow. "Come on, we better get home. I shall need something cold for my hand."

"So," began Tallulah as they walked briskly back the way they came, "tell me more about this Nicholas?"

"There is nothing to tell," shrugged Cassandra, inspecting the hedgerow, plucking a piece of honeysuckle, "he is the steward's son. We used to know each other as children. He moved away to study. I don't really see him anymore. That is all."

Chapter Twenty-Two

~ Cassie ~

Cassie was the last to eat lunch the next day. Miss Blythe had taken Huxley, who looked a little hung over, on a tour of the park. Doctor Brown was administering a fresh batch of leeches to Lord Miller. Cassie shuddered at the thought.

For once, she was enjoying the solitude of the dining room. She had dismissed the servant, telling him to take five. He had looked blankly back at her, before bowing, easing the door closed gently behind him as he left.

Cassie sighed. Last night's efforts had exhausted her. She still remembered the fear in Huxley's voice as he cried out in his sleep. Whoever this Harcourt person was, it was clear he terrified Huxley.

The door of the breakfast room creaked open and a serving girl entered. She bobbed a curtsy. "Excuse me Lady Cassandra," she said quietly, looking at a spot on the rug, "There is a gentleman to see ya. He is in the drawing room."

Cassie nodded her head once and returned to her cup of tea. As soon as the girl left, Cassie smiled and pushed back from the table, wiping any crumbs from her mouth with the edge of her napkin. She wondered if Charles had any news for her. Hopefully he would be in a more forthcoming mood today. She crossed the hallway and pushed open the door, a smile coming unchecked to her face.

He had his back to her, standing by the window. Before her mouth could pronounce the first syllable of his name, the tall, broad-shouldered figure turned around. He had brown hair, russet sideburns and a neatly trimmed beard. He was wearing a long coat and his feet were covered in a type of galosh, to keep his trousers and boots clean. The way his hazel eyes examined her face made Cassie uncomfortable. His unchecked gaze held an accusation.

When he spoke, his voice was low. "Are you not even glad to see me, Lady Cassandra, no greeting for me today?" He turned and moved to the opposite side of the room, standing in front of the mantle. He looked into the newly lit fire, its virgin flames devouring fresh timber. "You have no time now for a lowly steward's son."

Cassie did not know what to say, she had no idea who this was, "Sir, I…" she began.

He spun around, a flash of anger marring his features. "I am no Sir. You can reserve that title for your new friend, Mr. Stafford."

Cassie frowned, "Mr. Stafford is not my…"

"He must be something to you. You were seen with him, in the dead of night, alone."

Cassie kept very still, her brain racing. How did he know, who had seen them? What else had been reported?

"No matter, it is not my place to council a lady on how she behaves."

"I'm sorry, I…" Cassie took a step towards him, her hand outstretched in apology.

He looked at her as if her hand was diseased. She gasped at the intensity of his revulsion.

The door to the drawing room flew open and Molly tumbled in, out of breath. "Oh," was all she said when she saw the two of them at first. "Oh," a second time. "I am sorry ma'am to bother ya but…" Molly's eyes darted from Cassie to the gentleman standing at the fireplace, his back half turned.

Cassie was desperately trying to signal for some help but Molly seemed equally as paralysed. "I came," she continued, after taking a deep breath to gather herself. "I came to see if ya would like tea, Lady Cassandra. If *you*, Mr. Weston," she emphasised his name, labouring over it, Cassie could take the hint. "…if ya would like some tea?"

"No. No, thank you, Molly," was the abrupt response she received. The girl bowed and made to leave. Cassie mouthed the words, 'help', but the servant could do nothing, closing the door behind her as she went.

Cassie took a deep breath. "Mr. Weston," she began. His laugh caught her off guard. "So it is Mr. Weston now. Whatever happened to just plain Nicholas, Cassandra? I thought we were friends, capable of greeting each other as such."

"Nicholas," Cassie began again and the door opened a second time. Miss Blythe advanced into the room, the tea tray gripped firmly in her hands. She was supposed to be walking in the grounds, Cassie thought to herself. There was no way it could have been readied so quickly, unless the governess had spied the guest from the lawn and hurried the tea tray herself.

The governess's beady eyes took in the view of the room in one sweeping glance, and before Cassie could stop her she addressed their guest. "Mr. Weston," she gushed, the insincerity in her greeting evident, "how lovely of you to call. You are back from London I see. Here to pay your respects to the house before going on to visit your father?"

Cassie's brain was scrambling to make sense of the situation. Nicholas Weston was the steward's son. He was clearly annoyed with her for some reason. By the look and actions of Miss Blythe, the governess was doing everything she could to keep Mr. Weston occupied, to remind of his station in life and to distract Cassie. She looked at the man again. He was not like Charles in anyway yet there seemed to be a calm sincerity about him. Molly had some serious explanation to do about the extent of his attentions towards the lady of the house.

Nicholas was bowing, very deeply towards Miss Blythe. "I cannot stay, ladies, I am afraid. I simply came to pay my respects to Lord Miller and to wish him a speedy recovery." He shot an accusing glance towards Cassie. "Now, as you have pointed out, I must be going to see my father. Thank you for your hospitality." And with that he left the room, not uttering another word.

Cassie stood stunned, unsure of what had just happened. Miss Blythe was saying something about his manners being much dis-improved. It was obvious that the governess had no time for the son of the estate's steward. However, Cassie was not listening, a frown crossing her features. Is this the person Cassandra wants to marry?

"Shall we, Lady Cassandra?" asked Miss Blythe.

"What?" Cassie replied sharply, irritated at Miss Blythe's untimely interruption.

"Shall we proceed to get you ready for the ball?"

Cassie looked at the governess. She was dressed as usual in severe dark grey muslin, her hair pulled back into a non-descript bun, the tip of her beak-like nose slightly red, her eyes beady and too close together. Cassie disliked her for a moment and then remembered that her role was to protect Lady Cassandra, to oversee her development and Cassie realised that Miss Blythe must be very lonely.

"Yes, Miss Blythe, I think it is time." Cassie was not really referring to the ball and perhaps the governess knew this as she stepped wordlessly out of her way.

Upstairs, across the end of her bed, a mountain of magnificent material had been arranged. It was ivory in colour, made from taffeta and lace. The detail to the skirt was breath-taking. The bodice was cut in a heart shape design, the sleeves puffy but tasteful. Cassie walked to it and fingered the ruffles absently, thinking about what had happened downstairs.

She had to get home. She could do a great deal of damage to these people's lives. She wondered for a moment if Cassandra was doing equal damage to hers. She smiled to herself. If anything, her mother would be ecstatic that Cassie had magically sprouted excellent manners and a propensity for wearing dresses.

She missed her mum, had been trying desperately not to think about it, about that night in the hallway, the rain pounding on the window, the look of horror on her mother's face right after she had slapped her. Cassie knew she hadn't meant it, knew that she had been provoked. In that instant, as she touched the fabric of a dress which probably cost the equivalent of half a servant's wage Cassie realised how badly she had behaved, realised how angry she had become. If Miss Blythe was all that Cassandra had in terms of guidance or affection, then Cassie's home situation looked like winning the lottery in comparison.

She turned quickly and moved to the window. "I have to get out of here," she said, savage with determination.

Molly found her like that, at the window, her forehead pressed against the cool glass, her hands folded at her waist. "Miss," began Molly tentatively, closing the door softly behind her. "Miss, are ya well?"

"Yes," she murmured half-heartedly.

"Oh, Miss." Molly came and stood beside her, placing a hand gently on her shoulder. "Do not fret, it will get sorted, I am sure. Mr. Stafford will know what to do."

"Mr. Stafford hates me. Miss Blythe hates me. That man, today, Nicholas Weston, he definitely hates me!"

Molly took a step back and cleared her throat. "Yes well, Miss, I wanted to…that is…I should have…" Cassie turned and looked at the servant, her cheeks were red, her eyes downcast.

"Yes Molly, spit it out. You have been holding back on me?"

"Well, Miss, Lady Cassandra and Mr. Weston have been friends since their infancy. They grew up together as children ya see. They have a special kind of…relationship." Molly fidgeted with her apron, "Miss Blythe thought it inappropriate for the lady of the house to be associatin' with a servant's…"

"A servant?" interjected Cassie, "But Mr. Weston Senior is head of the estate, a very respected position, quite a well-paid job?"

Molly nodded. "Yes, but he is still a servant."

Cassie huffed, before turning from the window to pace the room. "That is totally ridiculous. What is wrong with you people?"

"It is not proper, Miss, And Lady Cassandra could see that too. Anyway, Nicholas went off to London to pursue his studies. Then he went to Europe for a while, to travel. It was for the best."

Cassie went to sit on the bed, crumpling the beautiful gown. "He thinks there is something between Charles Stafford and me, I mean Lady Cassandra."

"And is there, Miss?"

Cassie shook her head. "Don't be silly, he is an arse and he thinks I'm a spoilt brat. That goes for me and Cassandra. Ugh, forget it. I'm sick of trying to figure these people out. Let's just get this monster dress on, pull my hair up into a mountain of painful pins and get to this stupid ball where I'm bound to make an even bigger idiot out of myself."

They dressed her in silence, Molly's deft fingers pulling and pushing, poking and probing until Cassie was safely encased in the cascade of ivory lace. She felt like something out of Cinderella. She was afraid to touch her hair after Molly had plaited and coiled it into an impressive design on the crown of her head. Molly had added some colour to Cassie's eyes and a small touch of rouge to her cheeks and lips.

"So?" Cassie asked, as she stood by her dressing table, teetering on new slippers of cream, "How do I look."

Molly grinned from ear to ear. "Why Miss, if ya do not outshine that new Mrs. Thornton, then I do not know my place!"

Cassie smiled. "Really Molly! That is very unlike you, to say something bad about a lady. You are spending too much time with me."

They both laughed as they crossed the room. At the door, Molly touched her arm, "Be careful tonight now, Miss, Mr. Wrix of Crompton Hall will be there and he has taken a special shine to ya."

"What do you mean?"

"He means to have ya."

"Excuse me?"

"As his wife. He has made it known that he wishes to marry ya."

"Do I not get a say in this at all or is it decided by the other residents in the neighbourhood?" Cassie asked coldly.

Molly shook her head. "I just want to warn ya. Lady Cassandra has no intention of acceptin', but there will be protocol."

"What's wrong with him?"

Molly would not answer for a second or two and Cassie could see her trying to formulate the answer. "There is nothin' wrong with him, Miss, he just has a bit of a reputation…"

"What kind of reputation?"

"He is a cad," she said softly.

"A what?"

"A dandy."

Cassie shaking her head, still not understanding.

"He has a likin' for servin' girls, Miss." Molly looked to her feet, her embarrassment evident.

"Oh." Cassie thought for a minute. "How much of a liking."

"They say, well the servants say that he got a young girl in the family way, and left her to the master…"

"Left her?"

"Yes, Miss, left her, at the house he was staying in. Oh, he never touches his own servants, Miss, makes a point of that."

"What?" Cassie asked incredulous, "he only goes for other people's servants?"

Molly nodded.

"Why, that little…"

"Oh, Miss, he is a very pleasant type of gentleman, by all accounts quite handsome. I just thought I would warn ya about his indiscretion, so ya are fully aware in case ya happen upon him."

"And is Lady Cassandra really expected to marry this idiot?"

Molly shrugged her shoulders. "It is the best option so far. Mr. Wrix is very rich."

"But he is a man-slut," Cassie said loudly, clamping her hands over her mouth, afraid that someone had heard her. "Sorry," she apologized. "What happens if I—Lady Cassandra marries him? Does he get the house?"

"The house goes to the husband's care. That is the way of it."

"Damn it, Molly! That is ridiculous! Ludlow Park would be at his disposal to do with it whatever he pleases? Why doesn't she marry Charles?" It was out of Cassie's mouth before she could control the words.

Molly looked at her, her eyes big and round. "Mr. Stafford?"

"Yes. He is single, he is not a total tyrant, he lives next door, their lands are adjoining? Why doesn't she marry him?"

"He would not have her, Miss."

Cassie frowned, folding her arms across her chest, "What do you mean, he wouldn't have her? What's wrong with her?"

"Nothin' Miss, nothin', but Mr. Stafford and Lady Cassandra, they are not like that. They tolerate each other, but they are too alike. Too stubborn. Anyway, he is rarely at home, havin' cause to travel a great deal. He is destined for the law, they say. Lady Cassandra does not think of him in that way, not like…" Molly stopped herself.

"Not like what Molly?"

The girl looked at her from beneath her pale eyelashes, "Nothin',

Miss, I forget myself sometimes."

"She's in love with Nicholas, isn't she?" Cassie's brain had gone into overdrive. "That is why he came today to see me. He thinks Lady Cassandra and Charles Stafford... Oh crap. He saw me by the orchard the other night and now he thinks..."

"Oh, Miss, do not fret. It is not yer fault, I am sure..."

"Why don't they get married?"

Molly shook her head, her hands lifting up. "It is not possible. The lady of the house cannot marry the steward's son. It is just not done."

Cassie was silent for a minute, thinking, trying to logic out a solution. She didn't have anything to say. She heard the sound of a carriage coming to the front of the house. "I better go."

Molly took her hands and squeezed them gently. "Good luck, Miss."

They parted company on the landing, Molly disappearing quietly through the hidden doorway in the corridor. Cassie continuing as daintily as possible down the stairway to the hall.

Mr. Huxley was waiting for her, his hat in his hand. "Well, well, Lady Cassandra, what a vision. What a vision!" His chest puffed out like a bird and Cassie had to smile. Huxley was wearing an overcoat, the tails of his dress suit poking out from beneath the heavy material. His stature and girth did not suit his outfit. He looked more ridiculous than regal, but Cassie remembered her manners and greeted him with as much civility as she could muster.

The carriage was called and George and the driver brought the horses to a halt at the front of the house. Cassie wanted to talk to George, to ask him if he had said anything to anyone about the orchard but she kept her features blank as she was handed in to the carriage.

The carriage journey was a little more comfortable than the last time. Cassie supposed it would be a bad idea to suggest that she rode on horseback, so refrained. She wondered where Miss Blythe was and then concluded that she probably had not been invited.

Cassie wanted to just sit quietly for the journey, but Mr. Huxley insisted on talking the whole way. The only reprieve was that he was content to have, more or less, a one-sided conversation. All Cassie had to do was nod and smile, throw in the odd ohh and ahh, or yes and no, and the man was happy to prattle on.

She was busy thinking of Nicholas Weston and the look of anger on his face earlier. If the wrong people found out that she was not the Lady of Ludlow Park, then she, the house and the family were in a lot of danger. Had he told anyone?

The carriage trundled along and Cassie thought about the ball and what would be expected of her. She dreaded the prospect of having to dance. She went over in her head some of the tips that Molly had told her. Don't take off her gloves. Don't drink the punch. Don't refuse to dance. Don't voice too many opinions or people will think you are too free thinking. There were so many don'ts that Cassie thought her head would explode. She resolved to forget them all and concentrate on just surviving the next few hours.

Chapter Twenty-Three

~ Cassie ~

The assembly hall in the village was not as large as Ludlow. Cassie caught a glimpse of it as the carriage trundled across the square. It was a relatively new building. And it was one of the rare structures in the village made from actual cut stone. Miss Blythe had mentioned to her that Mr. Thornton, Jane Stafford's new husband, was a man interested in development, new thinking. This idea seemed pretty novel to the locals, but Cassie could see that his vision for the advancement of the village made sense. First step assembly hall, next step shopping mall. She smiled to herself.

The hall was three stories tall, with walls constructed of large slabs of granite. There were columns to the front and a large entranceway. The structure was blocky, like a big square box, but there was no accounting for taste Cassie thought as she clambered out of the carriage, pulling her skirts with her.

There were people milling about, standing in a kind of disorderly queue waiting to catch a glimpse and to be greeted by the new Mrs. Thornton and her husband. Cassie stood on tip-toes to get her bearings, to catch sight of the woman who was supposed to be her frenemy. At the top of the queue, with a plume of ridiculous looking black and white feathers sticking out of her head, was a girl of about nineteen or twenty. She was slim and of average height, chestnut coloured hair, piled on top of her head. She wore a dress of stark white with trimmings of black along the hem, the bodice, and the cuffs. She was monochrome, but Cassie had to appreciate the affect. You could not help but stare at her.

The reception area was pale and airy, several windows opened up on to the front driveway and the chandeliers with their hundreds of candles had been lit. Cassie could just see beyond the reception room in to a long, wooden floored gallery. A tickle of nerves ran through her at the thought of dancing.

The queue was moving forward steadily and before she knew it Cassie was standing in front of what must be Mr. Thornton. He smiled at her in a friendly sort of way and bowed over her outstretched hand. "Lady Miller, how lovely to see you again. It has been some time since we left for our travels. I am glad to see that you are looking well."

Cassie smiled politely before moving on to greet the new Mrs. Thornton. Jane Thornton looked as thorny as her new name suggested. She cracked the smallest of smiles, the corners of her mouth pulling up at either side and curtsied to Cassie. "Cassandra." Cassie did not miss the insult though she was relatively new to this game. Mrs. Thornton had used her first name. Well, thought Cassie, two can play at that game.

"Jane," she began, taking pleasure in the flicker of annoyance she could see in Jane's eyes, "lovely to see you. Married life has certainly," Cassie laboured a look at Jane's outfit, "...brought out the colour in you."

She bowed her head once and moved on, not looking back to see the effect her words had had on the new Mrs. Thornton of Thornton Manor. Huxley was there beside her in an instant, puffing to keep up. Annoyingly, he offered his arm again, and Cassie was obliged to take it.

"Shall we deposit our things?" he asked, nodding his head towards a servant who loitered in the hallway. Cassie was not sure what he meant, but she assumed he was referring to her shawl and cloth purse. She willingly gave them to the servant who installed them as directed into a large cloak room, men's attire on the left, ladies on the right. Cassie craned her neck to see into the cavernous room but Huxley pulled her forward towards the other guests.

He led her in the direction of the food and drink. Cassie was not sure what to do as she did not recognise many of the dishes and did not feel like eating. "Some refreshments, my dear?" asked Mr. Huxley.

"Yeah, thanks. I think I'll just have a drink." There was a bowl of something fruity at the rear of the table. There were apples and pears, cloves and berries of some kind in it. Looks safe enough. "I'll have some of that please, Mr. Huxley."

She received a glass of the liquid and downed it in one. Mr. Huxley looked at her perplexed and went to fetch another glass. Cassie felt the burn of the liquid hit her stomach and realised why there was so much fruit in it. It was to hide the alcohol.

So, this is what punch tastes like. She downed the next glass quickly to give her some much needed courage for the dancing ahead. Her head felt exceptionally light. She smiled at nothing in particular as she surveyed the room and its guests.

Many people smiled and nodded in her direction. Huxley prattled on beside her, admiring the furniture, the pictures, the food, the dresses, the candles, admiration for the whole damn place practically radiated from him.

A gentleman approached and bowed before them both. "Lady Cassandra."

Oh, crap, thought Cassie. Who the hell is this?

"May I say how lovely you look this evening."

Cassie smiled politely, turning to admire the dancers who had lined up in front of her. The truth of the matter was that she knew the gentleman was looking for an introduction to Mr. Huxley, but she couldn't give it as she did not know his name.

She pretended to be enthralled by the music and the dancing and the man was forced to turn to Mr. Huxley and bowing before him said, "Mr. Huxley, may I introduce myself, I am Mr. Babcock."

Cassie took her cue. "Oh, Mr. Babcock, how terribly rude of me. I'm sorry I should have introduced you, but I was distracted by the lovely dancing. I'm very sorry."

The gentleman bowed graciously. "No matter, Lady Cassandra. I will not hold it to you."

Hold what to me, thought Cassie? The two gentlemen began to talk about boring topics like the politics of London and the price of coal. Then they began to talk of cards, Huxley's eyes growing bright and Cassie lost complete interest. She had time to glance around the room and then she saw him, standing at the opposite wall, staring, bold as brass, straight at her.

He was bright, like sunshine, full of health and vitality. His hair was blond, cut short, falling in an appealing way across his forehead. He had light coloured eyes and a sun-tanned face, as if he had been out in the fields all day. His lips curled in an alluring smile and Cassie realised that he was a 17th century predator, the most dangerous kind; a virile unmarried man.

She wanted to look away but couldn't. She was trapped by his gaze. A slow blush began to work itself up along her neck, across her cheeks, flaming into her temples. He moved towards her, melting through the crowd, not stopping for anyone till he was right in front of her. Cassie's heart was beating fast and she looked into his eyes, the deepest amber, almost gold. Her ability to talk seemed to have deserted her.

He bowed low, taking her hand in his, kissing her knuckles, lingering for what seemed like an inappropriate amount of time. Cassie felt the last ounce of oxygen leave her system. She was staring at him and unconsciously holding her breath.

"Lady Cassandra, you are looking ravishing this evening, if I may say so." His tone was complimentary but something in the glint of his eye, some flash of hardness, like flint drew her from her stupor.

"You may say whatever you like, Mr. Wrix. You always do, if rumours are to be believed." The tone of her voice made him pause. Cassie had no intention of falling under this person's spell. He was a use and discard type of guy who reminded her of Dwane.

"Come, come Lady Cassandra, are you in poor form this evening? A dance perhaps would ease you into a better mood." He went to put his arm around her waist to lead her to the dance floor and she stiffened in response. She couldn't dance, had formulated the excuse of a sore ankle to get herself out of any trouble. But it looked like Mr. Wrix would not take no for an answer.

She found herself being propelled forward, the pressure of his arm around her waist. He patted her ass discretely, away from the prying eyes of the other guests.

"Get your hand off me," she hissed, keeping her words low. She tried not to growl at him, but what she really wanted to do was punch his lights out.

He smirked at her, as if she were a mere bauble to be played with, an accessory that one has necessity of when in polite company.

Cassie straightened up to her full height and glared at him. "Mr. Wrix, I would not dance with you if you were the last man on earth." Her admission made him pause, a frown fleeting across his features. "You," she said and leaned towards him for emphasis, keeping her voice low, "are a total ladies man. Your reputation as a..." Cassie searched for the right word, "cad precedes you. I won't be dancing with you, I won't be cavorting with you, and I certainly won't be marrying you." Her voice had risen to a higher octave. "Stay away from me. And stay away from my servants!"

She couldn't resist the last comment, had tried to refrain from insulting him beyond necessity. Her cheeks were burning crimson she was so angry. She noticed that a number of people standing nearby were staring at her.

"Damn it," she muttered under her breath, scanning the room for Huxley, the only other person she knew. She spotted the back of his balding head over by the cards table. He was in the middle of a game, completely engrossed and Cassie realised that she was on her own. Her heart sank. She could not turn around, could not look back at Mr. Wrix, could not move forward towards the onlookers, their mouth's slightly open in, what Cassie assumed was shock.

"Would you do me the honour of dancing, Lady Cassandra?" She turned around and said a silent thank you. She nodded as Charles Stafford held out his hand. His features were marble solid, but Cassie didn't care if he was annoyed with her. He had just saved her from certain social suicide.

She gripped onto his arm, tighter than was necessary, avoiding catching anyone's eye. Charles led her to the furthest end of the room, away from the people who had just witnessed the scene with Mr. Wrix. He stopped and indicated that she should stand in front of him. Cassie was beyond panicked. She wasn't a good dancer and here she had even less of an idea of what she was doing. Charles was looking above her head, at the wall behind her. She tried to catch his eye, tried to signal that she was in trouble, but he ignored her. The music started and she began to follow, stepping in and out as she could see the other ladies doing. Then they moved to swap partners. She was stuck with an older man, with large greying whiskers and beads of sweat forming on his forehead. Cassie smiled sympathetically at him when he went to move the wrong direction. Then she stepped back into line, moved once more and was faced with Charles again. His body was rigid, his hands closed into a fist when not needed for dancing. He would not look at her.

Sod this, she thought. They had swapped over partners again and sweaty head was in front of her. "I'm sorry," she said, pointing to her foot, "I have hurt my ankle. I need to sit down." The man bowed as gallantly as was possible and led her to a nearby vacant chair, mumbling his concerns. Cassie dismissed him and assured him that she would be just fine. As soon as his back was turned she stood up and pretend-limped out into the hallway.

She pushed her way into one of the rooms off the reception area, closing the door behind her. The sound of the party faded and she immediately felt calmer. It was the study room, bookshelves lined the walls and a large easy chair was situated next to the fire. The sash window looked out onto the street. She made her way over and stood there watching the evening light begin to fade. "Red sky at night," she said to herself quietly.

The door behind her opened and she turned to formulate an apology, to excuse herself for entering a closed room but she did not get the words out.

Charles was standing there, his features cold and still. He closed the door softly behind him.

"What do you want?" she asked, in no mood for whatever was coming.

"Are you well?" he asked, his voice strained with politeness.

"Yeah I'm fine."

"Your ankle?"

"It's fine. I just needed an excuse to get away from that awful dancing. Come on, out with it."

"With what?"

"Whatever chastisements you have for me, whatever behavioural issues you need to address, get it over with. That's all you seem to do.

It's the only thing you have to say to me." She folded her arms across her chest and waited.

"You," he began. He shook his head in frustration. "You just cannot help getting into trouble. Mr. Wrix, he..." Charles was having a hard time formulating a sentence.

Cassie walked forward and stood in front of him. "Stop right there," she said, her voice rising, "are you telling me that I am expected to be polite to that man? That man who thinks he can have me as if I was some kind of breeding cow?" She paused, trying to keep her temper in check. "I am not a possession. I am nobody's possession. I am my own person. I will have Ludlow Park for myself."

"You cannot do that. This is not the place or the time for you. You do not belong here. Your radical ideas..."

"My radical ideas are common sense if only you would treat people as equal. It is just simple logic, if you weren't so stupid..."

"You cannot call a whole society stupid. We live by conventions, by rules."

"Then those rules are ridiculous!" Cassie was losing her temper. They were standing very close to one another. She could make out the dark shadow of early stubble on his cheeks

"That is the way things are," he continued, looking at her intently. "You cannot change them, you are only..."

"Only what?" Cassie stepped towards him, her face inches from him, "Only what?" she pressed.

He did not flinch. His voice was steady when he said, "You are only a woman."

Cassie wanted to slap him, wanted to punch him smack in the mouth. She understood the frustration that her mother had felt. She pushed past him making her way for the door, too angry to carry on the conversation.

"Cassandra," he called after her.

"My. Name. Is. Not. Cassandra!"

He followed her, taking her forearm, trying to stop her from leaving.

"Get your hands off me," she hissed.

"Cassie, please." He let her arm go, and she pushed away from him, out into the hallway, past the few guests who were conversing quietly, through the front door and down the steps into the fading light of the late evening. She wanted to be swallowed up by the solid masonry of the assembly hall, to disappear into the shadows.

She moved along the side of the building towards the rear and the small pleasure garden, hidden from view. The ground was wet in places and water soaked through the fabric of her flimsy shoes. She could not be bothered to lift the ends of her skirts, instead leaving them trail along the ground, caking them with dirt.

She walked through the little beds of herbs, the fragrance mixing in the air to form a nice smell, reminding her of Sunday roast dinners. At the opposite side of the garden there was a tall iron gateway. She pushed her way through it, the creaking hinges complaining. She closed the gate behind her and leaned against the garden wall. The heat of the sun had left its traces on the stones. She took momentary comfort in the lukewarm feel of them.

What am I doing, she thought, the scenes from the last hour running through her head? She had mortally insulted Mr. Wrix in the ball, had embarrassed herself in her attempt at dancing and had argued with Charles Stafford. He was her only ally in this whole situation.

The gravel crunched on the other side of the wall. Cassie stood very still, half-hoping that Charles had followed her. She wondered if she should step back through the gate, wait for him in the garden. She was trying to make up her mind when she recognised a familiar sound.

"Yes, I know."

Mr. Evins's voice carried on the light evening breeze. He was talking to someone. They were coming in her general direction, the sound becoming louder, the words discernible. Cassie strained to hear everything they were saying.

"Huxley is running out of time. His debts remain unpaid," said the unknown speaker.

"This is what you had hoped for, Harcourt, was it not?" asked Evins.

Harcourt, thought Cassie. The name Huxley cried out in terror in his sleep. She edged closer to the gateway and peeped around the corner. What were they doing out here in the almost dark? In the dimness of the walled garden she could make out the stocky shape of Evins, his russet hair catching the glow of the setting sun. His back was to her. Standing talking to him was a tall man with a dark suit and a black top hat. In his hand, he held a cane, the top of which glowed golden. Cassie gasped and pulled back, bringing a hand to her mouth, stopping herself from emitting any further sound. The gold cane was the same as the one she saw at the Horse and Hound. This was Harcourt. And he was in league with Evins.

"He is caught," she heard him growl, his voice threatening. "He put Ludlow Park up as collateral. It is his as soon as Miller dies. Then as the terms of the bet stand, it goes to me. He cannot pay what he owes, the house will be mine. I want it done. Now! No more waiting."

"Yes," she heard the apothecary mutter. "I have increased the dosage for the final tonic. I made it up earlier this evening. I will administer it myself..." The words were growing fainter.

Cassie heard the crunch of footsteps on the gravel, heading in the direction of the assembly rooms. After a moment or two there was silence. She sagged against the wall, her breathing returning to normal. Huxley was terrified of this man Harcourt and well he might be. The man Ludlow Park was entailed to had a gambling problem.

It was all clear to Cassie now. Huxley's repeated inference to card games. He has offered his inheritance to back a bet. No wonder he was so anxious to hear about Lord Miller, no wonder he was nervous for his health and for Lady Cassandra's marriage.

If Lord Miller dies the house goes to Huxley. But in reality, Harcourt would own it. Huxley could not afford to have Lord Miller unwell. Harcourt on the other hand, could wish for nothing sweeter. Cassie pushed herself away from the wall. "Oh, my God."

Evins was going to murder Lord Miller. Tonight.

She picked up her skirts and ran.

Chapter Twenty-Four

~ Cassandra ~

The rain had returned, confining Tallulah and Cassandra indoors. Neither of them minded much but every time there was a noise from the direction of the front door Tallulah would jump, her eyes darting around.

Cassandra knew that she was worried about Becky. They were in the drawing room. Judge Miller and Jonah had gone off for the afternoon to do some shopping, spend some quality family time together. Cassandra had not been invited. Given her supposed bad behaviour at the fair, she took her punishment silently with a jerk of her shoulders and very little remorse. If Cassie's mother could not be bothered to speak to Cassandra about what happened and believe her when she spoke, then what was the point?

On the table in front of her was this strange thing called an iPad. The reception was strong for a change and Tallulah had spent a great deal of time showing her how to use it. But Cassandra was not convinced. It seemed to have a mind of its own. She kept asking for explanations as to how it worked and Tallulah would start talking about computers, the World Wide Web, the *In Her Net*, all these things that Cassandra could not understand. So instead she stopped asking questions and just began to press buttons.

She was reading an entry about the history of the town land from a local online newspaper archive. Cassandra had not tried to look at any entry about Ludlow or her own family. She did not want to witness the text disappearing from the screen in front of her.

She had read about the demolition and erection of a new church in 1847, noting with interest that the main patron was a Mrs. A. Weston. Cassandra felt a little funny for a minute, having read that name in print. She thought of her steward, Mr. Weston Snr. He was a lovely man, a wild mop of curly salt and pepper hair, a beard as fierce as his deep voice. But he was as gentle as a dove. She had seen him nurse little lambs to full health when they had been left without a mother. He was the best, the kindest man, next to his son.

Nicholas was in Europe.

Cassandra never mentioned him but she had not forgotten him. She wondered now, looking at the print on the iPad in front of her, the little sliver of information about a Mrs. A. Weston, the patron of the local church. Who was this descendant of the Weston family? Had Nicholas conceded to marry? She felt a stab of jealousy and closed the cover of the machine, determined not to think on it.

She stared despondently out the window at the drizzling rain. Tallulah had fallen asleep in the big easy chair next to the old fire place. The sound of her deep breathing was surprisingly soothing. After a few minutes, Cassandra's resolve wavered and she opened the cover again and flicked to the search page. She kept coming back to the article about the missing girl. Something about the story bothered her. She slowly pecked out the name of the town and watched as the search results ordered themselves onto the screen in front of her.

She clicked on one entry, scanning the headline, *"Girl Goes Missing from Ludlow Mansion"*. The date at the top of the archive was October 1747. Cassandra read it through once, then again at a slower pace.

A servant girl, Millicent Clayton, went missing one evening in a very bad storm. The people of the neighbourhood and house had spent several days searching for her, looking to see if she had taken shelter in any of the outbuildings, the farmhouse, the abandoned workers' cottages but nothing. The girl, aged fourteen, had disappeared without a trace.

Cassandra sat back in the chair, her hands clasped together in front of her. That name, Clayton, it was familiar to her, very familiar. She could not recall; then it came to her. "Molly," she said out loud as she sat bolt upright in the chair.

Caroline Healy

She knew what to do.

Cassandra found Mrs. Rivers in the kitchen, on her hands and knees, a pail of sudsy water in front of her, a wire scrubbing brush in her reddened hands. She looked up as Cassandra entered, her green eyes regarding her with distrust. Those eyes, there was no mistaking them. They were the same as Molly's eyes, the same shade, the same shape, the same sparkle of insolence in them.

"Mrs. Rivers," she began cautiously, "What is your maiden name?"

The woman did not answer her, just kept on scrubbing, round and round, sudsy dark circles on the stone floor. When eventually she did speak, her voice was dry like tinder, "I told you to stay out of the east wing."

Cassandra felt her knees go weak so she moved to the large oak table and pulled a stool out from underneath it. The woman sighed and turned towards Cassandra, her face betraying nothing.

She rose from her position on the floor and plopped the scrubbing brush into the pail of water before slowly moving to the fireplace. There was a kettle sitting just off to the edge, a black iron kettle. Cassandra remembered a similar pot from her childhood when she would seek refuge in the kitchen on a rainy day, to sit amongst the servants, soaking up their chatter as if it was rays of warm sunshine. Miss Blythe, when she came first, put a stop to that within her first week. Mrs. Rivers lifted the heavy kettle over the small flame of the fire and took down a battered teapot, its spout chipped.

In typical fashion, she said very little as she moved around the kitchen. She chose two cups from the dresser and made a pot of steaming hot tea. Cassandra watched, fascinated by the gnarl of the fingers on her hands, the slight stoop of her shoulders, the lines on her forehead. The woman sat down at the table and poured tea from the pot. She settled back into the seat and looked at Cassandra, the scar on her face standing out in sharp contrast to the rest of her features.

Cassandra's resolve swayed a little at the prospect of confronting one of the servants; especially one as terrifying as Mrs. Rivers. "What is your maiden name, Mrs. Rivers?" she repeated.

The woman tried to smile but the movement made her scar stretch tightly across her cheek. "Why you askin'? Don't you know?"

"Your name is Millicent, is it not? Millicent Clayton?" The woman nodded once, keeping her eyes focused on Cassandra.

"When were you born?

"1733".

Cassandra paused for a moment, "Tell me what happened."

Mrs. Rivers sat very still for a minute, then began her tale. She spoke softly, her voice low and serious.

"I was fourteen. I worked in the kitchens as a scullery maid. There was a storm, a vicious storm. So much wind. So much rain. I had to bring a tray to the master. His room was in the east wing. The wolf mirror. I must have banged my head. When I woke, the storm was still raging. I was disorientated."

She stopped, as if remembering for the first time.

Cassandra leaned forward, anxious to hear every word.

The woman continued, "I went down the stairs but the kitchen had changed. I did not know what had happened. I walked into the garden, to the gardener's cottage, where my father worked. I did not know that there would be railings. I could not see in the dark. I fell."

Cassandra tried not the stare at the scar that ran the length of her features.

"The next time I woke I was in a bed in a strange yet familiar house. My face and head were bandaged."

Cassandra interrupted, "The master of the house at the time, he took pity on you?"

Mrs. Rivers nodded. "I was unwell for some time. The masters kept asking me questions and I stuck to my story. The doctor wanted to have me committed. They looked for my parents, they advertised in the papers. Nobody claimed me. The master would not send me away and so I began to work in the kitchens."

Cassandra sat very still, thinking. "They closed the east wing after that?"

Mrs. Rivers nodded. "After the storm the roof was leaking, the family had not enough money to fix it. So, they decided to close it up. I spend my life here, working, living. I married Tom Rivers, the head gardener and moved to the old gate lodge. I've been housekeeper here now for nigh on thirty years."

Cassandra did some quick calculations. "That must have been the sixties? When you came?"

The woman nodded. "1963, that's the year I came through the mirror."

Cassandra did some quick calculations. Cassie's grandfather was the master at the time. Cassandra did not know how long he had been dead for. She knew it was not possible to ask him any questions. "That night. The storm. What was it like?"

"Wild. I thought the house would come undone."

Cassandra heard the front door open. Judge Miller and Jonah must be back. "And you never could get back?" Cassandra almost whispered her last question.

The housekeeper stared at her for a minute, a fleeting look of pity crossing her stoic features. At the sound of Judge Miller calling from the hallway Mrs. Rivers pushed back from the table and poured her half-drunk cup of tea down the sink before returning to her task, kneeling down on the floor, scrubbing the soapy water in constant circles.

Cassandra got up slowly from the table, taking her cup of tea with her, moving automatically towards the door, her thoughts rushing around in her head. Millicent Clayton, Molly's daughter, had gone on to become Mrs. Rivers.

Cassandra walked slowly back to the drawing room, the sound of the T.V. drifting out to meet her. When Tallulah saw her, she sat bolt upright in the chair. "What's happened?" the girl asked, concern edging her voice.

Cassandra slowly reiterated all that she had learned. "She said that the east wing was closed after the storm, a tree or something had come down through the roof."

"The residing Lord Miller didn't have the money to make repairs?" asked Tallulah.

"Yes. What does that have to do with anything?"

"Well, if the east wing was closed then people would have no cause to be near the mirror in a storm. So, no one would get sucked in."

Tallulah got up suddenly from the chair, going to the box in the corner. The screen was fuzzy with grey images. She hit the top of the box with the palm of her hand, causing the screen to go completely blank then fade back with an almost perfect picture. "I heard in the news that there was a hurricane in the south east of America."

Cassandra looked at her, not understanding what she was saying.

"It hit the Florida coast last night."

Still Cassandra did not understand.

"The tail end of that storm might be coming towards us." She turned up the volume button on the television, the sound of the small man on the screen reaching across the room to Cassandra. *"Storm warming, Hurricane Arlene crossing the Atlantic at..."* The sound dipped in and out. Cassandra leaned in towards the television set, her hand gripping the side of the couch.

"What is he saying? When? When?" She could not hide her impatience.

Tallulah shook her head, "I'm not sure. I didn't hear..."

The door of the room opened and Jonah came bounding in. "There is a storm coming. Mum has brought in candles and told me to close all the curtains, make sure the windows are bolted properly. What are you doing?" He looked from one worried face to the next, frowning.

"Nothing. Go away, Jonah. I'm talking to Cassie."

"Mum wants me to give you these." He threw two pale candles across the couch at them. "Keep them by your bed in case the electricity goes out."

The girls glanced at each other and picked up the candles. Cassandra went to the window and drew the heavy drapes across. The sun had set and was disappearing behind the hills. In the distance the sky was dark, brooding and Cassandra could see the roll of black clouds. The countryside seemed quiet as if it was holding its breath. Cassandra knew what was coming. She was afraid but there was no room for fear. She had to be ready.

It was time to go home, time to make Ludlow Park her own, something she should have done a long time ago. She had a duty, a duty to do what was right, not what was proper.

Chapter Twenty-Five

~ Cassie ~

Cassie stumbled in her silk slippers as she jogged up the stairs to the assembly hall. She had a head start, but how much of a head start, she did not know. Somewhere in the distance she could hear the roll of thunder. The night was closing in and there was a heaviness in the air, as if the weight of the blackening clouds were pressing down on the earth.

She made her way into the reception area, conscious of any other guests loitering. The servant who was supposed to be looking after ladies accessories was standing at the entrance to the ballroom, completely engrossed in watching the dancers.

Cassie scanned the hallway to make sure nobody noticed then slipped into the cloak room. It was packed to the brim with coats, shawls, feathered hats, gloves, umbrellas, all manner of accessories; men's accoutrements on one side, womens on the other. Cassie did not have much time. She hitched up her skirt and with fumbling fingers ripped the ribbon ties of her hoop open. She tried to step out of the contraption but it was caught. Frustrated she doubled over and gripping the hooped frame in her hands she pulled it asunder, snapping the boning in two. She kicked it away from her and her skirts billowed down around her legs. They trailed alarmingly to the ground but Cassie didn't have time to care, she needed to cross the green and get to the apothecary before Evins. Losing some of her heavy clothing was a necessity.

She kicked off her loose slippers and jammed her feet into a sturdy pair of boots, one size too small. Pulling on a dark coat, the pale material of her skirt was somewhat covered. At the last moment, she reached for a dark shawl, tying it under her chin. She may as well make some attempt to hide her identity. If she were caught there was no telling the consequences.

In a few easy, unencumbered steps she had crossed the hallway and made her way down the stairs out of the assembly hall, the noise of the party following her as she moved into the darkness. Cassie glanced to the sky. There were no stars to be seen and she felt the cold wind blowing around her. It was going to rain.

She pulled the shawl down lower over her face and jogged up the laneway in between the buildings, flattening herself against the shingled wall of a house. It had only taken a few minutes to cross the village to the apothecary shop. There was no light in the window and Cassie hoped she had enough time.

If Mr. Evins was paying his respects to his host and hostess, she had another five, maybe ten minutes before he would be back. She moved up the street and cut down a side path, coming around to the rear of the building. Thankfully, as she remembered, the windows to the back workshop were at ground level.

She stooped low and moved quietly. She rubbed a patch of dirt from the glass with the sleeve of the heavy coat. She could not see anything inside—she would just have to take a chance.

As she suspected, breaking, and entering was not a common crime in the sleepy hamlet so the window came undone with a gentle tug. She glanced over her shoulder into the darkness of the alleyway and slipped one foot, then the other, followed by her legs and torso into the gaping hole of the window. Her skirts bunched beneath her and snagged on the latch as she slid into the room.

She knocked into several bottles on the way in. The noise practically pained her. She slid to the ground, holding her breath, counting the seconds to see if anyone would come. Nothing happened.

The glow from the dying fireplace illuminated the room. There was enough light to make out the workbench next to the window. Slowly, she made her way to it.

On the workbench, she saw the wooden bowl, a cloth of muslin still draped protectively over it. Beside the bowl was a glass bottle, brown with a stopper. It was labelled for Ludlow Park. She recognised it. It was meant for Lord Miller. She undid the stopper and took it over to the fireplace. She tipped the contents into the grate, in a blaze of firey red the contents of the bottle fizzed on the hot coals. Cassie stepped back, shielding her face from the heat. With shaking hands, she refilled the bottle from a jug marked brandy. She added a couple of drops from a bottle of feverfew and the other innocuous bottles that lay about the table. She replaced the stopper, confident that her potion would do only good.

She paused in her task, imagining that she had heard a noise in the street. Rain began to pitter-patter onto the basement windows. The sound began soft and gentle but grew in intensity. Somewhere in the distance she heard thunder. She knew that she did not have much time left. She lifted the muslin from the bowl and peered into it. Mandrake root; the most costly of plants. Mr. Evins would not be able to source another root for some time.

The bulb, shrivelled and gnarled like twisted limbs, made Cassie shiver. She jammed the wreathing plant into the pocket of her coat.

There was a noise at the front of the shop. Someone was coming. Cassie moved as quickly as possible. She kicked a bottle that had fallen on to the stone floor, sending it spinning, the noise echoing off the silent walls. She gave into the panic and rushed blindly towards the window, not caring if she made noise. Her knees scraped against the timber of the counter as she scrambled up on to it, fumbling with the catch, her skirts slowing her down. She pushed the leaded glass out and up, forcing her head into the open air. She wriggled on her belly, kicking off with her legs, trying as fast as she could to heave herself out of the basement.

She heard the shout from the workshop, her body, half in half out, trapped like a wriggling worm. A hand gripped her foot and she could hear cursing. Strong fingers dug into the flesh of her ankle. She pushed herself up with her free hand, grunting with the effort. She managed to flip herself around, her body now facing upwards the weight of the glass window pressing into her tummy. The hand was clawing at her leg, dragging her, inch by painful inch back through the window. She braced her free hand onto the wall pushing against it, pulling her body out. Her strength seemed to be leaving her, the fight going as waves of panic gripped her.

She pulled back her leg, bending it at the knee and kicked out with all her might, aiming her boot for his head. She heard a terrible crunch, followed by a loud crash. The hold on her leg loosened as the apothecary slid to the ground. With one final heave Cassie pulled her legs clear.

A dog was barking furiously in the distance and she could hear someone shouting. She did not wait around to see what would happen next. She scrambled to her feet, skinning her hands on the sharp stones of the broken cobbles. She ran down the alleyway and into the night, fear making it hard for her to wheeze a breath into her lungs.

The rain was coming down in torrents. It made the material of her dress heavy so that it clung to her body in wet masses. She was glad of the weight. It distracted her from the throbbing of her hand, the parcel of mandrake root tucked to the pocket of her coat. The taste of fear on her tongue was unpleasant.

She looped around to the green and scanned the open space. Another clap of thunder broke the sky and she yelped in fright. She wondered if Evins had tried to follow her once he regained control after her kick. She had better get a move on. She aimed for the shelter of the large oak tree near the tie posts for the horses. She was nearly at the middle of the green before she noticed the figure of a man, crouched beneath the branches of the tree.

Her heart almost stopped in her chest. How had he found her so quickly? She could not see his face, just the bulk of him, crouched low to the ground, as if ready to spring. Another thunder clap stung her ears, followed by a lightning bolt, the flash illuminating the green for an instant, putting her in sharp relief.

The man stood up, his body unfolding, his figure becoming clear. *Charles*. Cassie exhaled a sigh of relief and jogged slowly towards the tree. Her clothes were drenched, her hair limp under the wet scarf, her knees and legs covered in dirt. *What will he think of me?* She brushed a dirty hand across her forehead, pushing the material back from her face.

He took one look at her as she huddled under the shelter of the tree. "Where have you been?" he demanded. "I searched for you everywhere. I thought Wrix..." Cassie remained silent, the outcome of her actions sinking in. "You are bleeding?" he said, a tinge of concern softening his words. He took her hand in his and examined it closely. "Are you determined to find trouble at every impasse?" His tone was reproachful but at the last word his composure changed, his good breeding and manners giving way to his emotions. "If he has touched you, I will kill him."

Another thunderclap broke the sky.

Cassie shivered; she was unable to explain, the words lost.

He cared about her, beyond the proprieties of society. Heavy sobs rattled from Cassie's chest as she began to cry.

Charles pulled her towards him and wrapped her in an embrace. He smelled of wood smoke, horse and new leather. Cassie sobbed into his chest. He stroked her hair and murmured into her ear. She did not know if they were words, she did not care. All she cared about was that he was holding her. That he would keep her safe.

Chapter Twenty-Six

~ Cassie ~

The storm loomed in the distance as Cassie and Charles raced across the hills along the road to Ludlow Park. Cassie had wanted to stay under that tree in that exact moment forever, but the sound of angry voices in the distance meant that it was time to leave. They moved hastily towards the horses that were tethered on the green, Charles untying Bryon.

He helped her up into the saddle, saying nothing when she hitched up her skirts, exposing damp bloomers, to straddle her legs across the horse's back. With one deft leap, Charles jumped up behind her, hooking his feet in to the stirrups. With expert horsemanship he guided the animal across the village square and along the roadway. Cassie was beginning to shake, the cold of the night tightening around them. Charles urged the animal forward.

The ride was heart stopping. Wind and rain lashed at Cassie's face, at her clothes, soaking every fibre. The horse seemed to feel their anxiety and pushed on through the brewing storm. Every now and then a streak of lightening would illuminate the sky. Cassie kept a tight hold on the pommel of the saddle, the reassuring presence of Charles's warmth at her back.

It seemed like no time at all before the grey boundary wall of Ludlow Park rose up to greet them at the crest of the hill. Cassie said a silent thank you as they slowed down, her nerves stretched taut to breaking point.

The animal skidded to a halt before the garden wall, Charles drawing the reins in tightly. He dismounted, offering to help Cassie from the saddle. With much tugging and pulling she managed to get down from the horse, dragging her wet skirts with her. They had not said anything to each other since the village green. Charles's silence was making her uneasy.

They led the animal through the gate, across the yard and into the stables. It was dark inside with only the whinny and shuffle of anxious horses breaking the silence.

"George," she hissed into the dark. She pulled back the dripping shawl from her shoulders. No sign of the stable boy. There was no chance that he would have gone to bed, leaving the horses alone in the middle of a storm.

Charles was behind her, a hand on her shoulder. She turned and squinted at him in the dark. "He's not here. The stable boy, he should take your horse. I need to explain, I have to…"

She didn't get to finish her sentence. He moved towards her and she took a step back. Drops of rain fell from his hair, down along the plain of his cheek to his collar and then disappeared. Cassie could see the whites of his eyes, feel his breath on her skin. She moved again, uncomfortable with the intensity of his gaze. Her back found the timber of the stall. She could go no further.

"You are determined to disgrace yourself?" he repeated, moving a strand of soggy hair from in front of her eyes.

Cassie was not able to breathe properly, her lungs filling and emptying in short puffs. She did not trust her own voice so instead she shrugged her shoulders.

"You are determined to disregard your duty as a Miller?" He was so close to her now she could see the dark outline of his perfect lips. His hands came and snaked around her waist pulling her to him.

She gasped at his strength.

"You are determined?" he asked.

"Yes." Cassie could barely get the words out.

He inclined his head in acknowledgement as if surrendering to the inevitability and then he kissed her.

Cassie was glad he was holding her so tightly. She would not have been able to remain standing unaided. She melted towards him, wrapping her arms around his neck, meshing her rain soaked body closer to his.

"You insolent…"

Cassie felt a vicious tug wrenching them apart. A lamp had materialised, the light blinding her dark-accustomed eyes. She stumbled to the side, banging into the timber of the horse stall.

"I will have your life for this, you cad. Get your hands from Lady Cassandra before I run you through."

Oh, crap, thought Cassie, recognising the voice. She blinked her eyes furiously, raising her hand to shield them against the glare of the lamp. Nicholas Weston stood there, a lamp held high in his hands, the glow encasing him. George cowered behind him. She could see that he had a swollen lip and would not look her in the eye.

Nicholas was livid, his whole body radiating anger. He took a step towards Charles, the lamp swaying in his grip.

"Nicholas," she hissed, trying to get his attention, trying to defuse the situation.

He glared at her from beneath his blonde lashes. "You, my lady, should think on your actions."

"Oh, for the love of god, you total idiot, get over yourself." Cassie had had quite enough macho behaviour for one evening. She was wet and cold and had just been kissed like nothing she had ever experienced before. She needed a bath, a warm bed, and some time to reflect. She stalked over to Nicholas, planting her wet messy self in between the two men.

"What," she emphasised the words with as much gusto as she could manage, "are you doing in my stables? And what, may I ask," gesturing to George behind him, "have you done to my stable boy?" She hoped that she was getting the tone of authority just right.

He was about to respond when Cassie raised her hand abruptly. "You have no jurisdiction here. You are the steward's son, not the master of the house." As her words sunk in Cassie saw the spark of anger begin to ebb in him. His shoulders slumped, he lowered the light.

"You are right, Lady Cassandra," he said dejected. "I have no rights here. I am just the steward's son."

Cassie could see real hurt in his eyes. "Nicholas," she began, sighing, knowing that he would probably not believe her. "I am not Lady Cassandra of Ludlow Park. I am a nobody."

A nearby clap of thunder seemed to shake the stables. The horses whinnied and stamped their feet. Charles had stepped nearer to her, she could feel his reassuring presence at her back.

"Nicholas," she implored, "this is nothing to do with you. It's more than you, it's bigger…"

The doors to the end of the stable creaked loudly. They stopped and all looked towards the end of the stable. The door groaned on its hinges. Someone was trying to open it. Charles stepped in front of Cassie, pushing her behind him, blocking her with his body.

She gripped his arm, terrified that Evins had recognised her; that he had come for her. The doors heaved open and a man stood there, dressed in tight trousers and a coat of some kind. Cassie squinted into the darkness. Another person was jogging behind him. They stepped into the stables and closed the doors.

"Molly?" she called, stepping around Charles, who tried to hold her back. "It's okay, it's Molly."

The man with Molly walked towards them. Cassie frowned, there was something familiar about him. He stepped into the light cast by the lamp, taking off his hat as he moved, his hair tumbling to freedom down his shoulder.

"Lady Cassandra," whispered Cassie.

She could hear a strangled gasp from behind her, could imagine the looks on Nicholas and Charles's faces.

The girl in front of her was slightly smaller than her, with the same coloured eyes, the same shaped face. Her hair was fairer, longer, stretching down to her waist. Cassie moved forward and reached out a hand, touching her ancestor, a slow smile spreading across her face. "You are real. You came back?"

The girl laughed quietly, drawing Cassie in for a tight hug. She noticed the girl's clothing. "You're wearing my favourite jeans!" she exclaimed.

Cassandra was not looking at her any more, instead her attention was taken up by the two men behind her. She advanced a few steps and bowed the most graceful curtsy Cassie had ever seen. Lady Cassandra barely acknowledged Charles, instead, all her intention seemed to focus on Nicholas. She took his hand in hers and just stood there, silently, gazing up at him.

"Miss," began Molly, sliding up to her. "Lady Cassandra came back through the mirror. The storm, Miss. It will not last for much longer. It is time to go. Your friend, Tallulah, Mrs. Rivers, they are waitin' for ya."

"Mrs. Rivers?" The name sounded strange on her lips, as if it was another lifetime ago.

"Your mother as well, Miss. She will be wantin' you home safe."

"But Molly, I have so much to tell you, Mr. Evins, Mr. Huxley, Lord Miller."

The servant girl took her hand. "I will know most of the story now, miss," nodding in the direction of Charles. "Her ladyship will be told and she will know what to do. We have the medicine for Lord Miller, mould and all as it is."

Cassie was trying to think through the fog that cloaked her brain, and she glanced back at Charles who was watching her anxiously. "Yes," she said quietly, "the penicillin will grow on the bread. Wait till its blue and give it to Lord Miller three times a day. Don't let Mr. Evins near him, and insist that Doctor Brown makes up any medicine or tonic in front of you. I don't think he was involved, but it is best to be sure."

Molly nodded. "Yes, Miss. It is time now. You have to go."

Cassandra and Nicholas were talking quietly, her hand grasped in his as if it were his life's duty never to let it go. Cassie glanced at them a moment, smiling, before moving through the stables. The rain was still heavy, but the thunder and lightning seemed to have moved off a distance.

After a moment, Lady Cassandra was beside her at the door, shouting instructions, "We must go. I do not know how long the Wolf Mirror will work for. We must hurry."

Cassie looked behind her. "Charles? Where's Charles?"

Cassandra shook her head. "I do not know. Come, Cassie, we have no time to waste."

"No! I won't go without saying goodbye. Where is he?" The wind twisted through her loose hair, whipping it around her face, pushing it into her eyes, her mouth, making it hard to see, to talk. The rain pelted down in big drops. She wanted to call out, to howl over the noise of the wind. "Charles," she cried.

"I am here. I am here." He was beside her, his arm around her, his other hand in hers.

She looked up through the wet and the wind. "I thought you had left."

He shook his head. "Not until the end. We have a few more minutes."

"Mr. Stafford," entreated Lady Cassandra, "We must go, now. She does not belong here—she must return home."

He nodded his understanding and urged Cassie forward, speaking low, "She is right, Cassie. You are too fiery for this world. You must return."

Cassie had not quite thought this part of the plan through. She knew he was right, but she did not want to leave him.

"Come with me?" she urged, stopping to face him directly. "I can show you the most wonderful things. I can..." He put his finger to her lips and shook his head.

"I have my duty and it is here. It was not meant to be, Cassie. It just..."

"Hurry," shouted Cassandra, over the boom of thunder, "the storm is moving off. We do not have time."

The five of them, Charles, Cassie, Nicholas, Molly and Lady Cassandra Miller, dressed in the clothes of a boy, ducked out into the fierce weather and half stumbled, half ran across the stable yard, through the herb garden, across the front lawn of Ludlow Park and up to the servants' door.

Cassandra and Nicholas pushed the heavy door open. Wet and bedraggled they landed into the kitchen, shivering and dripping all over the flagstones. "Quick!" Cassandra moved across the kitchen and collided with the cook, rolling pin held high in the air, ready to strike at any intruders.

"Lady Cassandra," she gasped, taking in the torn jeans, the trainers, the loose hair in one glance. She was about to speak when she looked past Cassandra and her eyes settled on Cassie. The cook's mouth dropped open, her hand stilled in mid-air. "But. But, I... Mistress," she looked from one girl to the next, unable to formulate a full sentence.

"Cook," commanded Cassandra, her voice brisk, "have the fire stoked up and make some tea. We will have need of it in a few minutes. See to it that there are dry clothes for everyone and get something warm for us to eat."

The cook stood still for a minute, then blinked. Knowing how to follow orders she did not ask any more questions, but did as she was told.

Cassie looked to Molly who seemed small and diminutive in the dull candle light of the kitchen. She was shivering with the cold, her skirts soaked though, her cap and hair drenched. Cassie went to her and took her hand, pulling her in for a hug. "Thank you," she whispered before letting her go, smiling kindly, "You have been a good friend to me. I will not forget you."

Molly smiled shyly, unused to such thanks or praise.

"Molly," Lady Cassandra asked. What is the name of the boy who has been courting you?" The servant blushed a bright shade of red and Cassie frowned, unsure how that question was relevant.

"Come along, Molly, we do not have much time," chided Cassandra, her authoritarian voice coming out once more.

"Thomas, Mistress."

"Yes Molly, but Thomas what?"

"Clayton, Miss," she whispered, mortified by the content of the conversation.

"Will you remember that?" asked Cassandra, taking hold of Cassie's hand.

"Yes," replied Cassie in surprise.

"Good. Now, we have to go." Cassandra took Cassie by the arm and led her up the steep stairs and along the kitchen passageway, passing through the hallway and up the staircase. Miss Blythe, in her night shawl stood at the top of the stairs. She gave one sharp yelp and proceeded to fall to the floor, feint with the sight of her mistress, times two, in such a state.

"I will deal with her later, do not worry. Come along."

Cassie glanced down the stairs, making sure that Charles was still following her.

They all drew to a halt at the junction of the east wing. Cassie could feel it, a cracking in the air, a heaviness that had nothing to do with the storm.

"You must go on your own. It would not be safe to risk the others. Mrs. Rivers, Millicent, she will be waiting for you." Cassandra drew her close and hugged her tight. "Thank you, Cassie. Thank you for what you have done for my family. I will see that Mr. Evins meets with justice. I will do my duty for Ludlow Park, even if that means breaking the rules. I must be strong, for my children, my children's children and all my ancestors to come." She hugged Cassie one last time, pressing a cold token into her palm. "Now go!"

Charles took her closed hand and bent to kiss it chastely. A bolt of energy zapped through Cassie, as if she had been electrocuted.

"I will think on you often, Miss Cassie Miller. I will remember you always." Drawing her close, he kissed her. "You are ready. Go now." He stepped back and turned away from her, walking along the hallway, down the stairs, not looking back once.

Cassie stumbled forward, down the hallway, tears of helplessness blurring her vision.

The wolf mirror on the wall glowed more golden than ever before. It seemed to hum in the darkness. She looked over her shoulder and could see Cassandra standing still as stone, her hand to her mouth as if restraining herself from calling out. Cassie took a deep breath and took the last two steps up to the Wolf Mirror. She saw her reflection there.

She looked pale, bedraggled. Her hair hung in a sopping mess, her eyes were large and saucer like, blotchy from crying. Masses of material clung to her like wet rags. She needed to go home. Cassandra was right, she didn't belong here. She looked back once and held up her hand, a universal signal to all humanity, a signal that said goodbye and hello and everything in between. She stepped towards the mirror and touched the glass, looking beyond it, looking to the future.

Chapter Twenty-Seven

~ Cassie ~

Cassie parked her car to the front of the house. She knew that Mrs. Rivers would be waiting for her, but she could not go in just yet. She had a job to do first. She saw the figure of the housekeeper in the hall window and she waved at her, smiling before pointing across the lawn and down towards a copse of trees. Mrs. Rivers nodded her head in acknowledgement.

Cassie had been back to Ludlow Park several times over the last few months. In the beginning, she could not bear to visit, claiming exams and study, an excuse her mother was hesitant to accept until she saw all the books spread out on the dining room table, her daughter pouring over past exam papers. All her hard work had stood to her. She had been accepted into several colleges and to Judge Miller's astonishment had chosen the one closest to London.

Cassie sighed, shaking her head, thinking about it all. She got out of the car slowly, reaching back for the bouquet of flowers. The day was fresh, autumnal, the leaves on the trees having turned a bronzed yellow, a burnt red and a dull green. Winter was coming but she did not mind. She liked the change in the seasons.

She walked across the dewy grass, leaving a trail of footprints behind her. Her shoes would be drenched by the time she got back to the house, but Mrs. Rivers would know where to find her a pair of warm, woolly socks.

Coming to a copse of trees, she pushed in to them, parting their branches with her spare hand, moving her way deeper and deeper in to the trees. The locals and Mrs. Rivers had long forgotten that this place even existed. It was through her final research project for history that she discovered it.

Cassie had become obsessed with the details of the Miller family, much to her mother's amusement. For her project, Cassie went to extreme lengths by contacting the London Library and the Society of Genealogists for information. Her mother had been secretly glad that Cassie was taking such an interest in the family. Of course, Cassie was doing it because she was desperate to find out what had happened to Lady Cassandra, to Molly, to all her friends. She had avoided the Stafford family history, instead preferring to concentrate on the Miller and Weston lineage.

With one last effort, Cassie pushed through the collection of trees into an oasis of green. The space was oval in shape, surrounded by tall deciduous trees. To the centre of the clearing, peeping from the clutches of long grasses was the ghostly shape of grey granite headstones. The trees and surrounding nature did not seem to want to colonise this place, being respectful of what lay beneath the ground.

It had been a while since Cassie had been here, the grass having grown tall and mottled. She picked her way carefully across the space, the crinkle of the flower wrapping sounding very loud. She stood for a moment, head bowed before two grave stones, still erect but eschew. The carving on them was simple, puddles of greeny-yellow lichen were trying to colonise the headstones. Cassie moved forward a step and brushed some of the new growth from the granite slab. The carving, long worn by years of wind and rain, was barely decipherable, but Cassie did not need to read it, she had stood here many times. She knew the text by heart.

"Here lieth the body of Lady Cassandra Miller and her husband Mr. Nicholas Weston, ever loved, ne'er forgot."

She smiled, as always, at the thought that Cassandra had never taken her husband's name. Cassie liked to think it was because Cassandra had been a revolutionary and not that she was ashamed of the rank of Nicholas Weston.

That night, almost a year ago, when she came through the mirror, she remembered it exactly. Her stomach had heaved, her head had throbbed, she felt as if she was going to pass out but sheer determination kept her awake, kept her standing. She turned and looked at the mirror, the glass rippling as if a stone had been cast into its pond. She stood and looked at her own refection, but it was not hers alone, it was Cassandra's too.

Tallulah and Mrs. Rivers found her there, slumped on the bare timber floor boards of the east wing, sobbing, her right hand clenched into a fist, her body cold and shivering. The housekeeper had led her patiently to her once familiar bedroom where she helped her undress with the precision of a lady's maid. She brushed out Cassie's long hair, plaiting it loosely before helping her into the softness of the bed. Cassie was too numb to say anything, happy to let someone else pilot her body, move her limbs.

Before Mrs. Rivers turned off the light, she leaned down towards Cassie, smoothing out her hair and Cassie had looked at her face, with its lines and weathering, at the scar which marred her poised features and at the eyes, ever watchful. There was something familiar there, in the slant of the eyelids, the colour of the lashes, the tint of the iris and Cassie had smiled, recognising a friend.

In the days that followed her mother had loitered in her bedroom, a cold cloth on her forehead, cooling Cassie's raging temperature. Her night time cries and delirious talking about Charles and Cassandra slid across Judge Miller's consciousness as feverish ramblings, a side effect of the flu that Cassie was fighting.

Tallulah had come to sit by her bed every day, just holding her hand, not saying anything except that she was glad she was back. Jonah, too, was on his best behaviour, leaving his Nintendo by her bed in case she wanted to play it if she was bored.

On the fourth day Cassie slipped out of bed, her knees knocking together, feeling rubbery after so much bedrest. She slipped on her second favourite pair of jeans and a hoodie and made her way slowly downstairs.

She moved silently down the cool corridor and the stone steps to the basement kitchen. Mrs. Rivers was waiting for her there, a pot of tea on the stove and some rock buns cooling on the wire rack. Cassie slid into the seat and waited until the housekeeper had finished drying the dishes.

"Well lass?" she asked, sighing as she sat heavily into the seat, "You're back?"

Cassie nodded, a barrage of questions waiting to be asked, but instead she took the cup of tea offered to her and a rock bun, nibbling at the currant on the outside of the cake. She did not know where to begin.

They had spoken many times since then, Cassie regularly visiting the cavernous kitchen, sitting companionably with Mrs. Rivers, watching as the housekeeper made bread or cleaned the silver ware, never saying much, just content to be in each other's company. Over time, the housekeeper had told many a story, recounting old and new.

Cassie touched the gold locket that hung from a delicate chain around her neck. She wore it always, never taking it off, Cassandra's parting gift.

Cassie straightened up from her position in front of the gravestones, shaking herself out of her reflective mood and lay the flowers on Cassandra's grave. She liked to bring something colourful for the Lady of Ludlow Park.

She glanced at her watch. It was almost lunch time. She would need to get back to London early. Her mother was cooking a family dinner. Cassie had made a huge effort to repair the damage done over the last two years with her mother, but she had laid down some solid terms herself. She had told her mother that she must leave her work in the office at the weekends and consent to spending some time with her family. It had worked out better than she had expected, Judge Miller taking a step back from her case load and leaving a great deal of the paperwork to Dobson, her assistant.

A rustling sound, some animal in the undergrowth, disturbed Cassie's reflective mood. It must be a fox or something, she told herself as she turned to leave, anxious to talk with the housekeeper. The cracking of a branch from the other side of the family graveyard caused her to swivel on her heels. Something was out there, in the trees moving towards her.

She took a step back, stumbling against the edge of a fallen grave slab. Some kind of crazed animal was pushing its way through the branches of the trees in her direction. She resisted the urge to scream and instead bent down to pick up a stout branch, gripping it tightly in her hand.

The beast cursed loudly, the sound echoing across the small clearing. Cassie exhaled and lowered her weapon, confident that the advancing noises belonged to a human.

He emerged in the next instant from the branches of the tree at the opposite side of the graveyard. His clothes were dishevelled, his jumper torn, a patch of pale skin peeking through the arm.

"Charles," she gasped, the stick falling from her fingers.

He stood at the edge of the clearing and looked at her for a moment and smiled. Cassie was too stunned to speak.

"Hello," he said quietly, taking a step towards her. "I'm sorry if I frightened you. I have just been exploring my grandfather's lands and I think I might have wandered off course."

Cassie watched him, the tilt of his chin, the way his hair fell, lopsided across his forehead, she noticed his eyes, a lighter shade of blue, not the same but almost. She realised she was staring and cleared her throat in an effort to begin to speak.

"I…" she started, unsure what to say, "I…"

"You?" he smiled at her, with perfect white teeth.

She could not continue. He moved a little further into the clearing and she noticed that he was not as tall. He stepped over some gravestones and came to stand in front of her. "My name is Christian. Christian Stafford. I'm down from London. I come every year around Autumn Fair time to visit my grandfather."

He held out his hand and she hesitated for a moment, memories of the past and present jumbling together in her head.

"Hello," she said eventually, "I'm Cassie Miller."

He smiled again, "Nice to meet you Miss Miller."

THE END

About the Author

Caroline Healy is a writer and community arts facilitator, living and working in Ireland. She studied creative writing at the Seamus Heaney Centre, Queen's University, Belfast.

She writes short stories and novels, and has won awards for her work. In 2012, her collection, *A Stitch in Time,* was published by Doire Press. Her writing has featured in publications such as *Wordlegs, The Bohemyth, Short Story Ireland, Short Stop U.K., Five Stop Story, Prole, Literary Orphan* and the Irish Writers' Centre *Lonely Voice*

Her second collection, *The House of Water,* featuring *Nun on a Bike* has been published by Norwich based publishing house Galley Beggar Press.

She writes Y.A. fiction and her book, *Blood Entwines*, is published by Bloomsbury Spark.

www.carolinehealy.com

www.ingramcontent.com/pod-product-compliance
Lightning Source LLC
Chambersburg PA
CBHW020418180626
46812CB00003B/1043